I0764176

Carlos Montoya

Also by John Paul Jaramillo

Little Mocos

House of Order

Carlos Montoya

A Novel

John Paul Jaramillo

Carlo Montoya Copyright © 2023 John Paul Jaramillo

This is a work of fiction. Names, characters, places, and incidents either are the product of the author's imagination or are used fictitiously. Any resemblance to actual persons, living or dead, events, or locales is entirely coincidental. All rights reserved. No part of this book may be used or reproduced in any manner whatsoever without written permission except in the case of brief quotations embodied in critical articles and reviews.

Published by Twelve Winters, a literary project.

P. O. Box 414 • Sherman, Illinois 62684-0414 • twelvewinters.com

Carlos Montoya was first published by Twelve Winters in 2023. All rights reserved.

Cover and interior page design by TWP Design.

Cover art copyright © 2022 Thom Whalen. Used by permission. All rights reserved.

Author photo copyright © 2022 Chris McDonald.

ISBN
978-1-7331949-8-3

Printed in the United States of America

For my love, Deborah,
and for my family

Special thank you to
Jennifer C. Cornell

Acknowledgments

Parts of *Carlos Montoya* first appeared in the following: “trip home” at *Fogged Clarity Arts Journal*; ; “highway motel” at the *WriteLaunch.com*; “wrecks” at *The Grief Diaries: A Magazine of Art and Writing About Loss*; and “poca loca” was a *Glimmer Train Stories* Finalist.

Contents

To the old men. To the good, old, dead, demented men we love. And to the west.

— Jack Kerouac, *On the Road*

Carlos Montoya

1950

lumber

Carlos limped to the worksite near South Fork, Colorado, out where he believed the early October air surrounding the San Juan Mountains held strange spirits. He positioned his double-bitted axe through the barbed wire fence and struggled his limbs between the razors.

"Viejo," the broken-faced Tony Sandoval shouted, pulling at the cigar beneath his harelip. "Too good to sign-in like the rest of us?"

Carlos shifted his axe from one aching shoulder to the other. He slapped at his deaf ear and scratched at greying whiskers.

Ahead of the crew of men, placed far in miles of green woods and down among a skidway of ten-foot-high logs, the saw engine ripped through the first of the day. The littlest man of the crew, Pifanio Jaramillo, stood there staring at the mountain of trees and then the surrounding wooded hills. "Less talk and more work, cabrónes."

Carlos rested his axe against a tree and hustled before any of the other younger men to help roll a chunk from under the saw.

About ten a.m., Tony slid a decrepit branch under the saw. Most of the logs were birch and beech and some maple, eighteen to thirty inches through, but this one was only a few inches. The thickset one they called Eddie took off his greasy denim cap and hollered, "Quit fucking around."

Tony grinned and laughed with the rest of the men. "Lookit what I am making for the old man. Carlos needs his cane to walk."

The blade bent and the branch kicked sideways from the track, rapping Eddie just under the jaw. By the time Pifanio stepped in and raised the saw, the blade had jumped free and hung spinning and shaking shredded pulp from its two-inch teeth.

"Ay, que cabrón!" Pifanio said. "What the hell are yous doing?"

"Kicked," Tony said, glaring at Pifanio. "Knocked him in the face."

Eddie chuckled, felt at his chin. Carlos slapped at his dead ear before finally running to clear the branch from the line.

AT LUNCHTIME, Eddie cut the switch, and the engine stopped with aching coughs. Tony sank his axe in the chunk they were splitting and collected his flannel shirt from the bushes.

"Come on, Carlos," Pifanio called.

The rest of the men looked and grinned, and then mud-footed, one by one, they made their way to enter the makeshift tent at the top of the hill.

Inside the tent Pifanio's table sat with lunch boxes and mason jars filled with water. By the time Carlos finished his smoke and sat down at the table, the men had finished washing up out of tarp-lined buckets. They ate their bologna slices and drained thermoses of coffee.

"We should have a radio, Pifanio," Eddie said. "What do you think, viejo? Carlos? We need a radio in here or no?"

Carlos stared as his ear buzzed and cracked, the voices not quite reaching him. Finally, he grunted with an understanding.

"You want music, get down to Main Street on Saturday night," Pifanio added and nodded.

"Hey Carlos, tell me what you were saying about the Indian hell," one of Pifanio's men said, laughing out loud. "What's this about hell's entrance, Carlos?"

"Sipapu!" Carlos finally acknowledged. "Mountain hell—"

"What language is that?"

"Tewa Pueblo," Carlos whispered.

"A mountain hell?" one man said. "Like the shit work of a life out here, Carlos! Que no?"

"Hey, Carlos," one interrupted. "Tells us about the war and fighting in the trenches."

"Yah, Carlos," another agreed. "Tell us about shooting Germans."

"Old man has some batshit stories," Tony laughed.

"Bullshit," Eddie whispered under his breath. "He's never been to no war."

"Sipapu is a place in the mountains," Carlos finally whispered. "It's a home—"

"Oye, Carlos. Old man," Tony interrupted. "I hear you got a wife out there in Monte Vista."

"I hear she's fresh from the looney bin," Eddie claimed. "From the institution. Not quite right in the head."

"Jesus Christ!" Pifanio said. "Give my Compadre's life some respect. Didn't none of you ever learn to respect elders? For Christ's sake!"

The men loitered after lunch smoking and throwing their vachas safely into a water bucket outside of the tent then walked silently down the skid road into the woods and their saw work.

The youngest man, Renzo, pointed at Carlos' half-smoked cigarette and asked: "Can you teach me to roll my own?"

Carlos shook his head at the simple boy, not registering the words directly. Before Eddie had his saw engine running and before he refilled the tank, Tony and Jake had their axes and hooks into tough and knotty wedges they had rolled aside earlier.

Carlos later answered the voices, slapping at the buzzing in his ears, "I ain't about to be no boy's schoolteacher."

franklin street

Carlos' woman, the skinny, teenaged thing of a wife, rested on the couch. With one stiff chair as a desk beside her, she sat with her lap covered with magazines and half-written letters to her mama and sister.

For a minute or two, the viejo Carlos stood in the doorway, stopped partly by the air and partly by the feeling of anger and perceived threat. The house he had framed and built seemed cold and strange around him.

"Damn, mujer," Carlos mumbled deep into the house. "How hard is it for her to fill the stove? I want to come home to warmth and coffee."

"I'm sick, husband," the curly haired Felipa announced after finally giving the man her anxious eyes.

"She's sick. Sick of what? Working? Cleaning? That's what she's tired of."

"Shut up, viejo. You talk crazy! Listen to me for once!"

Carlos crossed the room still fresh from paint and emptiness and sat down into the hard wood chair. And while rubbing at his aching lower back, he sat and listened to her. "What does the mujer have to say?"

"I never should have married you," she cried. She wore an evening dress covered in cigarette ashes. Her neck and shoulders were overly exposed.

"She'll freeze in this dress," Carlos answered. "Where's the sweater? If sick, she'll need something warm."

"Do you hear me, viejo? I walked over to the neighbors and telephoned my mama and she can barely answer. Can barely talk. She is so hurt by me. By me being run out."

Carlos slid his hand against her skin as she wept and coughed on wet tears. "Ah, this woman."

"She says the marriage ain't holy. That's exactly what she says. Ain't sanctified by God so she don't recognize it. Says I'm a ruined woman with you, Carlos. Says she don't have a daughter. Says the whole thing is shameful. And never going to respect us."

"Damn it," Carlos answered. "Keep the voices down. The vecina lady next door will think I'm killing the wife."

"Don't you hear what I'm saying, Carlos? Says she don't even want to think about me no more. She don't want nothing to do with me, Carlos! Can't you see that! She don't believe in marriage without the church. Says you're a thief of a man!"

"No need to scream! I can hear. I ain't too damned old to hear a woman."

"Well, this is the only way you can hear me! You have to get used to it! This is how I have to talk to you!" she said with her face up against one of the pillows, whimpering.

Carlos only heard the pattern and refrain and never the sense of her words. But even in her anger and craziness, her crying and pain upset him. He couldn't help but to kiss at her hand to calm her.

"A wife belongs with a husband," Carlos said. "I'm the father and you're the mother now! Did you tell her these things? I have a home here and I have money coming in."

"You have to work every damned day, Carlos!"

"A man has to work."

"You don't have what I thought. You have to work, and we eat worse than when I was with my papa, Carlos! You ain't what you said! You ain't half of what you said!"

At first, he tried stroking at her head until she pulled away from him in disgust and impatience. He said, "Then pack your clothes, mujer! Pack them!"

"I have brothers—"

"Never seen no brothers, mujer."

"Since I was two years old, I have brothers that would kill for me! You know they will kill! They'll string you up!"

"If the woman regrets!" Carlos said, trying to focus on her face, her eyes. "Then get her the hell out!"

Felipa sensed the stupidity and the anger of Carlos, so she ran behind the locked door of the bathroom.

Carlos limped out onto the porch to roll a smoke, abandoning the flawed attempts to light a match again and again. Finally, he returned to knock at the bathroom door.

"The woman of the house needs to eat," he begged. "For Christ's sake. She'll die half starved."

AFTER MIDNIGHT Felipa lay in bed pushing and pulling at Carlos. "Something flying around in here, viejo," she said, "Darling. You know I can't be with monsters in here. Please. Darling. Darling."

Carlos threw himself from the metal spring bed and then pulled on his overalls. "Goddamn it! This woman!"

"Don't kill it. Just let the window open and it'll find its way."

He smashed at the walls with his boot.

"If you fixed them we wouldn't have these problems," she said. "If we had screens like decent folks' houses—"

"This woman just hates to see me at peace."

"When aren't you resting?"

"I said at peace. Not sleeping."

He stood on the mattress swiping and following Felipa's imagined winged animal and then he surrendered. Suddenly he was enraged, and he slammed his aching body into the living room loveseat. He threw his feet up onto the arm and then wrapped himself in the tiny serape reeking of cat smell. “Goddamn it, this woman,” he answered to the saw buzzing alive inside his mind.

highway motel

After the sawyer Pifanio Jaramillo met up with the married Felipa Montoya, the moon-faced, roly-poly Jimenez boys, Juan and Renzo, sat in tar-stained coveralls, witnesses to the whole infidelity. They caught it all through a dirty motel room pane of glass.

The brothers had travelled to pull a tourist's car down from Hayden Pass and were sitting across the parking lot in their boss' diesel wrecker sharing a bottle when they caught a glimpse of the thin-legged Felipa and Pifanio. They laughed knowingly at the scandal and at the man Pifanio as he washed his pants in a sink. The man was ten miles from home with his oldest compadre's wife sleeping nearby in the narrow bed, and the brothers believed him to be vain and pitiful as he placed his wet trousers over a chair.

Later, from the next room over, the brothers drank whiskey and smoked cigars and put their ears to the wall to eavesdrop. They listened as Pifanio rolled into the bed sheets and listened to Felipa's soft breathing that changed into a mild snore. They thought for sure the young woman would wake and Pifanio would have to find the energy to carry a conversation or to console her.

In that moment the Jimenez boys thought of Pifanio's wife and children and the compadre Carlos sleeping miles away in the speck of a town that was Monte Vista. They thought poor Carlos might be sleeping after a night of drinking and perhaps passed out and waiting on his wife. They knew the old man had no phone and argued whether to spend the next day driving the miles to inform the damn-fool-of-an-old-man.

PIFANIO RECOGNIZED the Jimenez brothers from his worksite and closed the thin drapes. Perhaps wrong thoughts also influenced Pifanio to throw on damp clothes, to run out of the small concrete room, down past the ice and cigarette machines to cower and hide, past a stray dog sniffing around the laundry room and then past the lot and then down to the main office. The spirits and voices Pifanio believed to be observing made him shrink—dissolve, really—until he finally unlocked the passenger door of his truck and found more cigarillos.

For a long time, without thinking, with the eyes of a ghost, the man sat in his truck and stared at the dead bugs and then at the webbed cracks in his windshield. He felt the Jimenez boys and everyone else from his life staring down. He felt them search his mind for excuses and defenses as he punched at the dash and then at the gear shifter console.

Back in the room and the bed, after bathing his face in cold water and after wiping his face dry with his undershirt, he calmed.

"I thought you left me," Felipa whispered, coming out of her sleep. "I would've hated you my whole life if you left without at least saying bye, Pifanio."

The two lay there motionless and Felipa was the first to stand and put on her panties and bra, staring directly at Pifanio as she moved. She pulled the housedress over her head and had her wild curls pushed behind her ears. "Don't worry. I don't expect nothing, Pifanio," she said.

"Those men work for me—"

"I'm not ashamed of nothing. Let the entire valley see."

—

VOICES MOVE QUICKLY in the San Luis Valley, on the air, crawling over the dirt and along the highway, and so days later, standing at his door, Pifanio stared into the face of his oldest compadre in the valley, the Carlos Montoya. Rain pebbled the viejo's hair and pockmarked face. The leather collar of his denim jacket was soaked and so were his coveralls. Carlos said, "I thought maybe the patrón wanted to explain himself."

"Let my wife get some coffee for you," Pifanio answered.

"I want the man to tell us," he said, despite the warnings from the Jimenez brothers. Then he gave Pifanio a good look at the rusted Springfield pistola placed in his coveralls. Carlos held darkened and expressionless eyes. "I want the patrón to tell us the story."

"Get up out of the rain, Carlos," Pifanio said. The old man made no motion to clean his boots or clothes as he made his way into the living room. Carlos looked immense to Pifanio, who stood in his boxer shorts and undershirt.

"That rusted old thing, Compadre?" Pifanio asked. The walls were decorated with animal pelts and stuffed and mounted trophies, a temple to the outdoors and Pifanio's skill with a long rifle.

Carlos said, "I'm not hired to think or to ask questions, they tell me, but to only follow the patrón's orders. But I came here for the man to tell me to my face. Here to the house of los ricos. Aqui vienen los ricos!"

The two men were surprised to have the wife Delores enter from the hall. To this day folks in the San Luis Valley consider she is what saved Pifanio. "Carlos!" she said. "¿Cómo estás? What blew you in? Come for coffee?"

The voices in the old man's head gave him a self-consciousness, but he did not hide the iron from the husband and wife. The old man never lost focus on Pifanio.

"I wanted to come on over and get a couple of words straight," Carlos said in an almost complaining voice and tone. He slapped at his buzzing ear.

"How come you're not headed for the worksite?" Pifanio asked.

"A damned joke," he said. "Pifanio has a bunch of thugs and fools working. I guess it represents the patrón, que no?"

Delores moved towards Pifanio before he barked at her to leave.

"I think the wife here might want to hear how her husband runs his life," Carlos said. "So why don't the wife sit down here?" Carlos asked as he pulled the slide and cocked the weapon and pointed it at Pifanio's neck.

Delores' scream froze the room.

"Why don't the patrón tell Delores?"

"What's he talking about, Pifanio?"

"The patrón owes us for a week of work," Carlos said. He wagged the piece. "I think the patrón owes us, Pifanio. I think you owe the truth of what you've been doing with my Felipa."

Pifanio shook his head and just scoffed. He was practically spitting: "I can imagine how jealousy eats away at you."

"Ay, que cabrón," Carlos returned. "I am hearing it from the man himself. I want him to sit down here and tell us straight out."

"You're a drunk fool, Carlos," Pifanio said. "You're drunk and frightening my wife."

Delores was a light and shaky thing and insisted on understanding, nodding her head and repeating, "What in heaven's name, Pifanio?"

"Tell her!" Carlos lifted the gun to the ceiling and fired two times. Slam. Slam.

"Just a Goddamn minute," Pifanio yelled. To Delores he said, "Don't listen to this viejo."

Carlos shrugged. "I guess the man's got nothing to say to

me?" Carlos fired again. Slam.

Pifanio's ears felt as if they were burning from the inside.

"How this man gets everyone to lie for him all at once. So help me I ought to put a window through the man's head." Carlos' wet eyes caught Delores, who began to sob and fall to her knees with an understanding. Her hands covered her face and with this the old man felt shame. He straightened up without a word and then pulled the clip from the gun. Then he cleared the last cartridge from the chamber, and it jumped out onto Pifanio's fine stained hardwood floor.

"No patrón," Carlos said, making sure to collect the cartridge. He hid the gun deep down in his coveralls and then picked up Pifanio's blanket from the armchair and dried his face and neck before nearly cracking the doorframe with his exit. "This man is no Goddamned patrón of mine," Carlos spat out to the early morning valley air.

first dreams 1921

The man known as the Cocinero first came to young Carlos while in his days with the 28th Division, 110th Infantry, during the journey crossing the grey Atlantic. Carlos travelled from Camp Dodge, Iowa, Camp Gordon, Georgia, and Camp Upton, Long Island, New York, and sailed to Liverpool, England. From Southampton, England, he embarked for Le Havre, France. It was the first time the young man had experienced so many miles, his first time on the ocean, and the first time the man could remember dreaming. Never had the head for it, or so he thought. Dreams were something for children. But the man he would come to know as the Cocinero appeared to him while Carlos slept on a ship's deck.

In the dream the Cocinero was on horseback alongside his dog companion. The dog nipped at Carlos' feet and he stepped and jerked away from the animal. The mounted man with the leathered face and neck and unkempt clothes reminded him of a man's path, his family and the work going on at home in the horse fields of his father's lands. He laughed and spoke pointedly as the sun and skies surrounded the man on horseback. "Your home is calling, young man." Carlos could not speak but only walked and listened to the man who strode steady toward the horizon. "Where are your people?" the Cocinero called out. After waking Carlos became seasick and vomited onto the deck as he watched the ocean rise and fall. Volunteers were handing out donuts and mugs of coffee. Carlos heard one remark, "Look! They're sending babies to fight!"

years later, *after returning home, Carlos made the long, sad journey most former Army cavalry made in those days. He traveled across the white, snow plains of Colorado to Chaco Canyon, New Mexico, then through Arizona, out to the San Joaquin Valley of California for work. There he was hired on by Mormons as a hand on their journey to Utah, along with several other gavacho cowpunchers and drifters. The work was tiring, and the days were long though the treeless, grassy plains were quiet and peaceful. He enjoyed the simplicity of his workdays. After finishing his commitment, Carlos, the vaquero, was paid 12 silver dollars, respectable money for a young man. Then, foregoing the advisement of the viejos of his youth, Carlos lingered and neglected to point his mare towards home.*

In the faint light of morning Carlos reached Taos, New Mexico, and a small stone morada plastered over with adobe emerged on the horizon as if in empty space. By this time it was late January, and the ground appeared as a sea of blowing snow to Carlos' tired eyes. Slipping and panting, Carlos felt his horse needed rest and grain and especially warmth if he was to make it through the storm. As Carlos approached, he understood the building was only one of many hidden in a dark cold and fog, a village of homes and decrepit outhouses. Between each house ran a narrow valley, and the first he approached belonged to a man he would soon know as Lino, who was out in front of his home feeding his two scrawny dogs that were lying quiet and shivering in front of the door. Carlos approached the lair and its owner with a strange caution, a fear that comes after sleeping under western skies for months at a time with only the sky and imagination to speak with. To the young vaquero's eyes, the Cocinero looked to be in his sixties. He was tall and round, with a sad, dark expression. He wore a simple bolo tie and faded Levi's. The old man appeared as a man of power and was very friendly to Carlos, and to all Spanish-speaking men of the llano.

"Señor," Carlos, the young vaquero, said. His spurs jingled as he dismounted. He removed his wide hat with care and respect and wiped the snow from his neck with his handkerchief. He offered the man some tobacco and coins. "I cannot make it farther in this weather. My horse also requires rest and grain, and I would very much appreciate shelter from this storm's harsh wind."

"My people say this is the time when the sun stands still," Lino said. He grinned and nodded. He took the horse by the bridle and looked at the mare and the long, slow breaths visible in the cold morning air. Lino spat and kicked at the mix of mud and snow and then took Carlos' hand in his large, scarred dark fingers. He was duly impressed by the young man's tone and respect, as well as concerned for the poor vaquero's pale face and unkempt appearance. "My skin is my own, my friend, but my home is yours. Keep your coins and your tobacco," said Lino. "This land is lonely, and I have not spoken to a living soul from outside my village for a season."

Soon, Carlos was invited into the two-room house. Wrapped in his poncho, Carlos held his hat and slowly introduced himself to Lino's wife. The small woman's skin was scarred and wrinkled with age. Her body was hunched from life on the llano and scuttling around the small dirt-floored morada in only bare feet. Every now and then she would sigh and make light, feathery sounds, clacking her teeth as she swept her long dark hair side to side and stoked the adobe fire, preparing food for her husband and this stranger. It was there Carlos would take his meals over the next month, gathering strength and warmth; it was there he would bathe and shave in their bedroom, learn of their ceremonialism and commitment to the care of strangers. It was there the couple would mend Carlos' britches and chaps, his only two blankets kept rolled on his saddle and the one flannel shirt he kept alongside his silver dollars and bottles in his saddle bags.

Later that first night, Lino appeared from outside, from tending to the horse's needs and his own small chores, collecting wood and roots for his wife. He wore a tattered, red sweater that sagged from his wide frame. His graying hair fell in bangs down to his chin, and he pulled a long-bladed knife and cut long strips of pink meat that had been hanging over the fire and offered Carlos some to eat with his fingers. He squatted down, cross-legged with his wife and Carlos, around the cooking fire.

Carlos nervously made conversation as Lino poured dark coffee and his wife prepared bowls of rice and frijoles. "This snowstorm might last forever. I rode three days and there looks to be no end, Lino."

Lino laughed and said, "Nothing lasts long, vaquero. Only the mountain and the sky."

The woman never laughed and said, "I am not impressed by your wisdom, old man. It won't keep us warm or fed."

Lino ignored his wife, and then graciously accepted a bag of tobacco and rolling papers from his guest. He offered the young man tin mugs filled with hot coffee, to which the vaquero responded, "Thank you again for the hospitality."

Later Lino had questions: "Don't see too many folks riding horseback cross country no more. Most ride trains these days. Or drive trucks."

"Do not insult the young man, husband," the woman said. "He is our guest and traveled a great way."

Carlos smiled and tried to understand, tried to think of a response, as he smoked, but could not. He could only think to reflect and say: "Your name?"

The man grinned, and then sliced and swallowed down a large piece of lamb meat and laughed. "They call me Cocinero."

"Why's that," Carlos said.

"Because I am the Cocinero."

Carlos nodded and attempted to smile.

"At a ranch called the Cutoff they call me that. Most of the

year," the man continued. "But now I am here with you."

"I know you," Carlos said. It was then the young Carlos spoke nervously and had to reveal and recount his vivid dream and his time in the Great War overseas. How he knew the man was called Lino, the Cocinero, because of a dream.

"Perhaps we are all in a dream here together," the old man finally said as he ate and belly laughed.

AS INSTRUCTED *by his hosts, Lino and his wife, young Carlos slept in the morada, his bedding near the fire for warmth. And on this night, he was suddenly aware that there were two figures in the room. His first impulse was to jump to his feet and grab the pistola and cartridges in his saddlebag. But the men were already upon him and yet looked harmless, silent. One was dressed in a reddish-brown blanket, a serape, with his hands and large forearms crossed over his chest. His partner appeared in a rumpled dark blue version but with a tattered suit coat covering the blanket and missing all buttons. Their immense masks held faces and were adorned with beautiful animal pelts, feathers and turquoise. The larger of the two, the one in red, announced himself as a friend, and stood in a quiet respect for the vaquero Carlos. The other man in blue had no message or introduction and looked upon Carlos with impatience and disdain.*

The man in red reached forth a hand and introduced himself. "Don't be alarmed, cowboy," said the figure. "We are ghosts, but ghosts are just people and should not be feared. My partner here is old and lonesome, but he wishes you no harm or insult." The one in blue sat cross-legged with a stern outlook. "We travel in great migrations," the man continued, "through this traditional route from South America, and we have come to tell the Elders, Lino, that his morada home is right on the line we must travel as we head north. We will stop in from time to time to ask for food and water, blankets and necklaces of feathers for trade and for tribute.

If Lino's people leave, we worry there will be no one left for us to meet."

Carlos was stunned by the large glowing eyes and the long matted hair sprouting from the top of each man's head and mask. "Stay this route," the man said solemnly as he handed Carlos a beaded charm.

The next morning Carlos woke feverish, tired and thirsty, and he related the entire conversation to Lino and his wife over coffee and posole. Lino was impressed and excited that the spirits had revealed themselves to Carlos and demanded full detail.

"I do not remember their clothes or intention as much as I remember their faces, Lino. I could only tell their faces. I can only remember the darkness of their masks. I cannot or do not want to believe it was real, but when I woke this morning, the dirt floor was messed, and their immense footprints were so clear I could not deny them."

Lino recognized the two quickly as great medicine men, healers of sick and lost souls. Lino admitted to Carlos that the visitors had been the sacred Twins. "It is their duty," Lino explained, "to keep the Earth properly rotating on its axis, according to my Elders."

"They give news or warnings of the earth," the woman added.

"You have heard their messages, Carlos. You must see them through. Stay for our ceremonials."

"I am a Catholic," Carlos argued. "I pray to La Virgen. I pray only to her, Lino. I must get home. My family waits on me," Carlos said, "my father and my mother. My freedom to ride from here means more to me than religion."

"These spirits have lives of their own. Belief does not matter. You do not believe, yet they appear. What does that say of your belief, boy?"

marriage

Saturday night the viejo Carlos heard scratching at his bedroom window along with sounds of rousting chickens and the chomping of garden tomatoes. With no shirt and in only his boxer shorts, after falling out onto the grass, he stood rubbing at his patchy beard, thinking of ways to communicate with the voices. With the sunrise the wife called out, "For Christ's sake."

The old man told her, "What can you do?" The woman's bare heels stepped across the wooden porch, her presence sending the visitors away from the crawl space and then out across the property.

"Where are your clothes?" the wife scolded. "Cabrón, you have got to know health."

"Ah, woman," the old man said. "They've travelled such a long way."

Finally, the viejo and his young wife argued over his attendance at Sunday church. "I have guests," the old man argued. "I can't leave them out here all alone."

"Guests?"

"That's what I'm telling you."

"What about your God?" she said, moving from the window to the porch. She held her hands around her belly.

"What about him?"

"What voices are these with no church or God?"

He didn't mean to be rude because he valued courtesy, yet

suddenly and spontaneously, he recited The Parable of the Good Samaritan as his wife whimpered and slipped into her sister's primer-colored Invicta. "Love your neighbor as you love yourself, que no?" he cried out.

THAT MORNING Carlos' visitors rifled through the old man's tools and fishing equipment, his stack of lumber and saw legs. His tools and buckets of nails from old jobsites. They bit and tore at the metal. They bent screwdrivers and wrenches with bare hands, which made the old man shout and then laugh. He praised them.

They discovered his beer stashed under a raggedy tarp and then they made their way through his saws and collection of axes left abandoned and dusty.

"Can't work as I used to," the old man lectured. "As I once did. When yous first found me." And then, before they removed the leather guards and the littler ones touched at the saw blades naively, "A man'll bleed like a pig!"

The strange crew sat unhappy and drank and slept most of that first afternoon before they borrowed the old man's 29 Model A and before they removed the engine and liquid coolant with the newfound tools. Even to the viejo this seemed excessive until the crew rebuilt the greased monster.

Afterwards they moved through the wife's garden, digging into her cucumbers and peppers. They moved up and down the rows of vegetables pulling at leaves and then more aggressively at roots. Many took bites of under-ripe buds of corn spitting the waste into the air and at the old man's feet.

"Those are too green to have any taste," he taught them.

They resigned to the house while the old man's back was turned. Even more of the visitors and voices had entered and soon they had the cushions of the sitting room couch ripped and clawed and spread in thick layers around the entire house and floor, while in the bathroom a few went through the wife's seashell soaps and towels, the good towels picked up on the old man and woman's wedding day gifted from her people in New Mexico.

They clomped over wooden floors and went through the wife's closet and tried on all of her costume jewelry; they pocketed most of the actual gold and silver. The viejo arrived to watch them dance around in the wife's best shoes and long winter coat. It took three of them to fit inside and re-create the wife's height and weight. The little ones stood on the bigger ones' shoulders and pursed their lips, rolling on thick layers of lipstick. They tossed around the woman's wigs and scarves.

"Yes, I remember when she used to 'dress to kill', as they used to call it," he told them.

"Yes, yes, yes," they finally whispered to the old man, mocking what they'd heard from the radio before taking the contraption apart and spreading the components across the bathroom floor. They poured the man drinks, and the younger creatures sat in his kitchen and pulled the food from the refrigerator and the icebox. They poured the ice on the tabletop and opened each and every can from the cabinets. One even poured milk onto countertops. They guzzled cans of soup and their digits flipped the garbage cans near the door and examined each piece of the contents.

In the bedroom they found the old man's best suit and also the wife's wedding dress and they couldn't resist trying them. They stood side-by-side and stared into the wife's dressing mirrors. A smile crept onto the old man's face, and he prompted them to hold hands and then to kiss and to dance. "At my wedding I danced and hollered," the old man announced. "That's what you do. You just don't fuck a woman in a room. You take her before God and prove your love. You build a home."

Hands pulled picture frames from the walls and wanted to understand the old man's story. They were told a few details.

They knew about the love of baseball and the work in the Army and serving near Los Alamos in New Mexico. They knew about the man's several visitations and his connections to the government and later Oregon work camps. The months and months of axe strikes and sweat as he learned his trade. They brought more pictures to the man, ones he'd forgotten and put down into shoeboxes hidden away.

"What can I tell you about who I used to be or what I've seen?" the old man confided in his guests. "All I've known is work and calluses."

Finally, they lit cigars and tamped the old man's pipe and all settled on the porch for a smoke. Towards lunchtime they fried an immense pan of onions and bacon. They listened to his drunken stories and accepted his elder advice. They offered to drive him what may have well been miles and miles down the valley highway, and in minutes they were flying past red brake lights and yellow warning lights.

THAT EVENING old man Carlos drained beers and rum and RC Cola down at SLV Bowl, just outside of Hooper, Colorado. Under his finest grey Stetson, he drank with his visitors to be friendly and then also to be agreeable, then to learn more about man's mistaken victory over nature after splitting the atom, most things Carlos could never understand. And then later while the young voices lectured and then threw spares and slapped hands, the old man drank over his young wife's habits, and he drank over his lack of dollar bills. Finally, he got the idea again to drink to be free from the voices.

Out on the highway, after all the dollar bills had been spent, the passing headlights burned at the crew's eyes and filled the cab of the truckito with strange shadows. The night skies along the empty llano reminded Carlos of dark grey, snowy roads, though the heat rose off the two-lane flat top. Headlights pinched between passing cars, when his engine, like his own breathing, coughed and hiccupped and then recovered before finally dying.

In its middle age the truckito failed him despite being recently reconstructed, just some dirt in the fuel line or maybe his visitors had miscalculated the level of gasoline, maybe a short circuit with the battery or distributor points, maybe the plug connections. "Something you all can cure?" he felt compelled to yell out. But turning off the lights and trying at the starter again and again brought no result, and he waited for the smell of gasoline from the flooded carburetor. That was when the hood's flames licked upwards.

Eventually he opened the truckito up to the night and let himself out onto the sand and chipped gravel where the warm air surprised and dizzied him. The headache seemed to radiate out through his jaw to the ends of the hair on his chin, so he cursed the night and cursed the visitors and good Samaritans and their damned opposition in the universe. He watched headlights passing and his eyes stung with water and ached in the harsh luminescence.

Seeking assistance, he searched for and found his semi-automatic pistola and cartridges, waving the gun at passing cars with no luck, and then he paced and walked up the road. Soon there was no sign of life around him. Back at his truckito, he lifted his hood and searched for wires and connection amongst the red-hot flames. He held the metal weapon in his armpit as he worked.

Who'n the hell are you? he thought into the black emptiness around him. Not a busted coil or a distributor, he thought. Who'n the hell are you to come to me like this? To leave me alone to all of this world? Go ahead and burn me to death!

He pulled and leaned on the fender. He kicked at the gravel and then unlaced his stained boots and then freed his aching feet. He sat back down in the driver's seat and switched on the headlights to see what they revealed on the empty shoulder. Even in his drunkenness he knew the highway as the lifeblood of the valley. Soon a compadre or a farm worker would be passing by and stop to give a push or a tow.

That was when the voices crept further in, and the flames touched him. He felt the heat on his face and along the seams of his pants. The sparks gave him gooseflesh he hadn't experienced since he was a small boy in New Mexico. The Blanca Massif, the great mountain to the east, loomed above him as the flames came from under the dash and as he pulled himself free. He struggled to his feet and then struggled for air to breathe. His legs ached and his bare feet burned beneath him.

The bright burst of his weapon flashed in the night sky. He emptied the weapon and staggered and then fell to one knee. Lungs filling with the smoke and ash, the old man coughed and gagged, nearly vanishing into smoke and fire.

WHEN THE SHERIFF dropped him off on Franklin Street, the young wife Felipa bathed him and then kept the sickly man on a cot bed pulled close to the wood stove. She covered him with a quilt, and as he breathed deeply, she wiped at his forehead and at his cheeks. His grey-whiskered cheeks seemed sunken, and the man looked so far from their first car ride and from the first weeks of marriage.

"Has he woken at all?" Felipa's straight-faced sister said, when she entered and found the two in the kitchen.

"No."

"Where'd they find the viejo?"

"Out on the highway. Passed out with no clothes."

Felipa moved away from the stove and her feet ached from standing over the man. She looked and could tell he was helpless in his fever and in his sickness. "I'm relieved you came, sister," she finally answered.

The sister asked, "Should we drive him somewhere? For his burns? The hospital in Alamosa?" She watched Felipa's expressions closely. "In this damned valley you're miles from the world. How long are you gonna stay with this cabrón?"

"Shush, sister!"

The man's sleeping breath and snores filled the small, overly warm kitchen.

"I don't care. The drunk of a man. I could care less," she answered. "He don't worry about you when he's out drinking half the night. I don't see him care. Destroying your home and your possessions. Now I know how you've been living. Now I know."

"Don't worry, sister," Felipa said. "He's my husband. What can I do?"

"But your clothes, sister."

"Don't worry, I said."

"He should've killed himself out on that damned highway. He's twice the fool of a cabrón than what you told me."

And as the two women drank tea and watched the sleeping viejo, Felipa admitted what the County Sheriff told her, the story of his nakedness, drunken stories about gunfire and burning stars. When Carlos finally woke, Felipa warned her sister not to speak of the bastard child, her own alien life, she had found to be growing inside of her.

poca loca

Felipa's oldest sister stepped into the kitchen on the old house on Franklin Street after travelling three-and-a-half hours in her powder-blue Buick Invicta. She found Felipa crying and scraping dinner plates and the husband Carlos yawning and draining coffee alongside her in the kitchen.

"They pushed me down into the car wearing just my house-coat to run me off from the neighborhood," Felipa informed her sister. "I had no idea the nun—Sister Giordine, remember they called her?—had turned on me and had me sent away."

The story was that the girls' father Gilberto had driven Felipa down to Our Lady of Guadalupe Parrish Hall for a disciplinary meeting. The led to the separating of the sisters for years and years until that very night's conversation and reunion under Carlos' roof.

"*Felipa?* they called at me over and over," Felipa explained as she sat and held her long lost sister's hand. "They had me at the rectory and questioned me: *Why did you scream at the Father and your Sister Mother? Why don't you respect the class and lessons? Why do you run around with boys and flirt with the Father? Have you had relations with boys? How many boys? Why do you sit quiet now when you yelled and screamed for attention then? Was it all just for attention? Do you do all this for the attention?*"

"Oh my god, Felipa," the sister said.

"I heard the Father or the Sister Mother saying they were taking me to a home for girls, sister."

"That was the longest and hottest summer of my life, Felipa," the sister said. "I missed you so! Were you terrified, my sister?"

"I pulled my hair and hurt myself in the girl's room in the stall where they found me bleeding," she explained. "I hid from them but of course they found me out and dragged me. They said I had to get right with the Lord. The Sister Mother gave me tea but the Father was so stern and questioned me over and over. *Why do you do such things?* he asked me."

Felipa explained how that Saturday had begun with the girls' mother walking the floor. Her husband Gilberto was not at home, so she dressed at first light of Sunday morning, leaving Felipa and her sister alone and behind. But the thin wisp of a girl Felipa could not asleep and followed her mother, who was at the door and then the porch by the time the girl screamed for her mother. Then the mother ordered the daughter to settle into bed. She put her hands on the girl, pushing and cursing at her to return. It was the night the family finally splintered into nothing.

"*Mama! Mama!* I yelled over and over. *Why are you leaving?*" Felipa explained. She boiled water for tea and told the dramatic story as she set the table and scraped crumbs into her hand. "Mama was up all night with no sleep and tears. She lost track of her husband and was losing her mind, I think."

"It was Joey Munoz, Felipa," the sister said. "The crewcutted Joey Munoz told the whole group at Sunday Mass and then Sunday school, and it was Joey who told each and every boy and girl but most importantly he told Evo Moralez and the cruel Ethan and Oralia Montes. They are the ones who told on you."

"They teased me and hurt me so," Felipa explained. "*What's the matter with your mother? they asked me. Was she abandoning you? Was she drunk? What is wrong with your mother? Does your father touch you? Does he beat you? What can we do to resolve all this?* the father repeated until it meant nothing to me, sister. That's when they sent me away, sister. From my home and my people. They sent me to Ridge Home. They left me alone and I never heard or spoke to yous or anyone from home. I thought yous had disowned me. Had sent me away to rot."

LATER THAT NIGHT as the bare-chested Carlos woke to take his sledgehammer and axe to the southernmost wall to add a second bedroom, Felipa sat and explained Ridge Home.

"Rusty old beds and furniture was all they had," Felipa explained in between Carlos' crashing blows. "Damned Godforsaken place and folks. Like a Hell on earth, sister."

"Ridge Home found you for me," the sister interrupted as she raised her voice slightly to compete with Carlos' sweaty work. "They told me where to look for you and that you married, Felipa. They had an address for me."

"They asked me if I was on marijuana. They asked me if I understood what was happening to me. The doctors asked me things and talked to me for days and days, sister. They had leather in my mouth and wires to my head, sister."

Slowly and steadily the kitchen filled with dust and broken boards. "Oh, my poor sister! the sister cried. "What is this man doing to you, poor Felipa! My poor sister!"

"The woman assigned to me, the gringa I called her, her name was Mary and she told me I was beautiful and that my name was beautiful and she saved me," Felipa continued, ignoring the chaos and noise, the dust flying and billowing around the doorway. "She took care over me and felt pity for me, sister. She explained to me my parents had gone and were not coming. She explained to me I was to rest and I was to follow the rules. I was to always do as I was told."

"Did they feed and clothe you, Felipa?" the sister asked though she was growing more and more concerned with Carlos' grunts and smashes.

"I had my night clothes in a paper sack, a hairbrush, two

dresses and mama's robe," Felipa added calmly.

"What did you tell them?"

"I couldn't talk, sister. I could only sleep for days and days. I am telling you I couldn't talk and couldn't respond. I just sat and listened to the hallways and the slamming doors and wheelchair wheels. Girls crying and wailing on half the night. They told me I was in the city of the sick."

"I can't hear you, Felipa," the sister said. "This man of yours is demolishing the whole damned house around us! What did you say?"

"I say, the girls standing and doing nothing, smoking cigarettes and staring out the windows, all told me the same. The same thing."

"Oh, Felipa!"

"Welcome to the city of the sick," Felipa repeated to the sounds of hammer cracking and slamming at brickwork.

no horses kept in town

Carlos would escape the house at dawn leaving pregnant Felipa to wait for him in the kitchen with her shoes off and breakfast dishes rotting. The city had recently threatened shutting the electricity and so she worried she would have no light for her magazine reading other than a few candles and an old kerosene lamp.

She would wait for Carlos while he tended to his mare Carmelita, and today, on the morning after deciding she would tell her husband of two years that she would not wait for him any longer, she was still waiting. She made a gesture of impatience as he laced his boots and buttoned up his flannel shirt. She fixed her worried eyes on the apples he bought for Carmelita and wrapped in handkerchiefs that he kept in his coveralls, but he did not speak or pay much attention.

"No one keeps horses in town no more," she announced. "The neighbors and the women down the street all speak of it as a disgrace."

He wiped at the knees of his work coveralls and at the lap where the material was worn from use. "Did you hear? No one keeps horses in this county, viejo," she repeated.

"Listen to me, mujer. When I was training for the war in Fort Riley, Kansas—"

"That's when you were a boy. Hundreds of years ago."

"I swear, this woman. Talks to us like we're damned dogs. I produce."

"You 'produce'?"

"I produce. I bring electricity into this house," the old man said, flipping switches on the wall of the kitchen. "If it weren't for me, this woman would starve."

"Shush, old man, my sister will hear you. She's sleeping."

"This woman wants me to feed and house all of her people. I bring home the money for her food and for her clothes. I produce."

"Shush, cabrón. Sister will hear."

"If they don't want to hear they shouldn't listen. I produce! I produce!"

"She'll live here as long as I live here, cabrón. Look around at what you 'produce'. One sickly mare and one tiny house. That's what you produce."

"The Montoyas and my whole family kept horses. My people down through the generations. This woman never understands—"

"Women laugh at me," Felipa said.

"Who? What women laugh?"

"At Solo's Market."

"Solo's?"

"When I cash your check. They laugh at me. Tell me to buy oats and grain for my husband. They laugh at your horse, cabrón. They laugh at you. They laugh at me for marrying such a cabrón fool-of-an-old man."

"This woman should pay no attention to people. When I was a boy in Costilla, New Mexico—"

"Ay, here we go. This ain't New Mexico, old man. And I ain't your mama."

"She would do her sweeping and have everything all bueno when the men arrived. She cooked and cleaned for the vaqueros and that was her life. She knew her place."

"This ain't New Mexico. And this ain't my life. I don't want to be laughed at. And I know I ain't your mama. Oh, Mary Mother of God," Felipa sighed. "Help me with this Goddamned horse man."

"WHAT CAN YOU DO, Sister?" Felipa spat to her sister over tea and the newspaper. I tell you this man cares more for his horse and his ranchero friends than his own home or family."

"Who keeps a horse in town anyway?" she continued. "You know, when I met him he had that big black Cadillac. And he was wearing a new suit and off to the dances in San Luis. His friends were in the car and they were all musicians. Guitaristas, mariachis style, you know. He had gold jewelry. For Christ sake, a gold watch."

"Gold?"

"Yeah. And he was all combed and washed and lotioned. Guapo. And now I can't get him to shake out his pants or change that same flannel shirt once a week."

"I know, huh."

"He came with his cousins and took us out. Out dancing. He bought me dinner in a restaurant and we drank cocktails. We danced. Oh, sister, I haven't danced in so long. A real dance. With real music. Not that pinche jukebox at the bar and grill he takes me to with those borachones—those losers he hangs out with. Those losers. Rancheros with their clothes all ripped. Not one of them is married. Most of them live with their mothers. Their mothers! Like little boys. And you know what he did with that gold watch?"

"He still got it?"

"Hocked it for a damned saddle."

"Oh my god, Felipa."

"He didn't hock it for a ring or nothing like that. Not even a radio. No, for a saddle and some oats. And the car was borrowed. The cabrón. You're not married, Sister. You don't know."

—

WHEN FELIPA finally arranged to sell the mare and saddle to Pifanio's dark-haired and green-eyed son, Pifanio's favorite son, the bare-footed boy took the reins of the mare and threw his leg over with a kick. He'd been waiting for weeks and hours to ride. His lips widened and then he nearly let himself giggle as the mount kicked and strode away from Pifanio and the fieldwork the father demanded. Carlos stood and told the boy and his father the horse needed brushing and grain, and so the boy bit at his lip and clipped onions until twilight. And after a day's work the boy's nervous energy rivaled the horse's, and the boy lurched with each powerful jump and nearly uncontrollably for hundreds of yards. It was the first time, in that moment with the boy, that Carlos had thought about the loss. When the boy finally thought to turn and check, old man Carlos stood with Pifanio and wiped at his forehead and at his neck. The old man's face was small and worrisome. And the boy's face glowed for the horse and the horizon ahead.

six-armed cross

When the tires of Carlos' delivery truck crunched to a stop near the six-armed cross at La Garita, the dark-haired altar boy stood where the headlights pinched between three-foot high plowed snow and the dark walls of fence line.

He sat and stared up into the hills to the distant peaks of the Sangre De Cristo Mountain line where the Utes and Comanche had a lookout hundreds of years before, according to his father. It was so cold and the only view was the church and the six armed cross, the two additional horizontal arms giving a complete cross no matter the side of the church, one arm extending toward the hazy hills and mountain passes beyond Saguache, another pointing across to the church's snow-covered picket fence to the cemetery and the mountains.

He waited and let the flooded carburetor rest and then tried again and again. Nothing. Eventually he opened the door and stepped out onto the packed snow. He exited the cab and opened the hood before lowering it to seek help from the altar boy. Just a little moco, the old man sighed to himself. The boy set his lantern onto the cleared entranceway of the church, and between the upturned collar of his flannel shirt and his denim work pants, the boy and the old man were unlikely mirror images. The boy's eyes were enormous and youthful. The old man could only stare and almost smiled as the boy foolishly held the lantern high and tripped over uneven ice and snow underneath his dirtied cowboy boots.

The boy swallowed and wiped at the newly wet and slick top of his head and then at his nose. "The men left me," the boy insisted.

"Your father?" the old man repeated. "Your father have a telephone?"

"No, sir."

"Where's the next home?"

"My Tia Jordine. Two miles, I think. They come on horseback."

THE OLD MAN stopped answering and talking because the man couldn't hear and because for minutes at a time Carlos and the boy were sitting on hardwood floors in Costilla, New Mexico, in 1910 before statehood and before Pancho Villa ever raided, arguing with Carlos' own Jefe and Jefita.

"Don't be a lost soul in this world, mi hijo," the Jefita would tell her boy. "A man needs knowledge and religion."

On the first day of his Catholic schooling, as he stood in white collared shirt and corduroy pants that was the uniform for boys, his Jefe sat in his chair and laughed.

"You should be in coveralls, boy," the Jefe remarked. He had his cigarillo burning in his ashtray.

Carlos as a boy never complained despite the teasing but he had to endure the days and days of silence from the man. It was in those days that Carlos perhaps learned to drift further and further into himself. At least until the day he dressed and walked to the door.

"When was the last time you worked out back, boy?" the Jefe said.

"Leave him be," the Jefita answered.

"I'm not talking to you, mujer. I'm talking to the boy," the Jefe said as he dropped his paper. "I'm asking you, boy. When was the last time you worked out back? When have you walked down to the river and cleared the wood I asked you to clear. When was the last time?"

"I have school, Jefe. I can clean down there afterwards. After I walk home."

"Oh, you mean when you want to do it, boy," the Jefe said. "I'm talking about when I want it to be done. I'm talking about what I want, boy."

Then the Jefe slapped at the boy's chin and mouth, more pushing the boy onto the heels of his church shoes and clothes.

"You know the boy has to get to school, Jefe. Doesn't he look like he's headed for the nuns?"

"Dammit, mujer. I'm not talking to you," the Jefe said. "Don't you start getting forgetful on me, boy. I'm telling you to get out there and do your chores. You want to eat? Then you work."

The boy looked at his mother and his eyes played a confused game for a long second.

"Don't play dumb with me, boy."

"I'll clear your wood, Jefe," the mother said with a tone of finality, hoping to appease the man and change the subject.

The Jefe laughed, cackling and hacking at his cigarillo and then he flicked his ash onto the wooden floor.

"Go, Carlos. Go," the Jefita said, and it all sent the boy into a trot out the door. He ran down the street past the Jefe's truckito and past Ketchum Road and then he laughed and ran on.

THE BOYS' study room at St Joseph's Church where the dirt was blessed had a corner window that overlooked a yard, and beyond that a sunken lane between snow-covered pine and spruce trees out to a low stone wall that surrounded the place. Beyond the school's wall, above the trees and narrow gates where the llano opened up leading to the horizon, Carlos could see the mountains between road and sky with a band of brown road.

Writing and working every morning with his books and

longhand lessons the boy would glance up and read the notices posted along the wall as well. The duties for altar boys were simple and he read them between his breaths alongside his friend and cousin Benito Martinez. We could do this easy, Benny whispered after mouthing gun rifle and car engine sounds.

The rules for Altar Boys typed and posted in Spanish were to be memorized:

1. *No unnecessary talking during services.*
2. *No eating or drinking permitted in the Altar.*
3. *Always wear collared shirt and neck tie and dress shoes.*
4. *Walking behind the Altar should be kept to a minimum.*
5. *No Altar boys in the vestry at any time. All boys must stand at the front of the Altar or in front of the chairs.*
6. *Before leaving the Altar at any time the boy must ask the Father for permission and his blessing.*
7. *Accept your assignment without complaint.*
8. *No pushing, fighting or clowning around accepted at any time.*
9. *Be on time.*
10. *When offering or receiving something from the Priest, always kiss his right hand.*
11. *When you vest, ask Father to bless your belt before putting it on.*
12. *If you must be absent, please contact Father ahead of time so a replacement can be found.*
13. *Our meetings will be held 3 times a month. Times to be announced in the Sunday Bulletin.*
14. *All Altar boys must register and participate in Sunday School.*

CARLOS STOPPED his work and his writing to speculate on what his mother might say as she sat in Sunday Mass listening to Father John's words and before she received the Communion. How proud she would be to see her boy there assisting the Father. Carlos didn't think of the work or the time before and after mass; he only thought of how his Jefita would approve.

"We can get to the wine, Carlos," Benito whispered before being shushed and cracked by Sister Manuela.

CARLOS HAD BEEN working as altar boy hardly a week before he found himself putting on his jacket before Mass and going out to join Benito. "Good morning, Señor Montoya," Benny said playfully, sharing his chew. The other boys acknowledged Carlos with a nod and sometimes a handshake.

He knew Benito's vice from mass to mass just by glimpsing him. Loose-leaf tobacco from Red Man and sometimes plug, whatever Benny stole from his old man. Sometimes Benito even had his old man's pipe and sometimes, if they were lucky, they rolled their own cigarettes.

Benito put his hand on Carlos' shoulder and bent backward to look up into the canvas blue sky above. "And good morning to you, my Lord."

The boys stared and said nothing and then shared chew. As Carlos glanced at the thin Valdez kid, Benito met the kid's eyes coldly and then with almost contempt.

"I'm tired of sharing with you, kid," Benny said. "You never share nothing with me or with my compadre Carlos here."

The kid shook his head and regarded him with humor.

"I gave you something to smoke last week, Benny," the thin Valdez boy said. "I seen you last week and gave you some. You member?"

"The sun's so warm out here and probably twice as warm for liars, no? What say you, Carlos?"

"I don't remember him giving you nothing, Benito."

"See," Benito said. "See. You see. We all know how you are, kid."

Benito was short and stocky but all the boys knew he could

hold his own. And he could care less about the danger of smoking behind the Rectory. It was dangerous but Father John smoked and the smell was in the air.

"Father John!" one of the boys yelled.

Whenever he caught them, he would light up a cigarillo of his own and then he would send them home to their parents. The first time Carlos chewed he kept it in his mouth before the second service and then after the third service he put a larger piece in his mouth. As he walked home he felt light-headed and dizzy, unstable and reached for the side of buildings to balance himself. Benito could only laugh. Carlos was amazed how fast the chew affected his body. He found the old woman Rodriguez' flowerbed just blocks from home and he fertilized them for minute after minute. Then the chew hit his stomach and he had to run to get to the outhouse. Benito teased Carlos for weeks after that. He never let Carlos forget and it turned into a point of pride for Carlos, who chewed more and more after that. He promised himself he would never be made fun of like that again, so he stole his old man's chew and cigarillos and tobacco or whatever the old man kept in his bureau. Father John laughed when they told him and then came out once in a while to watch over the boys. The boys each respected and trusted Father John for that.

"You're lucky, boys," Father John said in English, observing the boys quietly. The only times the boys ever spoke English was in church and in school. "You lucky it's me and not Sister Manuela, Benito. I hope you not doing anything other than chewing, boys."

THE BOY'S FACE was thin and anxious. "Señor?"

The old man stepped inside to the empty church and looked out over the stained wood of old pews and slouched into the last seat aware of his helplessness. His feet ached and his thin legs shivered. “How far you say to the next home?”

“Two miles. At least.”

“You got people there? If I walked down is there anyone to let me in?”

“I could go.”

“Someone older? A brother or a tio?”

“I could bring a horse. I can walk.”

The old man thought of sitting in this warm place as the boy waded into the blowing cold and drifts. And the boy had intelligent eyes, the old man thought. So, the old man watched the boy with interest. “How old are you?”

“Ten years old.”

“You a strong one?”

“Yes, sir.”

“Crazy not to have phone wires out here, no?”

The boy shrugged.

The old man suddenly remembered his father riding and plowing. The strength he once had and how he worked until his father had to yell out from the truckito. Once he himself had been the boy wanting the responsibility away from the village of his Jefe; he wondered if the boy found himself out all alone at night away from his family and responsibility only to find much more.

“You shouldn’t walk,” the old man said. “Too damn cold out there.”

“I can walk,” the boy answered.

“Yes, I am sure you can, boy. Maybe you should get me a tarp or a blanket,” the old man ordered from his resting place. “I need to cover my load of wood and tools. You can help me with that.”

Pulling a wool hat from his pocket over his disheveled head, the boy slipped out the door to find a cover for the old man’s tools and protection from the newly falling heavy snow. The old man sat alone for minutes and stared into the immense height of the church and straight into the estandarte. He felt weak and raised his eyelids to fully comprehend his surroundings. He contemplated the unfamiliar figure of Christ and the Virgin across from him. The place smelled of moldy wood and wood polish, supplies from the wood box and the smell of what he assumed was newly painted walls. The room had no windows and the room despite being warm gave the old man chills. He considered the night outside, the snowfields and the dead truckito and his night soon to be filled with chill and aches and a walk among the cutback under the crumbling overhand of cold frozen trees. He sat bemused with the ways a man can push himself into curious and complex nights such as this.

And when he heard the creak of the door again, he buttoned himself tighter into his coat and pulled his hat tightly down over his head and then wrapped his shoulder with the boy's buffalo blanket and then slowly stepped to the yard. And for a moment the old man and the boy faced each other in the trampled and broken snow. The old man took the boy's hand into his grip and said, "I'll go, boy. Stay with your church."

"Are you sure you can make it, Señor?"

ONE SUNDAY MORNING Father John became aware of another kind of disruption. One of the boys had apparently been into the Sacrament Wine. Whoever had done it must have watered it down, though Father John never saw anyone do so and must have noticed rather quickly. All he saw was those boys smoking and Carlos and Benito completing their chores. All he really heard was some uproar from some of the parishioners, Mrs. Quintana and Mrs. Deherrera. Mr. Palmer's teeth were on edge, and he complained as well, and Father John almost called the boys in immediately. In fact, all he heard for two whole days after Sunday Masses was the uproar. On impulse he slipped on his coat and headed down to Carlos' home, down across the lane and up the other side of the neighborhood. He walked the unpaved and narrow roads and found the Montoya home quiet and lifeless. The front door was open, and the doorway revealed Carlos' Jefe. His cheeks flushed red as he put out his cigarillo. He looked as if he hadn't slept and had a blankness that comes from a man tired and fatigued from work. He took his bottle off the chair next to him before standing to approach the door.

"Hello," the Jefe said in a sad and bashful fashion. "Por favor, siéntese, señor."

"Thank you," Father John said. He let himself in and then sat down into the slanting wooden chair and adjusted his jacket and pants. "It is a good evening, Sir," he said warmly. "Quiet and beautiful."

The Jefe's neck jerked into a curious pose. His throaty laughter was low and restrained.

"I came to talk about your boy Carlos," Father John said.

After a moment, Carlos entered to translate for his father who only spoke Spanish. Carlos' hands shook. Father John noticed the boy's lips were chapped and bloodied. As if he had been slapped repeatedly.

"I should think you are proud of your boy and his studies," Father John said and after a quick translation the Jefe nodded and smiled.

One of the Jefe's eyebrows bent, and he shot the boy a sideways look.

"He wants to know why you came out here today, Father? What'd I do?"

"I think you know why I am here, Carlos?" Father John asked, slightly annoyed at the question.

"No, Father. What?"

"What has the boy done?" the Jefe repeated in Spanish.

The Father leaned on the arm of his chair and said, "Tell your father I know you've been drinking as well as smoking."

The Jefe looked at the two quizzically. "What is this all

about?" he repeated with authority.

"Tell him, Carlos," Father John said. "How long has this been going on, Carlos?"

"What the hell is this?" the Jefe said, thinking of his words and regretting not having the words in English to respond or understand. He felt small and ignorant and then he felt angered and annoyed as well. He yelled at Carlos and then also the whiskey in his system caused him to yell at the Father. His booming voice filled the small house and at once frightened Carlos and also Father John.

"Mr. Montoya, there is no need for any of this," Father John said, immediately regretting coming over and not calling the family down to the rectory. And for a moment Father John's eyes were fixed on the Jefe's and he believed the man might strike him or the boy after the Jefe rose with a nervous snap and paced the small length of the area rug. "Perhaps I shouldn't have come, Carlos."

"I haven't done nothing," Carlos said. "Everything is Benito. Benito does everything."

"What has he done, son?" Father John asked. It was obvious to him Mr. Montoya had been drinking and his eyes revealed it all with the redness and whiteness.

"Goddamn it, boy!" the Jefe said. "What in the hell are you talking about? Are you getting your ass removed from the school or no? Dammit, Carlos?"

The boy's chapped lip was shaking uncontrollable. He turned his slightly wet eyes to the Father.

"My Lord," Father John said. "Carlos. Tell your father I am only here to wish you well. Tell him, Carlos. Tell him now." Then Father John stood and extended his hand out for the Jefe and the Jefe stood indecisive and confused. "For heaven's sake tell him, Carlos."

For a moment they all stood and talked over one another until Carlos' mother entered and stood in the doorway from the kitchen with her mouth wide open and a dishrag held loosely in her hand.

"Ah, Carlos," Father John said. "This must be your mother."

By the time the whole mess had been diffused and the Jefita had distributed glasses of water and iced tea, the Jefe was firm in his decision to take his boy out of school in favor of working in the campos alongside Carlos' older brothers.

OLD MAN CARLOS climbed over the first fence with a long groan and then pulled the blanket tightly around himself. Then he rested his hands familiarly onto the boy's shoulder as thank you. "Keep yourself warm," he told the boy. "Get inside."

"I should go. I should be walking for you," the boy whined and nearly cried.

It had been years since the old man had felt the steam from his breath surprise him and then he could not help but to smile. The anxiety and cold of his body for a short time quieted. Nearly fifty years ago he had dreamed of riding into nights like this. And for a second, he was frozen in his thoughts and memories and then he slapped his legs for warmth. As he slid onto the road the old man moved into a trot and the icy flow of air and snow smashed at his face and eyes. The old man looked to the boy as he walked for the unknown village ahead.

market

The bank was open when the voices had Carlos driving himself over. He had the worksite dog in the passenger seat, which went out the window as soon as he pulled to the curb. Carlos yelled for the dog and chased her into the bed of the truckito as he entered the place.

"I lost my work so I come down here to talk about this letter you people sent," Carlos said, sitting down hard at the branch manager Gil Solis' desk.

"That right?" Gil's voice strained, as it was clear Carlos, whom he had met many times in the office of downtown Monte Vista, Colorado, had been drinking and was, in fact, quite drunk. Short and trim with his thin moustache and his thin combed-over hair line, Gil's fresh face now had a look of concentration. "Can't have you quitting work. We could've handled this over the phone though, sir."

"I didn't quit," Carlos said. "I said I lost it. Look what you guys have done to me. You know how much money I have out on my mortgage and on my land. I can only spend a dollar a week because of your Goddamn bank. No money for nothing."

"We could've handled this over the phone, sir."

"I don't have the money for no phone."

"Yes, sir," Gil said. "How can I help you today, Mr. Montoya?"

"You should do something to help me?"

"Well, yes, sir. What can I do?"

"I should have gone to a lawyer."

"Sir, do you have the letter from your lender?"

Carlos dug thoughtfully between his coveralls and his flannel shirt where he had his important papers collected. He hummed aimlessly and searched for the official letter. He coughed. "You plan all of this?" he said.

"What's that, Mr. Montoya?"

"Here's your Goddamn paper."

"Take it easy. Let's just take a look at your paperwork and get through this."

"Damned papers," Carlos said. "Who owns this damn place anyway?"

"Robert Corson is the bank manager, Mr. Montoya. Do you want to wait for him to speak with? He won't be in today."

"No way to run no kind of business."

Gil's hands became nervous as he took the letter from his aged customer and then he slowly read. He slipped deeper into the chair.

"I should think you would bless your life, having a nice office to work in every day," Carlos snorted.

One of Gil's eyebrows bent and then he shot Carlos a sideward look. "No need to be cross, sir. I'm trying to take care of you. I ask that you please have a bit of patience with me."

Carlos leaned on the arm of Gil's modern office furniture and gave the man a quizzical look. "How long have you been stealing from the working men of this valley?"

"Excuse me, Mr. Montoya?"

"You heard me. I said how long you been stealing?"

"Do you mean how long have I been with the bank? If that's what you mean I have been with the bank going on two years. I've spoken before to you and your wife."

"That's a long time to be stealing," Carlos answered. He thought of the last two years of his life and his marriage to Felipa and how they'd survived with one another. Three years would be too much, he thought.

"Mr. Montoya, this here is a notice of foreclosure on your property. This looks like a third notice from our parent company in Denver. They warn of a lien on your work wages and your government benefits if payment is not given within 90 days of receipt of this letter."

"See what I mean," Carlos said, the nerves growing in the sound of his voice. "Stealing. Two years of spirits stealing my soul."

The man behind the desk was quick to laugh: "Your soul?"

"You laughing at me?"

"Sir. My advice to you is to submit a payment today or as soon as possible to show the company you are working and trying to pay off this note."

"Are you saying I do not work?"

"Sir. Mr. Montoya."

"You're a Goddamn fat cat of a spirit."

"These outbursts do not help the situation."

It was then that the security guard came up behind Carlos and made eye contact with Gil.

"I've changed my mind," Carlos announced after a long pause. "I don't want nothing more to do with this pinche bank. You hear me? If you have something to tell me you come to my home and talk to me like a man. You don't send me registered letters and give me this shit. Who in the hell do you think you are to come at me like this?"

The guard started his job, led the old man to the door, and Carlos was still arguing and talking as he was nearly lifted off of his heels. It wasn't until he stood in the sun under the hanging sign out front that read "Rio Grande County Bank" that he screamed and wailed. He cursed and focused. Then he unsnapped his wallet and pulled a wadded bill and held it vaguely in his hand. He walked to the truckito and swigged from his bottle behind the long bench seat. He looked up the street past the rows of parked truckitos and new model Chevys. He settled himself near the sideboard and swigged. He laid the money down at his feet, unzipped his coverall and let fly a stream of blood-stained piss. "Goddamn pinche bank."

ON A DRUNKEN IMPULSE Carlos threw on his jacket and drove out across town from the bank past the construction work on the old highway and then picked up his young wife Felipa. Where the dog had lain in the passenger seat, he swept dirt and dog hair quickly with his hand.

Felipa walked out to the truckito and lifted her head and smiled softly at her husband. Her cheeks were painted, and her clothes were clean and fresh though her eyes looked as if she hadn't slept. She held her pregnant belly and as she lifted herself into the cab Carlos stared with a drunken blankness and then pulled a pack of cigarettes from the case next to him.

"Good evening," Carlos said. "Have yourself a seat, my dear."

"Thank you," Felipa answered. "I didn't know you'd be home so early. We have to get to the market."

Carlos laughed and wiped at his neck and freed a cigarette and a match from his coverall pocket.

"That damned dog," Felipa said. She wiped at the dog hair clinging to her skirt and her nylons.

"She has to know I can't leave the dog," Carlos said. "Someone has to take care of the thing. And he don't want to be without me."

Felipa wiped her hair behind her ears. To Carlos her face looked tired and nervous.

"Think of them dogs out at the worksite with no people to give them food or nothing," Carlos said.

"It's not your worksite," Felipa said. "This house is your responsibility. And there's a baby on the way no matter your feeling on the matter or not so you have to make sure there's food in the house now that I'm down and out, old man. I checked the icebox and all we got is your damned beers. You gotta take care of these things. Not be messing with no dogs."

"I wasn't messing with dogs, mujer. I was out at the bank taking care of business."

"What kind of business?"

"I took care of it so I don't want to hear nothing about it."

"Was it about that registered letter? I know it was about that letter. We're losing the land, aren't we? I knew it. My sister told me but I didn't want to believe."

"Goddamn it, mujer. I haven't even started the engine and I already want to drop you somewhere."

After a short time Carlos sat sweating and tired from listening to Felipa's list and wants for the trip and the pregnancy. He nodded and almost laughed out loud at her mad blathering of words and orders.

"Back is so sore," Felipa continued.

"Call the sister," Carlos answered at the end of the ride to town. He sharpened his mouth and eyes. "Have her come and help."

"She went to Denver for work."

"Call her."

At the parking lot across from the grocery, Carlos made the brakes cry and then he jumped from the seat. He looked for Pifanio or his Compadres from work before he helped Felipa from her seat. He looked fretful and tired.

"Are you coming in?" Felipa asked. "You have to come."

Carlos raised his eyebrows and then kicked at his tires. "I'll be here."

AFTER LEAVING FELIPA, Carlos found he was older than anyone who had ever sat in the Wagon Wheel Bar and sat on a counter stool and stared at the emptiness of his glass. He was quick to misunderstand and ask his compadre, "What happened. I thought you were running off to the city for work? I thought you were married?"

Tony paused, adjusted his dark sunglasses and then drained his wide glass of tomato beer: "She's dead. She was shot."

"Ay Dios," Carlos said. "What the hell happened?"

"I told you. Somebody shot her."

"Who did?"

"Goddamn sheriff's deputy. This is what I've been telling you."

"The Sheriff?" Carlos asked.

"Deputy." Tony stood up with frustration and glanced over at the open doorway. There were mournful howls from the jukebox and above the door was an ancient and wide photo of the entire San Luis Valley of Colorado before it was settled, a background of the snow-capped power mountain of the Utes along flawless rolling land. To each side of the view stood two large beer bottles framing the valley. "He shot her while she was with some dude named Gilbert," the younger man continued. "Shot her right in the bed, Carlos. I was out at night working at the steel mill on a work crew out there like I told you and she picked up some man."

"No."

"She was fucking some cabrón and then this other cabrón, her latest one, came into my house like he owned it."

"Where was this?" Carlos said.

"Huerfano County."

"Mother of God."

"Engaged to a young girl and look what happened to me. I had to pay the funeral for the both of them too. Nearly three hundred dollars. Every cent I had in the entire world. I sold my truck."

"Shit."

"Her family didn't want nothing to do with her and left it all on me. I can count my family on one hand and she had a whole damn spread of folks. I tell you, Carlos. The Goddamn race of people in this country has gone down. Like animals, Carlos! Like Goddamn animals."

"I haven't been out there in years," Carlos said, adjusting himself on the stool.

"Cabróna met dudes at her work and at the place she went for her hair, you know. Her goddamned permanents or whatever. And brought them home while I was out working and while I was out bringing home money. I produced for my family. You believe me, right? Carlos? That I produced for her?"

"Yah. Yah," Carlos agreed, not really knowing for certain.

"And you know I caught him once and the little shit lied to my face."

"The Deputy or the barber?"

"The Deputy was the boyfriend. I'm talking about the hairdresser," Tony explained. "That little-assed fool used to come over when I was home and sit in my chair. Said he was delivering coupons for hair appointments. Can you believe that shit? He stands there and hands me a comb. The queer. The liar."

"A comb?"

"Yeah. Like I say. With his name on them coupons. Never asked for them. I can produce for the family, I don't need no comb. And I told him too. And she fucked this dude. In my home, Carlos. In my home."

"Fucking vermin," Carlos said.

"And one night the Deputy comes around for her I guess and finds her and then lets them all have it."

"What happened to this Deputy?"

"They found him running out to California in a squad car and then they shot him too out on the highway somewhere. I heard it all later on the radio."

"Why did you have to pay for the hairdresser?"

"Because goddamnit I'm a Christian. That's why. Because I'm a good husband."

—

FELIPA WAS out of breath. In the late afternoon sunlight, her eyes squinted and burned with sweat. The bagboy had her food boxed up and was following closely behind though he had to place them on the concrete when they found the truckito gone.

"He does that," Felipa whispered to herself before giving the boy twenty-five cents.

"He leave you dry, ma'am?" the boy said.

Half an hour later, when Felipa got in her passenger seat Carlos said he was sorry and explained how he met a Compadre down the block walking.

"It was so hot," Carlos said. "We went for a beer. I tried to tell him I was waiting for the girl but he had to tell me about his life, you know."

On the open highway he stepped down hard on the throttle and gripped the wheel, continually grasping and unclasping. His body seemed possessed of an energy that seemed electric. His eyes gave sparks, and his dark pupils were almost scary to Felipa.

"You left me, viejo."

"What's that the woman saying?" Carlos slurred.

The pregnant Felipa's face went pinched and mean. "Stop lying to me, viejo!"

Carlos hesitated and then he laughed for a good minute, not loudly but with a violence to his body. "Goddamn vulture of a woman," Carlos barked. "Mama vulture and soon we'll have a baby vulture."

Felipa dabbed her eyes and then concentrated on her breathing and then she caught her breath. "What?" she said confused.

Carlos stopped laughing and then he focused his hot, red eyes on his pregnant wife. "You heard me, Goddamn it. A Goddamn vulture of a woman. We've lived in that house going on 17 months and I have me a Goddamn vulture of a woman."

"Oh my god, Carlos."

Carlos' breath puffed at her. "She hears what I say. No kind of wife. I'll tell the woman that much. And that damned dog loves me more than this woman will ever do in her life. I took her in and all she has for me is mouth." And as he talked saliva built into the corners of his mouth. "So the dog ain't clean. So what. He cleans himself and he follows me and listens to me. Knows his Goddamned place."

"I ain't your dog, Carlos," Felipa said. She breathed heavily again before turning her head to the street and the passing lanes. Through the open window she watched passing cars and mile markers, the mountain view in all directions closing in on her and her thoughts. "Lord God," she repeated through her lips, the fear and uncertainty growing inside of her like the life that grew inside of her. "You're no man—"

The slap came very clean, sharp edged and quickly against the backside of Felipa's head. And across the lanes of empty fields and as they found the neighborhood and the dirt roads skipped past green lawns and gates, the scene seemed placid as she cried out and screamed. With the intention of leaving Carlos, Felipa opened her door and then stepped out as the truckito rolled onto Franklin Street. She had no intention of hearing any more of Carlos' bitter, drunken words.

Carlos swerved and then, alarmed, he grabbed for his wife. His tires slid across gravel to a sharp stop just a block from his alley and driveway. He reached for the door handle and pulled it tight against Felipa's leg and arm.

"Goddamn it, Felipa," Carlos said as the truckito slid to a stop.

Instantly Felipa was out of the car. Carlos saw her walking for the house and holding her belly as she moved. When she was twenty feet from Carlos and the truckito she turned and screamed out. "You fuck of a man," she shouted before heading for her front door.

When Carlos spilled from the truck, he had her wrist for a moment and neither moved and then Felipa's hands tore free. She threw her purse nearly at Carlos' face as she made her way up the front lawn and then onto the porch.

"Oh my God," Felipa screamed then she looked up into the sky in search of a way out of this marriage and this pregnancy. "How are you going to have the upbringing of this child? You drunk. You fuck of a drunk." Felipa's face convulsed and she looked in every direction at once other than at her husband.

A window had gone up across the street and then several boys walking by had stopped to stare. The boys stopped and then edged around the yard when Mrs. Nava yelled from her window. "For the love of Christ!" she shouted. "Leave that poor girl alone!"

"Keep out of this, you old bitch!" Carlos screamed before continuing in on his wife. "Tell me to my face. I want the woman to tell me I'm a 'fuck of a man' to my face. Go on tell me, cabróna! Tell me!"

Felipa broke into passionate tears and then she convulsed in terrifying moans. "You're drunk, viejo. Goddamn it, you're drunk. I can see it in your eyes. Every Goddamn day you're drunk. You can't drink in front of a baby."

For a minute the neighbors and Carlos thought it would come to blows and the whole damned universe of the valley would have to come and pull the two apart.

the elders

It was not quite midnight when Lino and Carlos made the long walk out to the large stucco Kiva. The small village was already dark and lifeless, and the house the two men entered was equally sad and desolate. Five women sat on the floor, the elder's wives Carlos would soon learn, silently shucking corn and scraping the kernels onto a blanket with their small hands. Each woman's face seemed muted and sad. The only light was a dim kerosene lantern, and no one talked or laughed or made any movement at the entrance of the two men. The only sound was of one of the skeleton-thin elders, sitting at the head of the dark building, dominating the walls and floor with a chant, a song that Lino would not translate. Carlos just stood holding his hat and poncho with his head bowed with respect for the old man and his song.

Carlos finally, after hours of song, gave Lino a gentle nudge with his elbow and whispered, "What does the man sing about, Lino?"

"He sings of his past life."

"Past life?"

"He sings and dances a thankfulness for our blessings. He sings of your visions and how the third dream will come soon. He said your dreams are pure and marks your entrance to the larger universes of time, and he will line up all the elders to help us understand. That is all I can tell you, vaquero."

"Es eso universes, Lino?"

"We must be quiet and respectful of the old man's song."

As the two men walked home the next morning, Lino answered more questions for Carlos. "Your new duty to the Clan is to stay awake for two days before going to sleep. If your heart is right then the Twins will return, the clouds will part above us and the great winter ceremonies will give us more answers. This is what the elders' song has communicated."

"What are these ceremonies? These songs?" Carlos asked.

"The great ceremonies recreate the first dawn of my people's Creation—their birth. There we recreate the beginning of all life on earth—animal, plant and man. Your dream from this world is important to understanding the previous worlds that have existed for our people. The elders cannot speak with you, because they do not trust anyone outside of our clan, and also because they must stay pure for the coming sixteen days of ceremonies."

"I mean no disrespect," Carlos repeated. "I have my own family and my own people. My freedom means more to me than any ceremony or ritual here. I cannot stay on more days."

"I am sorry, Carlos, but the vision as told is important to these ceremonies and you must see them through. I beg you, friend. You must stay the sixteen days or face missing the messages from otherworlds. You must care for more than your existence. The ceremonies will teach you."

CARLOS STRUGGLED *and only had one night of restless sleep when the next vision came. He dreamed that he was riding his mare and it was not winter or snowing, but rather he was alone high on the northern mesas of the San Luis Valley. The grade was very steep, yet the mare was deft in handling the bend of the cliff face and walls. Then a semicircle of sheer rock face filled Carlos' view, huge boulders and debris slowed his pace home and yet suddenly a glowing light, beautiful beyond understanding, shed a level path thick with orchards of choke cherries, peach and apricot trees, very similar to those that Carlos had played in as a young boy.*

When Carlos woke the next morning and described the dream and its magnificence, Lino explained, "That's the place in Colorado where the sacred piles and shrines to the Twins are located, the shrines of the red and blue Kachinas, where the Ute's sacred rock writing is located. I knew you had a tie to the spirit of the land. Didn't I tell you, wife? Woman? I told you this cowboy had a tie to our brother Utes and Zuni of Colorado. Did I not tell you? The San Luis Valley is a sacred land of peace."

"No. You did not tell me," the woman answered honestly. She was sitting on the floor of her and her husband's bedroom, shucking corn on a blanket. "You never tell me—"

"Well, I felt it, woman," Lino answered. "But the visions are strong, are they not?"

THE LAST DREAM *came to Carlos as the entire village of Taos was making preparations for the great ceremony, Soyal or the great rite of the winter solstice. Lino explained that the ceremony symbolized the second portion of creation, when all beings came from within the earth in living form as man and woman and began their journey into the world. But Carlos saw nothing of the rites because he had been depriving himself of sleep and human contact for days, as instructed by his hosts, in anticipation of the dream. Mostly, he just sat to drink and smoke.*

On the third night without sleep, after finally passing out near the corner of Lino's morada, Carlos dreamed that he sat in the middle of a great cavernous Kiva on a low bench in the middle of the floor. The bench was placed over a line of cornmeal that ran east to west signifying the path of the sun overhead. An altar loomed at the far end of the room and yet there were no exits on any of the walls, as if Carlos had existed there since the day he was born.

All Carlos could make out were the hands that came from behind him. The hands were dark and both were women's hands, and they both proceeded to take off all of the vaquero's clothes. Around his waist they unfastened his belt and the buttons of his flannel shirt. The hands washed his body in amole, a soapy weed root of yucca, and hawk feathers were pasted to his forehead.

In a little while the gentle hands returned, offering on his right a bowl of paste to eat and an oversized bottle of mescal, Carlos' favorite, on his left. The paste smelled putrid and raw and made him feel nauseous as he sniffed. His arms and legs cramped and ached, and for quite a while Carlos thought he might stumble over if not for those hands. Those dark, strange hands suddenly seemed to be signifying to Carlos a choice.

And as his strength left him, as his senses dulled and as his body throbbed under the heavy amole that washed over him, and as he sat there gagging and cramping, the dim light of the kiva suddenly came up. It was suddenly clear that one set of hands, those hands that had undressed and bathed Carlos, belonged to Annacita, the vaquero's sister now passed. The other set belonged to the round Terricita, the dead wife who had gone not six months before to la gripa. Another pair was that of his cousin Benito, passed from Carlos' life in the Great War.

The sister to Carlos' left wore a yellow sundress, a flowered print, and her light brown hair was braided closely around on her head, all as her brother Carlos remembered. Her features were kind and humble, and her beauty beamed throughout the kiva like a warm morning light. The wife to Carlos' right stood silent and naked save for a white cotton manta thrown over her shoulder. She too was covered in amole with a hawk feather at the top of her forehead, like Carlos himself. It had been eighteen months since he had seen or spoken with her—or had the strength to even think of her, since her passing in their San Luis home, yet the woman showed no emotion, only a blank stare. Carlos hunched over to her feet and sobbed, tasting the sour amole pasted to her skin and legs. He sobbed as he had as a small boy in fields of lettuce and grass, when he was lost from his Abuelito and his cousin Benito, when they played tricks on him, when they left him to fend for himself. He cried until he was sick, until he became ill and wanted to vomit. He sobbed there on the floor, waiting to make his choice between ghosts and life.

BY THE TIME *Carlos mounted and urged his mare north towards the San Luis Valley in Colorado, as he headed out over the open llano and as he drained his bottle, he had not slept or eaten in days and days.*

The horse maneuvered farther through the blowing snow that seemed to double in intensity. The mountains and the surrounding pines turned slowly into white blankets, pure and deep, forcing Carlos to slow. The vaquero worried and emptied bottle after bottle and his mind slowed. He wept and cursed his ridiculous life and fortune. He considered turning around, but the snow covered the ground and created ghostly dark shadows, leaving the man directionless and tired. It was as if someone had carefully arranged the land against the man and his mare, or so the vaquero cursed under his breath. His mind ached with crudo thoughts. Then the poor mare kicked up new blends of earth and great wind and then tripped, throwing Carlos down to white-covered rock and snow. The move was violent and shook the man, nearly breaking his leg and ankle on rock growing from the mountain. The mare as brave and true as he was spooked and ran as if the mountainside had wanted the two separated. Carlos cracked his head to the ground, and he drunkenly cried out. He spilled his bottle. His vision whitened out, and hour after hour as he struggled to crawl and then walk onto his knees calling out the mare's name, the white grew bigger and bigger around him.

Hours passed and the man slipped further into unconsciousness. His temples hurt, and for a moment the vaquero could not understand what was true and what was dream. He saw his wife's face and then felt her sweet kisses down his spine before her flesh was left rotting and drained of life before his eyes. The through the image a white horse stopped beside Carlos, and for a moment he believed it to be more snow from the great western sky. The horse grew larger and larger. The horse and the man studied one another until Carlos heard Lino's great laugh and voice. The Abuelitos had taught the young man to be patient and days of war and hunger in Army times had also taught the man patience, but the drink and the freezing winds had softened his thoughts. He saw a dark figure on horseback.

"You have put your mount through his paces, no?" the voice called out.

"¿Quien es?"

"What are you doing sleeping in the wind, my boy?" Lino said, grabbing Carlos with his great arms around his waist and torso. "I've been waiting for you, my boy. It seems with these dreams you've crossed over. The spirits have you, no?"

The vaquero said no words but only hung on Lino's immense arms and strength.

THE NEXT MORNING *Carlos found himself back with Lino, under his tent and blankets enduring the storm through the night. Lino fed the man scraps of his wife White Bear's bread and bits of dried meat. Then he asked the weakened cowboy to explain why he would flee the village despite the dreams and the advice given to him by the elders.*

"I tracked you through the night to Pueblo Peak," Lino said as he ate. "I must admit I thought your ways with a mount would have left you in better condition. I forget how young you are, vaquero. I forget how much you haven't seen or experienced."

"I was US Army. I can sit a horse."

"Hold on, friend. I mean no disrespect. And I can imagine much worse than the open llano, I can assure you."

"For Christ's sake," Carlos said. "The storm came in on me too

damned fast. Horse ran off. I'm not used to being lost and wandering."

"Sit up," Lino said. "Let me have a look at you."

Lino examined the cowboy. Eyes, throat and face. His solar plexus and then the top of his head.

"What the hell are you doing?"

"You are not well, cowboy," Lino repeated. "You are not happy. That's what brought you to me. Your problem is from the inside. Too much of the bottle for you, no? And your scarred hands. Fist fights follow after time with the bottle, no?"

The large Lino pulled a crystal from his jeans and held it in a makeshift manner to the morning light coming from the tent's small opening. "The hearts," he repeated. "You have left your world in order to find the hearts that have been lost to you. I can't catch up to you even as we speak."

"My horse ran off and I took a fall," Carlos returned. "What the hell are you talking about?"

"Carlos. Cowboy," Lino answered. His immense hands took the man's collar and shoulder. Then he said: "I know you've intentionally wanted to harm yourself. To end your life here on the plain."

"What are you talking about?"

"I used to think of this place as a doorway myself out of the painful life you find yourself in. To become a ghost where nothing is hidden from you. You've seen it all in dreams."

"I have seen my loved ones, my sister and wife. Both dead and returned to me in dreams. Though they were as real to me as you are to me now."

"You found what was lost to you in the world of your dream, vaquero. You heard their voices?"

"This is impossible to believe—"

"Don't be so dramatic," Lino said. "You're simply a soul in New Mexico." After the fat Lino smiled coyly and ignored the more and more anxious questions, the vaquero finally slipped into restless sleep and aching dreams. It was then the round man searched

Carlos' pockets, helping himself to tobacco and rolling papers. "And the least I can do is find you your ranch work."

1951

trip home

The Greenline bus cried to a stop near Alamosa, Colorado, and dropped Carlos' oldest daughter, Lena, downtown. She was still holding on to her mama's rosary beads as the bus whined past. She grinned at her father and his primer-colored truckito parked alongside the ticket office.

Through the driver side window, the red-headed Lena threw her arms around his sunburned neck. "You getting so damn old, Papa."

Carlos shook his head while she hugged him.

"In the last six months I've had sores and weakness in my legs," the Jefe admitted to Lena's concern.

Lena threw her suitcase into the truck bed and ran around to sit beside the old man. "What's the baby's name, Jefe?"

"We named her Bruna after your Great Abuela from Chama."

"The poor thing has to live with a name like that."

"It is a family name and Felipa thought the baby should have it," the old man explained. "Tranquilena has served you, girl. So don't say no more about it."

Lena watched as he rocked his legs and rubbed at their poor circulation.

"You should have me drive, Jefe."

"You got a license, did you?"

"No, Jefe."

"How are you going to drive me? I'm not near half as dead as you think I am, Lena."

"Well, you got the sugar and I'm looking out for you, Jefe."

"Shit."

On the way to the Jefe's house, which seemed to be farther out than Lena had remembered, Lena closed her eyes, opening them only when the truckito stopped for a signal light on First Avenue, and again at the El Monte Hotel.

The Jefe had slammed the door and unloaded her suitcase before Lena noticed.

"What's this, Jefe?"

"Your stepmother wants you here, hija," the old man admitted. He wiped the sweat from his brow with remorse.

Lena's eyes played an amused game with this, and she thought she might cry and carry on. She thought she might lose all her courage right in the middle of downtown Monte Vista.

"If this works out for you, mi'ja. This might all be for the best, no?"

THAT NIGHT Lena called her love Jeri in Huerfano. First, she tried the apartment and the Army Depot where he worked for the Ordnance Corps. She also called The State over on Main where he drank. Lena walked from her single room on the second floor down to the lobby in between each call to ask the round woman behind the desk for change. She had to ring the bell on the front desk, and each time the woman walked through the door as if to greet a new customer.

"Phone hasn't seen this much attention in years," she joked.

When she finally got the boyfriend on the phone, he was at the bar, and she could tell he was drunk. She heard it in his slurs and in his laughter. Her lips pursed and her eyes glowed with tears, and she shook her head.

"I made it, Jeri," she said. "I'm at a hotel because Felipa don't want me there."

"Hotel?"

"Yeah."

"Who the hell is paying for that?"

"I had the money, Jeri."

"Jesus Christ. When do you get Felipa's baby?"

Instead of answering, she held the receiver tightly and she played with the phone cord. "If you have to go downtown to get something to eat, Jeri, do it. Go down to the lunch counter at the drugstore for a hamburger sandwich if you have to. You need to eat."

"You hear me? I said when do you get your baby?"

"I'll have her soon, Jeri. But I'm not going to see nobody 'til the morning."

"And the old man?"

"He drove me. He's gotten old, Jeri. Really old. You should see him."

"How long do I have here by myself? When you coming back, mujer?"

"Soon. I have to be back at work."

In her sleep that night she returned to Jeri and the apartment, and she woke wringing wet and feeling more tired than when she first slipped between the sheets. She stared at herself in the vanity mirror and for a good long while she thought she heard voices and a baby crying in the hotel. The contents of the room felt strange and sad: the suitcase, the table and chair along with the half-made bed. Around midnight she opened her door and stared down at the empty hallway and out the window and the view over Main Street. She put her head against the cold glass and whispered her prayer.

IN THE HOURS before dawn Lena had the night sweats and dreamed of her mother, of the night the woman passed from la gripe. The ground was frozen and Lena's own thick Grandmother, her mother's mother, had to lumber out to the woodpile. The supply was depleted but the woman worked quickly. The twelve-year-old Lena could only stand and stare from the cabin doorway through layer after layer of thick snowfall as her grandmother wearing only a housecoat and blanket slammed down her splitting axe over and over again.

That night Lena was not ordered to bed and was not ordered to sweep or wipe at the dirt floors as the grandmother worked. She could almost hear the words from the approaching visitor Martin's lips. The broad-shouldered young man wrapped in flannel and denim and wearing work gloves had the look of a cowpoke, and that night had made his own first trip by horseback to the village of Seven Mile Plaza.

In snow-smeared pants tucked into cowboy boots, he found the old woman struggling with her work and wood. After riding for hours, he nearly fell from his horse with fatigue. Nearly lost his thin-brimmed hat to take up the woman's chore.

"Oye, Martin. What has happened?" the old woman asked solemnly.

"Your daughter, Señora. It's Mara," Martin spat through visible breaths. "I am so sorry to say. They say to make her as comfortable as possible."

"You mean, that man, Carlos, says," the old woman corrected and to this the young Martin gave a solitary nod.

Lena's Grandmother stood solemn with her mass of grey hair and then nearly exploded with tears and lost her balance as the young Martin explained. Her hair fell in waves surrounding her face with the news. With no telephone it was left up to the rider to explain. Carlos had urged Martin to be careful with the old woman's heart and senses.

Over the next few hours, sitting at the woman's dinner table draining coffee, the young man, Martin, sadly explained the death and the suffering of such a young and once healthy woman.

"All for the best," the man repeated emptily, perhaps because of how he lost his own father in the remote village of the San Luis Valley and perhaps his own brothers in Taos, New Mexico, gone nearly three years. "She'll feel no more pain from this world."

Lena listened on, not ordered to clean dishes or sweep up after Martin's boots as she was most nights and not fully understanding. At that age Lena still held on tightly to her paper dolls and dreamed of her cabrón father Carlos' unfulfilled promises of department store shoes from Alamosa.

In the low sunlight of morning the young girl slipped from her Grandmother's side from the cold metal-framed bed, and she banged the cabin door behind her as she made her way the miles to Del Norte. As she moved, she held her Grandmother's thoughts, warnings of thieves and spirits who make their income from travelers along the mountain roads, dark and malevolent forces from the mountains. She stepped into deep snow at times up to her knees, and in each step, she experienced fear and loneliness as she had that day her father Carlos ran off. She remembered the words of regret and the harsh words from Carlos on the day he drove off.

The plain towards Blanca Peak became more and more an unseen world for the young Lena as she walked and found her mama's bedside. She stood cold and aching.

"For Christ's sake, mujer," Carlos said, standing and smoking near the woodstove wearing only an undershirt and boxer shorts. "You could've died and froze out on the road." He drained glasses of whiskey and cursed alongside his grieving compadres that early morning. She cried and her father put his arms around Lena's shoulder and gave her drunken words in hopes to ease her cries. She escaped and then fell to find her mother's hand. It was the girl's first experience with death and dying. She had no words to speak. She wiped at her mother's forehead as the woman appeared to sleep and thought of the cold snows of the Los Valdezes' Pass and the village where she had always been raised.

THE NEXT MORNING in Monte Vista the darkness broke while Lena held her first cigarette. Out in front of the hotel she waited for her Jefe's truckito. A honk sent her running inside for her suitcase and her coat. Carlos stopped the engine as Lena dropped into the dusty bench seat.

Carlos' face was expressionless even as it burned in the morning sun.

"What you got to say to me, Papa? What you come to say?"

"Your stepmother won't leave the room this morning and she won't stop crying."

"Well," she said with scorn and raised her hands. "Take me to talk to her. You're her man. Take me to talk with her."

For an hour and a half the two drove around the barren city in silence. The Jefe stopped for coffee and cigarillos. The old man filled his rig with gasoline, bullshitting with the boys at the garage. He bought some beer. Lena never moved a muscle, but rather sat in the truckito. Again, she grabbed her mother's rosary beads and said her words of prayer until the Jefe returned with his beer masked in a paper sack, placing it between himself and his oldest daughter.

As he fired the engine and looked over towards Chapman Street, he was half hoping it might be blocked or closed. He whistled loudly and sang a little into the deserted morning. The houses and trees passed quickly as they drove. Lena again had that sensation, as on the bus, that the earth pushed her towards an answer to her sadness. She stared outside. The unpaved streets, where there normally would have been trucks of men piling past, were empty.

The Jefe backed the truckito silently into his driveway and lit another cigarette before finally asking, "When does the next bus leave, Lena?"

"I don't know the time."

"I'm asking you what time the bus leaves for Huerfano County, Lena. You came and you gotta know the time for this. You've got to be quick, girl."

"9:15 I think, Jefe," Lena answered. "The bus leaves at 9:15."

"So we gotta be leaving for Alamosa by what time?"

"8:15 or so, Jefe."

"8:15 then," the Jefe answered. He looked at his knees and to his shaking hands. "I'm gonna sit here and drink one of these beers, Lena. Now get in there and get your baby, you hear? Get in there."

"Yes, Jefe," Lena said automatically. She opened her mouth and shut it again with shock. The Jefe pulled a Pabst Blue Ribbon from his sack and popped the top with an opener attached to his key ring.

Sometimes on sunny, cold mornings Lena had stood on the porch of her apartment staring at her neighbor's children and dreamt of this day. Ever since the phone call came that the Jefe wanted no part of this child's life, ever since the stepmother got on the phone and agreed quietly and happily, Lena had been thinking of this moment.

Slowly and carefully, Lena unlatched the side screen door and walked into the kitchen. The small wood stove was quiet, and the radio broke the silence with the morning weather and rancher report.

"You here for Felipa?" the stepmother's sister said in answer to the creaking screen door. She held a quiet baby in her arms.

Lena nodded and smiled. She stared across the room and tried hard to figure out the situation with her eyes. Maybe she was stunned, or maybe the lack of sleep caught her weak in the knees.

"Do you have everything you need at your house?" The sister looked at Lena with a furrowed brow.

"No," Lena said. She cupped her hands over her mouth and her weak eyes ran over with tears. She nearly fell to one knee.

"No?" the sister yelled. "How do you expect to have the baby if you don't have what you need at home in the house."

Lena's mouth was dry: "I didn't know I was even going to be here today. I work, you know."

The sister pulled the blankets from a small bassinet on the kitchen table around the baby and handed the baby Bruna over to Lena. The girl was in Lena's arms and she felt weak and nearly sick with the physical weight, the actuality of it all. They both stopped talking and listened to the baby.

"Where's Felipa?" Lena asked.

"She can't help crying. She doesn't seem unhappy about anything; she can't stop crying."

"Should I talk to her?"

"Jesus Lord in heaven, no," the sister said.

Lena shook her head and smiled, wiping the tears away above the bundle in her arms. She bolted out the door and raced over to the truckito and her Jefe. Bruna stopped the silence of the Jefe's drinking and staring with her soft cries.

The Jefe swore. He wiped his tongue over his teeth and spit out the window. "Here comes somebody, Lena," the Jefe said as he fired up the engine. "Well, you going or not?"

Lena set herself gently in the cab and slammed the rusty door. Her chest expanded and Brunacita trembled in her arms.

"Lena!" Felipa called from outside of the truckito, beating her palms across the hood. The sound went up and up. "Lena!"

"It's over, Felipa," the Jefe yelled through the windshield. He drained his beer and wiped at his mouth. Lena's voice went on caressingly to the baby in her arms as the truckito pulled from the driveway.

"You have her and it's over now, Lena," the Jefe repeated.

"Lena!" the stepmother yelped. She looked tired and ragged in her housecoat. Her face red, her eyes anxious and wet.

As the truckito accelerated, Lena turned and watched the Jefe's wife fall to her knees in a wash of dust.

haunting neighborhoods

Wearing a new Peachbloom hat, the loca Felipa Montoya rode for hours on the Greenline, then she was standing in the shady afternoon among crowds of steelworkers left in line for morning coffee in downtown Huerfano, Colorado. It was 5 a.m. and she was awake with the impossible task of walking from the Main Street station to find Lena Valdez and her baby Bruna. She found Main Street and then Santa Fe Avenue and then Union Avenue.

She saw men grumbling in alleyways and playing games of dice, and in the blue light of dawn, she found Junction Street. Then along Evans she passed boarding houses and hotels, the lawn and shade of Memorial Square and the Pantry Café whose doors were just beginning to open. Over coffee and eggs, she skimmed the paper and then went to study her address book and her handwritten notes. She put off calling her husband Carlos in Monte Vista to let him know where she had landed.

In a crowd of young men heading to the steel mill she smoked a cigarette and then asked for the whereabouts of Routte Avenue. "Say again," one boy in coveralls said. The boy had a wide smile deep with dimples, and Felipa consciously picked him out of all the boys waiting and smoking at the bus stops.

"Hey," she called while pointing at the notes in her address book, "Can you tell me how to find this street?"

"No, don't think so."

"You didn't even look."

Amid the humming of traffic and semi's heading for the highway she stepped from a bus after heading across town. She found the street on her own and then found the number of the apartment, but she kept walking past, afraid to ring the bell, choosing to walk around the street and find the alleyway. She dropped her bag behind garbage cans and wooden boxes from a cannery. On a vast paved area laden with weeds and rusted machine parts littering the path she moved past where an old woman was sweeping and putting out potted plants for the day. The woman was large and round but nimble on her feet as she stacked the empty pots and fed them water through a hose. She held a cigarette in her immense lips. The woman's pants were hiked up almost over her belly and at first Felipa almost laughed out loud.

As she neared the gate of the house she guessed to be Lena's, she stood almost awestruck in place. She stopped and placed her hands on her hips and then onto the metal fence. She kicked at the pavement and then at the loose gravel she created.

"Are you heading in there or not?" the old woman said as she worked. The sun had just begun to clear the roofs and the woman was sweating and wiping at her brow. She worked in the neighboring yard filled with dead walnut trees.

With a weary moan Felipa finally answered: "You know the folks here?"

"The man he drinks and the woman she has a baby," the woman answered.

Felipa feigned a smile and patiently turned farther into the fence. She clutched at her jacket and at her purse. She thought of writing a note and slipping it under the door. She thought of having the old woman letting her in and then finding her daughter. She thought of sitting at the porch and waiting for someone to come out.

"The woman stays next door with the cousin sometimes," the

old woman said to no particular question. She strained over the leaves and trash around her porch until Felipa finally gave in and helped gather piles the woman formed. “They argue in the alleyway and in the driveway. They lock each other out. But you didn’t hear it from me,” she offered. “Just how folks is these days, no?”

Felipa smiled politely and nodded.

Later, in the woman’s kitchen, over coffee and buttered toast, the large woman asked, “Are you the sister? I know she’s got a sister.”

Felipa shook her head and watched the house from the old woman’s window. She caught herself in the glass, the fullness to her throat and the tiredness in her eyes and mouth. She fixed her hair after removing her hat.

“I’ve never seen the sister but I know she’s got one. I watch everyone around here. The streets are so narrow and everyone knows your business, you know? I watched them bring in the baby and I say to myself: Where’d that baby come from, you know? I say it out loud just like that to myself.”

Felipa held her hat and drank her coffee with sugar and nodded.

“That baby is gorgeous, you know? Like Elizabeth Taylor. You ever see a picture with Elizabeth Taylor as a kid? National Velvet. Big eyes, you know. She brings her over here and I get to cook for them and they just sit and talk. I thought you were the sister. She’s always talking about the sister.”

“Is the baby,” Felipa asked. “Is the baby okay? Do they do right by her, I mean?”

“I don’t think I get what you saying, girl. Say what’s your name?”

“My name’s Felipa Montoya and I’m wondering if they are good parents for the baby? That’s all I mean.”

“Lena loves that baby. Gives her everything. You sure you not the sister? You look like you could be the sister.”

And later as she sat on the old woman's toilet and the old woman collected her bag, she stared at the contents of the bathroom walls, then later the medicine cabinet and the shelves above the sink. She devised the words. "Would I be able to stay on here?"

"I'm an old fool," the big-bellied woman said later as she smoked her cigarettes. "And I don't have no man the way other women do and so a soul here in the house again is something I wouldn't say no to. You wouldn't steal from me, would you?"

"No, ma'am," Felipa answered.

"You got money for rent and food?"

"I got a little."

"Good because I ain't offering charity. I'll expect rent."

"Yes, ma'am."

WHEN FELIPA finally found the courage to call Carlos collect, after the old woman fixed dinner and then a bed on the couch, and after the old woman snored and snored through the rest of the house, Carlos scolded his young wife. He was angry for having to walk two houses over to the Maldonado's for the call, and he yelled at his wife. He was angry that he had to worry and show that worry in the presence of strangers. Then he told her he loved her, all while she whispered the softest of responses.

"Is the woman leaving?" Carlos finally asked and the words very much surprised the young woman. "The woman leaving me for someone? The woman sick of me?"

"I'm coming back to you, old man. Is that what you think? I left you a letter."

"That's good. Who's gonna fix the woman breakfast and dinner? The woman got someone else to do that, or what?"

When Felipa put the phone away and rested in her peach oversized nightgown, she listened for crying babies and for drunken arguments, but she heard nothing that first night. She pulled the makeshift covers up over her shoulders and simply sat in the lowlight of the tableside lamp.

The next morning Felipa woke with the old woman patting her: "You keep the light on all night?"

"Huh?"

"I was asking if you kept the light on all night? On the table there. Do you drink coffee? My man always drank coffee and ate toast in the morning."

"If you are making some," she said, yawning and somewhat uncomfortable in finding her bearings.

"Did you talk on my phone last night?" the old woman asked.

"Yes, ma'am."

"You reverse the charge?"

"Yes, ma'am."

"Good. I don't like people stealing from me. I'll take you in but I don't like it when they steal."

"I would never steal from you, ma'am."

Later, she lay quietly as the woman brewed strong coffee on the stovetop, and the whole morning reminded Felipa of mornings with her father or with Carlos. Her thoughts from the baby were diverted now, and she wondered why she had made this trip. Why she had wanted to purchase the ticket and why she had wanted so bad to see the street and the house her baby would grow up on. It was if something guided her there from outside of her thoughts. She was given the place in her mind, and she imagined the street and the city of Huerfano to be dark and ruthless and larger than her room at Ridge Home or even her home with Carlos. And those thoughts seemed like a barrier to her happiness and to her sanity some days and nights, but now in this woman's apartment, she felt nothing but sleepiness and foolishness.

"You awake, girl," the old woman said. "You awake for breakfast or you gonna let the whole thing get cold on you."

—

THE DAY with the old woman was strange in the house under the dead walnut trees, and through the untrimmed shrubs Felipa viewed her baby and her baby's new mother for the first time that trip. She also saw Jeri for the first time and sized him up as a man and as a father. She watched him while the old man ran out to the market for fruit and vegetables and his razor blades. But Jeri parked his Dodge in the alleyway and held the door open for Lena who always held the baby close, always kept the baby covered and safe. That was one thing Felipa noticed right on. They appeared to be an attractive couple with Lena's made-up hair and Jeri's Sunday suit and coat. From the old woman's bedroom, she could just make out Jeri and Lena talking and laughing. She wept and viewed Jeri lifting the baby to the ceiling and then laughing, an immense laugh that filled the alleyway.

Felipa lay on her belly and watched out the window trying to make out the couple and their Sunday routine. She imagined her own sisters and their care for their own children and for their own homes and lives with one another and how it all felt so foreign to her. How the babies had loveliness she admired, yet she also feared for the responsibility. She had thought of this for several weeks before finally finding the courage to make this trip.

Later that afternoon she watched the couple sit down on the concrete porch to their house and sit a while with the baby and with one another. Again, Lena held the baby close in her arms and Jeri walked along the fence line of his yard smoking a cigarillo and chopping at branches and dead limbs from his spruce tree. In that moment Felipa's heart raced and beat erratically and so she tried to resist the urgency to leave the safety of the old woman's house and argue or steal her baby away.

She ate alone sitting in the old woman's kitchen, and then when the woman returned, she had peaches and milk. By this time, she thought, Carlos would have finished a half day's worth of work and been home and gone again. She thought of Carlos seldom until these moments alone with the old woman, and she missed her husband and how he catered to all of her thoughts and wants, and she felt something close to gratefulness for old man Carlos.

"You come to see your people?" the old woman finally asked. "I got a car and can drive you, you know? Or I'll let you borrow it. Hell, I trusted you this much, girl. I could let you do that if you wanted."

"No license."

"Can't you drive, girl?"

"I'm sad to say, no."

"My man had no license too. Said he had no use for cars and roads. Said they were all death traps. Said he'd rather haunt the neighborhood on horse and buggy than sit and miss everything sitting inside a metal box. He was strange like that, don't you know. He was Italian and cooked every meal for me. Spoiled me, really."

"Sounds like a man worth the time."

"He left me this house and his pension. So, you don't know the half of it. Loved that man until the day he stopped breathing and now I sit and think on him most days. Stare at pictures and think on the minutes until I am with him again. Not for a while yet, though, God willing."

"God willing."

"Like I said, I could drive you."

She finally answered before asking to work for the bus fare home, "Like I said I only have people in Alamosa."

IT WAS SUNDAY and the whole neighborhood gathered at St Francis on Logan Avenue and most folks were drawn to the re-enactment of Mary and Joseph's journey to Bethlehem—Lena

Montoya as the young Mary and Jeri Martinez as young Joseph. The couple wrapped in blankets and holding the infant Bruna as the savior of the neighborhood. The smiles beamed through the crowd.

There were many eyes on the procession heading across the parking lot and out to the street, steelworkers with days off to kill and families along with old folks in tow. Bums passing by on their way out to the highway to hitchhike east with the hopes of finding fieldwork.

An old sweaty woman and her new boarder, the woman in the Peachbloom hat, were also viewing and chatting the afternoon away. The woman pointed out the couple for Felipa and for a moment the woman in the Peachbloom hat cried and then focused intently.

"What's gotten into you, girl?" the old woman questioned over and over. "The difficult journey of La Virgen?"

the cutoff

Lino had work at the Cutoff Ranch, and as Lino and Carlos shared the mild gelding on the 90 miles to Colmor that early spring, Lino explained the Jefe Waddingham's operation.

"What can I tell you about Colmor, Carlos?" Lino said as they rode. He explained how the place was a ranchers' paradise from the 1850s when it was sold out from under the old timer Javier Martinez. The nearby town was named Colmor because it was between Colfax and Mora, the linking of the two nowhere places, stuck between Wagon Mound and the old Santa Fe Trail marker, Lino explained.

Colmor emerged from the llano and the place was a village of small comforts to the men working the Cutoff Ranch. The town was a collection of dirt roads in those years—a way-stop between Springer and Wagon Mound. The flat-packed earth between Cimarron Canyon and Kiowa Grasslands. The place was a creation of the Patrón Waddingham, as he had zoned it and personally petitioned the Governor for a Post Office, coming soon. Most mail came in from Wagon Mound through the Patrón's dog cart, and so the man had the word on all news of the ranch and the town.

The men stopped at a lodge and feedstore for some food as they made their way. This is when Carlos met his love Mara for the first time. These were the days he was back from the war and women were the last thing on his mind after finding work and coins. She poured the men hot coffee to drain and tortilla with beans to eat. She laughed at the wandering Carlos and at Lino for bringing him to work. Her large eyes and sad face brightened when Lino joked with Carlos. "I could be your damned mother," Mara said to Carlos as she pushed her hair from her green eyes. She laughed and then slapped at Lino's chest. "Tell me about your wife, Lino," the round-faced Mara said.

"What's to say?" Lino said as he munched. "She's still mean. I am still in love."

"You tell her to come to Colmor and I will visit with her and get all the dirt on you."

"I'll tell her," Lino said.

"Lino was the one always to tell me about the importance of family and marriage. More important than the rocks on this land, is what you used to tell," Mara said. "You still saying that?"

"Only to people who listen," Lino said.

"And what's your story?" Mara said to Carlos through piercing eyes.

He was smitten the minute he saw her. He couldn't say a word.

"Silent men," Mara said, smiling. "Got to worry about the silent ones. My father said that."

When they reached the bunkhouse at the Cutoff, Carlos watched the men work the cattle yards and watched the men break horses. He watched the men throw off their boots after a long day of riding and cowboying to sit in their long underwear to eat Lino's potato caldo and burned pan de campo. He sat and thought of Mara from that first day.

"Should you write her or call on her?" Lino asked.

"Foolish boy thoughts," Carlos said as he hustled to peel and boil potatoes for Lino's soups.

THE PATRÓN'S SPREAD *was only a few buildings, the horse-working pens and the bunkhouse with the Patrón's home a mile away, all on the edges of Ocate Creek. The creek was the reason the Patrón planted stakes here though he had men machine dig a well closer to his home. The Pueblo Indians called the Patrón's home the Bighouse because it was the largest structure, the shape of a C with a courtyard at the center, all hand built by the Patrón and his people. Many Waddinghams had come and gone but Wilson and his son Arthur stayed. There was a broken-down house in the back pasture where the top hands stayed and sometimes Arthur's women from Springer the Patrón Waddingham brought in.*

Carlos always remembered Lino's hole of a kitchen setup from those days. Screenless windows above the stove and wood pile, no porch but hard dirt and rocks to rest on out there. Rows of neatly hanging pots and pans and flour and grain sacks neatly piled in the corners; no sugar, though. "Never no money for sugar," Lino would say. "Little honey, though." There were simple brass light fixtures placed over 10 place settings between a front and back door. Hanging ristras drying red chile and Eddie's dog Sheba was always barking at the back door. Coffee boiling Mexican style, fresh coffee smell in the air. Lard-fried goat meat on a massive cast iron skillet. "No hats on the table and no guns neither!" Lino would yell out to the men. There were spider webs up into the rafters. "Spider webs are for the flies," Lino would say. "If you want to cook you have to enjoy killing flies."

At night Lino would walk down to the Ocate Creek and hold court after meals with the hands and Pueblo Indians who were working for Patrón Waddingham. They all stood by the collapsing alligator juniper tree to hear Lino's chisme. All except for Carlos, who believed in working a full day, sun-up to sun-down. He could only be spoken to in his bunk at night before bed. Carlos usually fell asleep to the sound of Lino's gossip and stories from the surrounding villages. "Why don't you come down to the creek for talking," Lino said. "We all want to know you."

"I'm not here for gossip or to be known," Carlos said. "I am here to work."

—

CARLOS' MAIN JOB at the Cutoff was to spend the hours in the morning doing the much-needed job of feeding cattle. The process had been the same for as long as Carlos' trainer and mentor Eddie Duran could remember. Eddie was hard and from the old time. Broad shoulders and always unshaved. Up early, Eddie would say, "Animals eat before people." And the sleds were hooked up and the horses would pull the sleds along the ground as the hands forked the hay from the holding bins. It was a few hours work just to hitch the horses and fill the sleds with hay. Eddie would joke and throw the yellow straw at Carlos, "Here's your breakfast so eat it up. Eat it!"

That Spring the New Mexico mornings were cool and dark until the red cracked the horizon and soon the sun was blazing down. Eddie would control the sled and direct Carlos to fork out the food for the cows. They would come down from higher country drawn in by their hunger and instincts as the men zigzagged the fields. When the feeding was done, Carlos and Eddie stood and drank coffee and ate Lino's pan de campo.

"You work with horses out there in Europe?"

"Yes, sir. Too much."

"What did they feed you in that Army of yours, Carlos?" Eddie said.

"Chipped beef," Carlos answered.

"What's that taste like," Eddie said.

"Cow shit."

"Well we got plenty of that for if you don't like Lino's bread."

CARLOS STOOD IN AWE of the blood red light over the Sangre de Cristos and the light through the trees and sagebrush at the Cutoff. Carlos lived for the smell of horse sweat and dust collecting on the brim of his hat and his shirt pockets; the light coming through the dust and dusk of the light of dawn; hands wringing and stretching and worrying about the cattle and work of the days, as well as the animal sounds and the ring of the meal bell. There was nothing better for him. Lino's coffee pot usually was the first smell of the day and the first sign of life from the bunkhouse. It livened the men waiting for the wash basin.

Carlos dreaded the smell of Lino, though. The vile smells of body funk and grease over a long month's work. It contrasted with the smells of coffee and the frying of eggs and the smell of baking bread and pies the old man Lino would work at. The day seemed to begin with that smell and funk.

"Why do I need to smell like roses? Why do I need to smell good? No wife out here and I'm not going home to Taos until the season is over so what do I care about bathing," Lino argued.

The men complained and spoke to Carlos personally and passionately about the issue at hand. Eddie and the Padilla brothers would all say, "Carlos, get him to wash. He can cook there's no doubt, pies and bread and summer stew, but the cabrón smells to high heaven."

Jose Diaz was the one who called him out the hardest: "Get him to wash or he's out." There was even the idea Carlos should become the cook, but Carlos quickly killed that.

"I'm no cook. I'm here to work my way up to buy a horse. I lost my horse. Lino's the cook. He's got all the knowledge and I just do what he tells me. I just follow orders," Carlos said.

Spring went on in that way, the hands complaining of Lino's smell and also his lectures on philosophy. The men did not believe Lino to be Christian or Godly, but they enjoyed his pan dulce or his pan de campo and chile and beans and his coffee. They enjoyed that Carlos was silent, and they appreciated his work ethic. During the day he worked and kept to himself and his own business. But at night Carlos and Lino would banter back and forth away from the other men.

Lino would calm Carlos' mind with the words, "The work has been this way for 100 years and it will be here 100 years on. You're part of a larger world. I'm sure you could ride with the rest of the men if you wanted. We all have to work the roundup in the summer, and I am sure you can work on horseback then. The work of running in all the cattle and branding and castrating the animals. Don't feel so quick to feel mistreated here, Carlos. You have food and drink and fellowship here. Don't be so quick to despair."

Carlos laughed off the wisdom, not knowing what to make of it, and went back to his days with his silence.

ONE DAY THE BOY *from town brought a bushel of cabbage. "Well, I guess I am frying cabbage," Lino announced to groans among the men.*

"Say, Lino," the men were beginning to complain, "Why can't you fry us up a steak and some Texas-sized potatoes."

"No potatoes." That was Lino's answer. "And no steak for the hired help. You need your minerals."

"What the hell, Lino," the men said. "We need steak."

"See the whites in your fingernails," Lino said. "Not enough leafy greens. Too much meat in your belly."

Later with plates of fried greens and plates of beans Carlos asked, "Lino, is that true about the minerals? They used to tell us that in the Army and then they only gave us chipped beef."

"Sure sounds good, don't it, Carlos," Lino said. "How the hell else am I going to get these muchachitos to eat their vegetables. Like babies. Too much protein and meat is hard on the kidneys."

"Is that true?" Carlos said.

Lino smiled and then the two men sat grinning. Later, some of the men asked why Carlos always ate everything up. Always gobbled down all that Lino served to him.

"Hell, I even seen Carlos eating a rotten moldy tomato," one of the men said. "All rotten and full of black spots."

"Hell, I even seen the man eat an onion like an apple like he was at the Stampede Festival. Like it was a candied apple," anoth-

er said. "What's the deal, Carlos?"

"Spent nearly two years eating what I could find. Whatever put in front of me and I was happy to have it. Try not to think too much on it."

"Maybe that's why Lino likes you so much."

"Ever eat rabbit or squirrel? I knew a guy always eating squirrels and rabbits."

"I ate a dog once," Carlos said. He didn't know why he said it. He didn't know why he admitted to it. He just said it.

One of the men called Eddie's dog from the doorway to joke: "Oh Carlos, how can you eat a Sheba girl?"

"Dog can't smell any worse than this cabbage," one man said.

Another gave Sheba some of the greens to eat. Another man said, "Look, Lino, she likes your greens to eat. Why'd you have to eat dog anyway, Carlos?"

"We ran out of cartridges and we ran out of coats and socks and we ran out of food. Nearly ran out of men. We couldn't eat each other so one of the nights one of the men fried up some meat. They said it was dog."

The table of hands got quiet as Carlos told the war story. One said, "Man, I couldn't eat no dog. Poor Sheba."

"Hungry enough and you'll eat whatever you can," Carlos said, and it felt like another man's wisdom or a lecture from his cousin or his father. Angry words from a Buck Sergeant or a Captain always screaming at Carlos in his memories.

"Lino's greens don't look so bad now, huh," Eddie said. "Maybe that's why you care for Sheba so much. My dog but she's always sleeping with you and following you."

"Maybe you're part dog now," one man said. Later, Carlos smirked and sat with Sheba a long while thinking on it.

SOON CARLOS *would find Lino to be an odd bunkmate. Lino rarely bathed and had long flowing hair thick as straw. And he was al-*

ways filling Carlos in on his life story. He introduced to the man he was from the east coast and was educated in the finest Indian schools where they changed his name and cut his long hair down when he was only nine years of age.

"I thought you was from Taos Pueblo," Carlos said.

"I live there but I ain't from there," Lino said.

Lino swore off haircuts or any kind of white man's ways and worked on cattle ranches and cattle drives all his life, and as he aged, he graduated to cocinero. Became a man of recipes and flavors. He carried boxes of spices and recipes in his footlocker and hid them away before he cooked. He lectured on how he was also a philosopher though Carlos had never known one, and he only knew Lino as a proliferator of lard and butter. Lino would repeat, "I am a man who only cares for my true personal friendships. I care about you and any man here. Epicurus teaches—"

"Who's that?" Carlos said.

"A philosopher. He teaches me to find my own personal pleasures. The pleasure of friendship. The pleasure of family. Oh, I tell you, boys, I am an educated bastard. I ain't no heathen or dumb as no horse. I am an educated man. I have a love for books and libraries, and they are all in my thoughts. Epicurus is a man who lived before Jesus Christ and taught me all I ever need to know."

Carlos got to thinking he only read one book and really only simple passages from his mother's leather-bound Bible.

"All the man cared about was personal delights and appetite," Lino would say to himself. Then Lino would spit or cough or fart and fill the air with oily smells and stink as the men plotted and schemed to force him to bathe. They took their pay to town and gifted him soap and powders which he refused and took as an insult. Lino cursed the boys and forced them to take the gifts back for their wives or girlfriends or their mamas. He even went so far as to go on strike from time to time from cooking or prepping coffee. The Patrón Waddingham got word and sent his boy Arthur to force Lino back to cooking. Lino had used the same tactic to get Carlos

hired on, or at least that was the rumor.

AT NIGHT *after the day's work of feeding cattle and prepping meals with Lino, Carlos sat in his bunk with his nuevo testamanto Bible, the same he had with him in France.*

"What do you see in that book, Carlos?" Lino would say.

"First Corinthians. The Golden Rule, Lino."

"I told you I'm a philosopher and a thinker. I been to school on the east coast as a child. I ever tell you this story, Carlos?"

"Every damned night, Lino," Carlos said smiling and returning to his pages.

That was the night Lino admitted to Carlos his birthname was Magdalino but folks always called him Lino. Carlos nodded and smiled. "When you get to the Sermon on the Mount, the parts of building your life on bedrock let me know, Carlos," Lino said.

Most nights the hands rode off leaving Carlos and Lino behind to talk. Carlos would go back to his Bible and Lino would sit and lecture and of course drink. "Too damned religious for your own good," the hands would say to Carlos as they headed out to Colmor bars and cathouses.

CARLOS SOMETIMES *made excuses at dinner when the boys talked of heading to town. "Saving coins and bills," he would say. The day's work grew longer with more sunlight, the hands got rowdier and lonelier. "Too damned good to have a drink with the boys," the Padilla brothers would each say.*

"Lost the will to drink and live?" Jose Diaz said.

"Someone has to have religion and quietness for the rest of you men," Lino said, defending Carlos.

"Tell him about his girl, Mara, Lino," the boys said.

"Yeah, tell your silent religious man about his love," the boys said.

Carlos was too busy reading to pay attention, to take the men seriously.

"He's gotta find out some time."

"I heard you rode out to her a few times," the Padilla brothers said.

"I rode past and talked to her once. Picking up supplies with the dog cart. What's this foolishness?" Carlos asked.

"Word is she's been asking on you," Jose Diaz said. And he said it with the sickest and most deranged smile.

"She's the prettiest in New Mexico," the Padilla boys said. "She belongs to the Patrón's son."

"Word is she's sweet on you, Carlos," Lino said.

"Gossip," Carlos said.

"I've taught school and I am an educated man, Carlos. I tell you this much. And one day you will need my wisdom," Lino insisted.

"Wisdom? You hands are like old gossips."

"I'm a romantic, Carlos," Lino said.

"I know my place. If I am competing with the Patrón's son, I don't have half a chance. I'm only human but I know my place. I don't have money enough for a horse much less a wife."

"Well, I'll be damned the man can talk and is alive. Tell me more about your Mara. She's a curvy thing. Thin frame but a curvy little thing. Her hair is dark and wild. She'd make a fine wife."

"She's always in a cowboy hat to block the sun as she works. She wears boots when she works."

She had the sweetest green eyes, and Lino would always repeat how lucky the Patrón was to have a woman of efficiency and business sense. "She can hold her own," Lino said. "Green eyes say she's unique to the land and her people." But Carlos cared nothing for all that. She could tell a gelding from a mare and could tell a 2-year-old horse from a 4-year-old. That is something that impressed him.

"Any woman who would take men like these damn hands in

for the night would have to be sweet and knowledgeable," one of the hands said.

"Take in?" Carlos said.

The Padilla boys and Jose Diaz began to laugh and carry on with those words. "I hate to tell you, Carlos, but the woman is a whore."

"Don't make no difference to me," Carlos said. "Makes me think more of her."

"I knew when I met you, Carlos," Lino said. "I knew since I met you, I said to myself there's a man who knows beauty and a light when he sees it. Epicurus teaches us to value friendship and companionship. That's the purity. The true wealth of this damned dry land," Lino said. "She's a rare flower is all I am saying to you, Carlos. There is nothing more important in this world than ethics and beauty and companionship. And marriage."

"I like you, Lino, but I don't know what the hell you say half the time. And watch your back; those men hate your stink and they will come for you."

"Come for me?"

"Force you to bathe."

"Bathe?"

"I've been working camps for awhile," Carlos said, "and I tell you I know stink and my friend, you have a great stink. I could care less but these men aren't going to have it much longer. They will come for you. By force, probably."

"All men desire to know, Carlos," Lino said, "and now I know."

THEY SAY MARA'S MOTHER *was the one that said it straight out. When the man Luis Valdez from Colorado had announced his intention to court the young girl. "Whatever he tells you," the stone-faced mother said, "and whatever he promises you the answer is no. Do you hear me girl? There will be no marriage for you."*

"Yes, Mama," the 15-year-old Mara said. She had not quite de-

veloped her own sharp tongue.

"Let him take you to the Stampede and the dances," the Mother said. "Let him buy you flowers. But there is no way in hell you're leaving this home." The mother's words soon became the father's words and then became Mara's words.

Luis Valdez was more than a farmworker like his father and brothers. He owned land in Seven Mile Plaza and had men working the lettuce fields. He was tall and thin legged with broad shoulders. He wore crisp white shirts and suitcoats. He wore a fancy Stratoliner Fedora. The word around the village was that Valdez had money and had status. He drove his own Model T Ford pickup.

"That festival is as far out from home you'll ever see," Mara's mother had said.

Lena returned home with a picture postcard made that captured her hand inside of Luis' hand. Mara's father tossed the postcard into the woodstove.

They sat her down in the living room and the cigar smoking grandmother was the one to warn out loud, "Everyone gossips and talks on you. So don't be spreading your legs."

"Only whores and tramps go out with men alone in trucks," the mother said. "The village is small and I am tired of hearing it."

"Hearing what?" Mara said.

"About you out with that man in the fields."

"I brought him water and food."

"And who asked you?" the grandmother said. "Who told you to bring him food?"

On the back porch Mara washed the men's Sunday shirts and then cut wood for the woodstove. She stared at the burned-up postcard she managed to save. After she cooked eggs and potatoes and the men sat to eat, she wiped counters and swept up before lingering out back to once again stare into the burned-up card for answers.

"Hello Señor Vigil," Luis Valdez said the first time he walked

into the house on 5 Mile Road West. The small size of the living room and the lack of comfortable furniture struck him right off. "I am driving out to the landfill, and I'm happy to drive out your trash," Luis said before he was even fully into the room and removed his Stetson.

"Oh, thank you kindly," the mother said and the words were as sweet as she could manage.

"I'm here to ask for your daughter's hand," Luis said to Mara's father.

"Yes," the girl said out loud.

The next month Mara was pregnant but still had no pin or no ring from Luis Valdez. In fact, months later after her belly swelled, the family saw less and less of Luis.

"You've disgraced the name of the family," Mara's grandmother said. She said it out loud over all the arguing and crying one Sunday dinner.

Mara's mother added nearly sobbing, "How could you do this?"

Mara's father drank coffee and sat silent while the grandmother lit her cigar and blew smoke rings into the air over the dinner table.

"A damned disgrace to the family. I don't want you in this house no more," the father said. "Your cousins are taking you to New Mexico. Luis has given us money for the trip."

"When did you talk to Luis?" Mara said nearly sobbing.

"Never mind," the grandmother said. "Never you mind. In New Mexico I won't have to see you and hear the gossip. You can work and wash clothes and send your money home. You can live with the rest of the whores. You have to go before the people find you out, the mother said."

"I'll have no more of you in this house," Mara's father repeated.

THEY SAY MARA'S BABY *was an infant when the Patrón's boy Arthur rode to her adobe home in Colmor. He went to look at her from a distance when she went to the water tank to bathe, and then one day he walked up to tell her how her breasts were sagging and her belly rounding, and how he could tell she had given birth to babies. Before Lino there had been no one to warn her about the Patrón's son.*

Soon when she saw the man's horse or his father Old Man Waddingham's horse-drawn wagon, she ran and hid in her house. It was Old Man Waddingham who offered her the job at his store in Colmor. "Whitewash the walls and keep it clean. I can keep you and your daughter's bellies full," the Old Man Waddingham said. "I have peach trees and need someone to care for them too," the old man said. Later the old man slapped his son's face for taking the Lord's name in vain in front of Mara. Or so that was the story. Mara didn't want the men to enter her world, and she thought of them as hunters. As Lino was fond of saying, she had no choices in those days in Colmor, she had no defenses.

WHEN CARLOS SPOKE *to Mara for the first time, he gave attention to her girl first. He spoke to her with kindness and a soft voice. He told her his name was Montoya. Mara then stood face to face with Carlos to get in between of him and the girl, and she immediately saw the loneliness in his face. He was just a stray vaquero looking for work, but he carried himself with a guarded manner. He asked her about music and if she danced. He heard that down at the church that sometimes the folks would dance on the hard-packed earth. The old polkas, he kept saying, do you know them? Later he asked her if she knew of the Cutoff Ranch where he had taken work. He had so many questions for her and her voice filled him with a memory of happiness. Something from before the war. He let her do most of the talking at first until Lino advised Carlos, You have to learn how to talk to people, Carlos. So again, he asked her about music and accordion music. It was his way of asking where the dance halls were or the festivals in Colmor. He had a hard time being straight out with her.*

"Not many dances, cowboy. Too many miles between here and Wagon Mound," Mara answered.

Carlos had passed the brutal expanse from Wagon Mound to Colmor, the gullies and mesas broken up by juniper and pinon trees. A lot of silence between the villages, was how Mara put it to Carlos.

"Not exactly Paris, France," Mara said. "I heard you been out there."

Carlos nodded. "Field hospital. Not much more."

"Did you go to serve the country or the flag? Or did you go to hurt people."

"I was just following after my cousin. Went looking after my family."

At first, she felt pity for the newcomer, and then with that answer she felt what she guessed might be affection.

"You need someone to take care of you and your little girl," Carlos finally said to Mara.

"I need someone to fix the windows and fill my wood pile is what I need," Mara said. "Men around here ain't worth much more than that."

"Maybe I'll see you in the church on Sundays," Carlos said. "I come to the church on Sundays."

"They wouldn't have me and my baby down at the church," she said.

"Like I say, I hear they have dances down at that church," Carlos said as his mouth slightly widened into a smile.

THE PATRÓN'S SON, *Arthur, was pulling up his pants and pulling his suspenders over his narrow shoulders when Carlos came into Mara's room above the Patrón's store. Arthur was bare chested and shirtless and found the whole scene to be comical. He laughed out loud to see the pain come over Carlos' face. "You think I'm doing this to you," Arthur said. "You think I'm the one hurting you and Lino's people. But it ain't me. It's the industry."*

Carlos stood and got lost in the pain for a moment. This made Arthur laugh even harder especially as Carlos ripped his cigarillo from his mouth and had him out the door and down the stairs by his neck and arm.

"You'll learn," Arthur said. "You'll learn who owns this land."

Folks aren't quite sure how many times Carlos hit or attempted to hit Arthur that day, or how many times Arthur hit Carlos. Folks remember the blood on the stairs and back and spoke on it for weeks, long after Carlos and Mara rode out. Folks remember Arthur's laughter and his shirtlessness. They remember the men rolling around in the dust and dirt of the Patrón's feed store. They recall Mara at the head of the stairs yelling after them as naked as she could be. Folks don't remember how it all ended, but they know Arthur's companeros, Ray and Paul Padilla and Jose Diaz, took him home that day because he was bloodied so badly, he couldn't mount his own horse much less ride himself. They remembered his pants and suspenders were tore up and useless. They don't know what made Carlos lose his mind with thoughts.

THE MORNING FOLLOWING *the incident with Mara, the Patrón's men came for Lino, everyone except for Carlos and Eddie, who were out feeding cattle. They came with a fence post. They roped and tied him down and carried the man out to the water hole for a good bathing.*

without

Under the bare bulb of Felipa's kitchen, in the midst of wine bottles, beer cans, mangled photographs, a scarred tabletop and an overflowing ashtray, the sick and quivering old man listened for another neighbor's call. Instead he heard the voice of the thin-faced Compadre Tony or maybe Jake. His first impulse that second week without Felipa was to avoid being seen but there was work, always work.

Tony approached Carlos, calling to him, the voice coming into Carlos' inner ear. "Oye, Carlos," Tony said and looked around the house blankly. "How's it going with you, viejo?"

Carlos sat with his head down on the table and the phonebook right in the middle of the tabletop. "The shit they say?" he asked.

"Where's the wifey?" Tony said.

"Your house stinks," Jake added, sitting across from Carlos and smelling out into the air openly. "Don't you think it stinks?"

"They should know the woman is out visiting her family," Carlos said. "I can get on without the woman for at least a week but they should know I am down with bad legs."

"Bad what?"

"Legs," Carlos repeated loudly. "They should know I got bad legs. Eddie told me to stay home. I can get on without working as long as I want."

"Don't you need money?" Tony said.

"Checks from the Army. Whenever I need money, I get them checks."

"Checks, huh?"

"Or the spirits provide."

"Spirits?" Jake asked.

"They probably brought you here today, no? Are you here with the men?"

"What the hell is the fool talking about?"

Jake ignored the question and focused on the mess of bottles and vachas. "How've you been living?"

Somehow the men managed to pull Carlos into the bathroom where spider webs filled dirt-framed windows. They held the man steady under his shoulders and damp armpits.

"You eat today?" asked Tony, leaning against the door. Jake soaked the old man, clothes and all, underneath the showerhead. "I said did you eat today?"

Scanning the men's face for the first time, Carlos sucked in his cheeks with pain and then spat a mix of mucus and blood down from his nose.

"I brought you some bread and a bologna, Carlos," Tony said. "Some chile and beans too. I'll wait and see when you done here if you need to eat. I'll brew some coffee too, viejo. How's that sound?"

"They need to know I have them checks and don't need to work," Carlos answered.

"Who the hell are you talking to?"

"You need to eat," Jake said. The old man stripped off his soaking flannel shirt and coveralls, revealing his blue sickly frame and dry gangrenous skin.

—

THAT VERY NEXT MORNING, two gabacho doctors amputated Carlos' legs at the knee, and his young wife and beauty Felipa returned from Huerfano County. First, she called the worksite and then Pifanio's home. She spoke to Delores and tried not to forget her shame or to quarrel. She looked down at her hands, her chin trembling as she asked for the foreman.

As Pifanio and Felipa later stood talking in the hospital, Carlos screamed in apprehension of the chapel priest who came into the antiseptic smell of the hospital room. Felipa and Pifanio nearly faced one another while Carlos continued to yell and carry on. There seemed to Pifanio only one thing to do as he exited the room and Felipa followed.

"It's gonna be okay, Felipa," Pifanio offered.

"How's it ever gonna be okay? We ain't from no money."

"I know."

"He's a stricken man!"

"I know!"

"Yeah, you know. He goes and buys my Blue Box from the corner store when I have my time. Ain't no man ever done what he's done for me and I can't even get you to call or talk, Pifanio."

"How can I call you if you have no phone, Felipa?"

WHEN THE PRIEST exited the room and asked for the wife, he acted surprised at Felipa's young age and held her shaking hands while they both recited prayers. He put his hand on her shoulder and whispered, "In the midst of life we are in death." And then he moved on down the hallway to the next room. Felipa's eyes watered, and she finally broke down into her handkerchief and into her hands before entering.

Later that night Carlos told Felipa, "Don't want me to die in no hospital?"

"You won't die, viejo."

"She don't want me to die here."

"No. Can't say that, my husband."

"Help me with my boots," the man said in a delirium. "They must help me with my boots."

And with those words Felipa wept and held her man's arm in a way she had not thought of since those first weeks and months of the marriage, when she had first moved from Ridge Home to Franklin Street. Suddenly she knew how to touch him and to comfort him. For two years she had done her best but now she remembered how he looked in the beginning and how she was proud to have a home of her own. A husband of her own. All those moments had not been wasteful but building to a necessity and hurt.

"My boots, cabróna," the old man, Carlos, repeated as he weakly tried to pull himself from his bed and then later from his first wheeled chair.

LATER HIS WIFE had entered the hospital room again, the door just shutting behind her. There seemed to be nothing left in the room but the man and his wife. He cursed and then moved on to punches to his thighs; the way he lay on the stained floor with piss and dust made him think of how the world had him and how further touches of change would kill or worse, deaden him. Torture, or something near it, was what he felt as he scraped and clawed the walls and then at the wheeled chair before he regained his seat. And yet as he started for the door again, he threw a sick and unapologetic glance at the woman.

"What do you have to say for yourself, old man?" Felipa asked.

"What?"

"They say you scream at the walls and carry on conversations and they have it up to here with you. Say you up half the night with your damned tears and cries."

"And where is the man? The Patrón?"

"Who?" she said innocently.

"I pulled a pistola and haven't spoken to the cabrón since."

"When?"

"He nearly pissed himself."

"When was this, Carlos?"

"Somewhere sometime. No how or never? I don't know."

"You're too damn old to be this damned stubborn. We are here to help and you yell and scream. I'm here and waiting to talk to you but you've been knocked out cold from what they give you because they say you're violent. I'm so sorry for all of this, husband. But they say you won't calm yourself. What do you have to say for yourself?" she repeated.

The old man Carlos sat with his sickened expression. He never said another word. He gave her looks and rolled his eyes. And Felipa who stood at the center of the quiet room endured the violent raps the man had made at the chair and at the walls before the woman whispered on and Carlos found the consoling softness of the woman's voice.

"I suppose we'll have to learn marriage all over, old man," she said, brushing the wet hair from his forehead. "I will have to watch over you now. What do your voices have to say about that huh? Viejo?"

boys in new mexico

The whole function of the months of September and October was to prepare for the winter, prepare for the coming of cold weather and the end of field work and side-jobs. They also knew the cow the father owned was being fattened and prepared for a final transition from fall to winter. That was the year the father planned on moving to the city of Costilla after hearing about work for the railroad and moving away from the rural life the boys had always known.

The boys had simple jobs of carrying the feed buckets and hay bales out to the corral every morning, carrying a stick to shoo the animal from the fence in order to pour the liquid and dump the food for the beast. Benito hated the work and hated the smell of the cow, hated that every morning the horses and the cow ate before the family.

"None of us eat before the animals," the boys' Jefe barked in Spanish.

From an early age Benito resisted the work and resisted the cow and her damn stupid ways, her encrusted nose. He hated how she broke from the fencing and how the boys had to chase her up the north grade before she hit the open road that separated the properties. Benito hated the way they had to mend fences to keep her in, and he hated the smell of shit under his feet. And most of all he hated the work the father made him and his cousin responsible for, hated the cow's fat belly his cousin

Carlos rubbed lovingly.

One day Benito fed her and then aimed an imaginary Springfield rifle, the kind his Tio Marquez let him fire on a hunting trip one year, and he pretended to shoot her right between the eyes. The cow was as good as slaughtered for the family in his mind, and it didn't hurt him one bit.

Mostly he hated how his cousin Carlos loved the work, reveled in the responsibility and the commands from the father. He hated the way his cousin called the father "Jefe."

"Yes, Jefe! Yes, Jefe!" Benito said, mocking his cousin's responses at night when they lay awake. "What should we do now, Jefe! Give us more work, Jefe! Whatever you say, Jefe! Take us to the fields to work us until we're dead, Jefe!"

In the double bed the boys shared with their Grandfather, Carlos would yawn and pay the cousin's teasing no mind. The ceiling above was plywood and unfinished, and as the boy yawned and woke for a new day of work, he laughed at his cousin.

"Shut up and get out to that cow," Carlos said.

"Don't elbow me, Jefe!" Benito said.

"Well, get up then," Carlos said.

And Carlos was always the first to the kitchen and the sweet smells of morning coffee and fried eggs. Sometimes bacon and tortillas were on the table if the boys were lucky.

Carlos huddled around the wood stove for warmth as their Grandfather finished his coffee and as he gave them the morning duties.

The Grandmother the family called "Skinny Grandma" had two bowls of oatmeal mush when she ordered the boys to get to their work and then to wash.

"About time yous wake up," the Grandfather joked. "Both of yous out and get that cow fed."

Benito jeered and staggered to the warmth of the wood stove.

"Soon that cow will be slaughtered, and you won't have this job no more but until then, get," the Grandfather said.

"Yes, Jefe," Carlos said.

Benito reached and grabbed at his cousin's hair and then Carlos shoved at him. Benito slammed into the wood stove and nearly knocked over a skillet from the stove.

"Boys," Skinny Grandma shouted. "You'll burn yourselves up."

"Goddamn it, cabrónes," the Grandfather said from behind his coffee cup. "Get to your work, boys."

THAT MORNING the autumn air felt cool, even in the north shed. The cow stayed near the corner of the shed on this particular morning because the old man's Compadres, the Marquez cousins, had come with their single shot rifle and their butcher knives wrapped in cloth in their arms.

Last day to mess with this stupid thing, Benito thought as he smiled and leapt up to the metal bars of the makeshift fencing.

"Quiet, boys," the oldest Marquez cousin said while the youngest loaded the weapon. "You'll spook em."

"Where are they gonna shoot her?" Carlos whispered to Benito.

"Where you gonna shoot them?" Benito asked out loud to the Marquez boy aiming the rifle out over the fencing.

"Quiet," the older man ordered before finally pointing his index finger between his own eyes. "Don't want to mess with the meat."

The youngest Marquez boy took a deep breath and then let it out again and again in an exaggerated way.

Benito was excited and Carlos was nervous. He must have

seen the Skinny Grandmother slaughter a chicken a thousand times, the flow of redness and then the woman making quick work of the body. He must have also seen a deer slaughtered and hanged in the backyard by the grandfather or his father a hundred times, but the cow was different. He had fed and taken care of this cow every morning for months before their ride out to the llano, before their work in the fields. This cow had some meaning to him he couldn't quite understand in the moment.

The rifle cracked through those thoughts and rang out into the north shed and into the inner ears of the Jefe and Benito. The cow leapt and then her mouth burst with a painful sound and then she was running and staggering all over the shed. There was a shriek of agony from the animal and then from the Jefe.

This running and drunken staggering went on and on. Benito laughed and the Jefe stood with his mouth open, his hands sweating and wringing together at first, then smashed into his pockets.

Then the men, including the Jefe and Benito's father, ran at the cow with their blades and their sharp tools. The Marquez boys followed and cornered the animal against a manure pile and fired a second and then a final third shot. And even though the young Carlos was scared and wanted to hold his face in his hands, he looked on as he thought a man should, every bloody minute of the chase and the shooting. He watched as the Marquez boys struggled with the rifle and struggled in the mud and manure.

The animal finally stood still and then finally came falling down to the earth and the feet of the panicked Marquez' boys.

"Ay, que cabrón," the oldest Marquez boy said. "Did you ever see nothing like that, huh?"

And as the men shook hands and slapped at each other's backs, the oldest boy, Carlos, ran over to the corral fence. He was hanging onto the metal bars and vomiting over the slick metal, his hands clinging for balance and for support as his stomach heaved.

"What's the matter, Jefe?" Benito said and then laughed.

"Couldn't stand it, huh?" the youngest Marquez boy asked, laughing and readying the blades wrapped in cloth and leather straps for the work of slitting the cow's throat and belly.

"Better get down to the house, boy," the father ordered. "If you can't take the man's work out here then get into the house with your Skinny Grandma."

Shame made the boy walk out of the shed and then out to the woodpile before he cursed himself. He couldn't believe he let Benito and the father catch him in his weakness. This feeling of weakness made him cry. His head ached, and his stomach cramped and spasmed with more than this first true sight of death. He couldn't stop thinking of Benito and the Marquez boys laughing.

On his way he met up with the Grandfather sitting on a stool at his own woodpile, chopping his thin spruce blocks for the woodstove. The old man seemed to know exactly what had happened, as if his years gave him the answer.

"I thought you were the Jefe," the Grandfather said, almost instinctively. "Thought you were firme."

Crying harder, he felt defeated, and he made his way into the kitchen where the Skinny Grandmother was cleaning her stovetop. There were no sounds in the house other than the Skinny Grandmother.

The Grandmother remarked. "You look as white as a ghost."

"I'm no ghost," the boy screeched, slamming his backside down at the kitchen table. Carlos was 9 years old that autumn when the Skinny Grandmother finally held the boy in her arms and poured him milk to ease his weak stomach.

los malos

Eddie and the hands in and around Colmor and even as far as Wagon Mound referred to the men who stole horses and cattle as Los Malos. Old Man Waddingham called them rustlers from the old times and ways, and Lino referred to the men as sinners because he knew Carlos had religion and had faith in his Lord. Carlos always read from his leather-bound Bible at night and believed all men could be saved. "Not Los Malos," Lino said. "Los Malos steal and cheat and feed their people and meet down near the river and sell to cabins and outfits right from under Waddingham. Or so the folks say."

Old Man Waddingham would ride down and meet the hands around the bunkhouse table as Lino served food and warned his men: "I pay your salaries and so these men steal from you. That's who they steal from."

EDDIE HAD ONCE *explained it all to Carlos: Los Malos were boys, really, and lived with their Grandparents and Fathers and Mothers in Mora. They slept most of the day and then drank coffee around dinner time, sharing their mother's tamales and sharing pots of coffee with their grandfather, telling their jokes and stories. Later they walked out to throw rocks as their grandparents went in to sleep. Los Malos had no work or schooling and had no real direction. Every bit of coin and scrap of money they could find was brought home to the Abuelitos and to the Abuelitas who cooked their meals and washed their Levi's hanging on the line in the backyard. Sometimes the Abuelitas took in some clothes for laundering. This would involve boiling water and then placing the cloth and stirring and then hanging them out to dry. The mothers and fathers were dead and gone, ran off for work or dead from the great sickness. In fact, the Abuelitos weren't really Abuelitos by blood but were compadres and friends to the boys parents. Los Malos got going after the old folks slipped into their iron-framed beds and that's when the boys came alive. They drove the Abuelito's horse down to Wagon Mound and then up and down the lanes looking for animals to hit with their rifles or maybe a deer to shoot.*

Los Malos in only undershirts played around until nearly 3 am and then found the Cutoff Ranch fences. They found cattle near a clearing right where they were told. They had a quick fist fight and then targeted each other with cow pies before collapsing to the ground and laughing until their sides ached. The trick to rustling or stealing was to wait for the legitimate world to sleep, is what Lino always said. The plan was simple: take a rifle and shoot a cow and then carve out the good meat, and they chopped and hacked and bloodied their undershirts before heading out and heading home. The Abuela always wondered what trouble the boys got into by bringing home blood-stained shirts and beef. They worked and carved until sunup, taking the meat in paper sacks to local folks. They took some meat to the Abuelitos and the villages near and around Colmor and Wagon Mound. By 8 a.m. Los Malos were back in bed before their Abuelito's first piss and smoke. The old man warmed his coffee and sat on his porch in Colmor and then found the coin and paper bills had magically appeared in his leather billfold.

"What's this, vieja?" the old man said to his aging wife.

"No se," the woman repeated. "Them boys of yours always thinking about you and your empty billfold."

The days following the raids Los Malos had great cookouts where folks served up steaks and great chops of meat.

"Quite a damned enterprise," Old Man Waddingham said to his boy and the boy's compañeros who arrived at the bunkhouse with their gun belts and Colt revolvers. The old man spit and pulled his hat from his forehead. "What in the hell am I paying you for if you can't catch these bastards?"

"The locals cover for Los Malos," Jose Diaz explained.

"Quien es Los Malos?" Ray Padilla asked.

"That's what they call them," the Patrón said. "But damned if I think it's just a couple of boys with a rifle and a butcher knife. Ain't you boys got rifles or knives?"

"They are up early, and the men fall asleep, Patrón," the men explained.

"Goddammit," the Patrón said. "Ain't you got coffee and rifles and supplies and men and you can't catch these boys. Have the men sleep during the day if you have to, for Christ's sake."

"Word is they have more horses and guns down in the valley protecting the cattle," Lino later reported to Carlos. "The Patrón needs your gun. Hell, I'd get on a horse and find those boys messing with the cattle, but I am too old and too damned tired. Besides I'm not sure I don't love those damned boys for doing what they do."

"They're thieves, Lino."

"What does it matter to you? You're getting your meals and food. That's the way the world works. The Patrón steals the labor and Los Malos steal for their tables. They steal to live and they steal to survive and they exist for one another," Lino said. "That's the thing the Patrón could never understand. They can't go to the law and they can't go to the Patrón directly so they make their own law."

CARLOS HAD BEEN *at the Cutoff a month when three boys were strung up for horse thieving and stealing. They had the boys in the Patrón's orchard as proof of what happens to thieves. The next night two more cows were stolen, and Lino explained it all again as the way the Cutoff worked.*

Carlos began to dream of the boys, and they began to appear in his prayers. And since the war he was in the habit of sitting up at night and reading his bible and meditating before sleep. He prayed for the boys to do right by their God and by their people. Lino called it meditating and said it was from Epicurus, but Carlos knew nothing of that. In fact, Lino laughed out loud when he heard Carlos speak the prayer aloud. Lino said, "These boys are sinners, but the people need sinners like they need their animals, their horses and cattle. The viejitos need sinners like los ricos need their money. Just the way of the world. They do it for survival."

EDDIE HAD INTRODUCED *the work horses and the draft horses to Carlos on his first full night out at the Cutoff. Lino was the Cocinero but Eddie ran the hired help, the work hands, and knew every bit of the work and livestock. Lino joked he could tell the horses apart in the darkness because most days the man bridled and saddled each horse before sunrise.*

"This here is Margaret but I call her Magre though she don't like it," Eddie began. "Just like a woman I knew." He tipped his hat to the animal. No matter the time of day he wore his large flat brimmed cover vaquero style. "And this is Molly and Doc—Molly is the fat one. This is Gina and Eva. This is Boss," Eddie said, and as he introduced each mare he rubbed and scratched at ears and mane. "This is Spotlight. She's an old one, the oldest on the ranch. Older than the Patrón maybe. This one here is Izzy and that is Bobby. And here's Ben. Ben is the spookiest. I mean easiest to scare. Saw a Mexican grey wolf one time when I was out with Ben, and he tossed me and ran off and left me with the damn biggest wolf I ever seen."

"What did you do, Eddie?" Carlos asked.

"I simply apologized for being out that far and I asked for the

wolf's permission to live in his world."

"His world?"

"These horses and that wolf are the real owners out here. They feed us and do all the heavy lifting and they are the ones who own the land, as far as I can see it. Not the damned old Patrón up there in his damned big house."

Eddie was accompanied on most workdays with his cattle dog he called Sheba.

"Called her that because she was lazy or so the folks who sold her to me said. Queen of Sheba and all that. But that dog works me into the grave, that one most days."

It was Eddie who taught Carlos the finer points of vaquero style. Carlos had been in the army but didn't know too much of the old ways of working horses. Eddie was gentle and spoke to Magre, his favorite, in the softest voice. Unlike the Patrón and the son, he never whipped or beat a horse. Never tied a fencepost to a horse to shoe the poor thing.

"The vaquero style is calm and gentle," Eddie instructed. "Pressure and force never beats out balance and signals. See how I move the bridle and the bit. Nobody threatening her or beating her or forcing her to move. We move together. The mare stays in balance and goes where I move my body."

"Always keep them calm and quiet, Carlos," Eddie said.

"Officers in the war beat and strapped a horse and lifted her up with pulleys and contraptions. It was all about speed and shoeing a horse with efficiency," Carlos said.

"Some men should be candlemakers," Eddie said.

"What's that?"

"Because they don't give a damn about what it takes to care for a horse."

Eddie was also the man who could throw a figure eight with a reata. Throw a rope to snag the neck and the front leg of a fleeing cow at the same time.

"A vaquero who can throw a figure eight is worth five hands,"

Lino later admitted to Carlos. "He should be running the whole damn outfit."

THE DAY THE PATRÓN'S MEN came for Eddie for being one of Los Malos, they roped him and some say they whipped him. They ripped his clothes from him and shot him in the neck when he fought. They had his scarf wrapped around his head in the box and had him propped up on a fence by the bunkhouse and everyone could see the man as they walked by. They had a sign up labeling him a cattle cheat. The idea was to make him an example. Lino said that's the way the Patrón handled his business if he caught the hired help stealing or playing on his land.

"They say he sold cattle to the families and to the people," Lino explained. "Said he led folks to the llano where the fattest cows were and left some out for money. Left out where Los Malos could find them. They say a cattle thief is worse than a horse thief, but Eddie was just feeding families. Didn't think the Patrón would miss one cow out of hundred. Eddie's the one in charge of the count."

"Where will they bury the man, Lino?" Carlos asked.

"Folks will take him to Ortiz, Colorado, where they have the Catholic cemetery. Always wanted to be buried in Colorado with his mother and father and his people."

"Poor man," Carlos said.

"He knew the trouble coming down on him," Lino said. "He knew the Patrón and that son Arthur of his would set his whole life on fire for stealing. He knew. But he didn't care and neither do I. Too damned old to care."

moving

After Felipa and Carlos finally loaded their clothes and furniture into the truckito, Felipa received word her sister had passed. The neighbor lady received a call from the sister's husband and walked over with the news. There was a crash and her Buick turned up smashed out and burning out on Interstate 25. It was then Felipa felt hollowed out and had the idea to burn every last family picture in her bedroom, all the photos her sister brought and had mailed.

"I'm gonna burn these damned pictures up. Ain't got no family I want to see them survive with," she wailed. "Ain't got nothing no more here."

In the weeks and months following Carlos' surgeries, she had gotten into the habit of taking the old man's place at the porch and hollering away at the neighbors. She found herself drinking Carlos' beers and smoking his tobacco out of his pipe. No one on the block took her quite as serious as she wanted.

And this was her mindset during the sessions of organizing and planning before the big move. After the mortgage was lost and after the money had all dried up, after the pinche doctors from Alamosa sent out their bills.

She pulled clothes and bedding back from the truckito and piled them onto the center of her bedroom after Carlos told her there was no room in the truckito. She watched as the men from the neighborhood broke down her brass bed and broke down her mirrors and dressing tables.

"Que paso, Felipa?" the woman from across the way mentioned as she swept out the carpets and spotted the mess of clothes and photographs.

"I'm finding places for all of them," she lied.

Later she found the kerosene in the shed and remembered how the old man had once cleaned the oil stains on his jeans. The matches were in Carlos' coveralls and alongside his cigarillos and rolling papers. She had also taken to the habit of smoking and even chewing as she worked in the garden.

She pulled the matches and calmly struck them along the pack. She walked solemnly to the bedroom and dropped the fire on to her clothes and family photos. Carlos was behind the truckito speaking to Tony Sandoval and Renzo Archuleta from blocks over and discussing the best routes north to Huerfano County.

"You sure you don't need me to drive you, compadre?" Tony asked.

"The woman will have to drive us out of here."

"She have a license?"

"No license. But she can drive."

The men smoked their cigarettes and laughed. Carlos asked about his smokes and his matches.

"The woman keeps them from me," Carlos complained. "I have to get them on the outside."

"It's hell to get old," Tony said.

"Que old," Carlos returned.

Just yards away in the center of the house where the woman poured her kerosene and drenched her bedding and photographs the flame and sticks of wood slipped from her fingers. The spark and flame surprised her and in minutes she fought the urge to throw her purse and then nearly her entire body into the flames.

It was the floorboards and abandoned rugs that went up first. Then the flames tickled the wood panels on the north wall. Felipa stood and watched mesmerized by it all. She giggled and stepped closer as the heat rose. Then she sobbed.

When the men came running from the yard, Carlos rolled over slowly in his chair and weeping, unable to enter the home, he nearly yelled, “My wife! My sweet, poor darling, wife!”

the projects

In those years old man Carlos lived off of his government check in a low-income, barracks-like complex of 212 units. His wife was working at So-Lo Grocery blocks away and wearing a uniform to clean Judge MacKinnon's house once a week, and so there was no one to get Carlos up some mornings or to help with his clothes and his wheeled chair.

He didn't know the Gomez family. They had moved in only the fall before, but one morning the wife said they were always home, and if they called they would help out around the house since they both worked for the local Catholic charity. Mrs. Gomez had a sloppy look, but she had been a nurse at the Army Depot, Felipa explained, and she spoke Spanish. The wife wanted him to call over and ask for help or if he needed to talk, and by the first week of July, Mr. Gomez was walking over to lift the old man in and out of the bathroom and driving out to Prairie Liquor for the old man's rum at least twice a week.

Mr. Gomez was an old farmer turned dishwasher and drank and played cards half the day, and more importantly he saw the old man as an elder worthy of respect and service.

When they sat at the Gomezes' dinner table that first time Mr. Gomez said, "Oye, Carlos. I may have a shot of rum for you!" The old man Carlos saw a Compadre to sit and bullshit with, but Felipa made a face when she tasted fried potatoes instead of chicken or cheese in the enchiladas. Felipa hated any meal she didn't see as proper and worthy of her. At first, she spent a few weeks complaining over Mrs. Gomez' kitchen arrangement and cleanliness. Then she was just happy to have a place to drop the old man off while she worked and while she finished her shopping.

But the Gomezes were Godly people, Carlos argued. They sat down with the man and showed him old photo albums and newspaper clippings from New Mexico. They listened to Carlos' stories curiously and poured the old man coffee. They played their antique Philco console radio for the man. "My God," Carlos once said. "I saw a radio as this when I was a kid in Costilla, New Mexico. I heard it once a long time ago. When I was young!"

The old man inspected it and reached out his fingers to touch the ancient wood and then wiggled the knobs and buttons.

"Let's find another station," Mr. Gomez said and then found a station playing old time western ballads. They all sat around the empty lunch dishes and the empty glasses of rum and RC Colas, and they let the old man listen to song after song.

About the time Carlos had listened to his third or fourth song off of the radio, Mrs. Gomez was singing "yo voy vagando en el mundo sin saber a donde ir." Mr. Gomez glanced at the old man and discovered that he was grumpy. He wasn't listening anymore but rather staring with his head nearly down to his chest. Mr. Gomez saw the old man as a little helpless. His eyes met Mrs. Gomez' and he motioned her over.

"What do you do all day, Carlos?" Mrs. Gomez asked. "Is there somewhere we can drive you?"

"No, hija," Carlos said, waking. "The woman works so I sit."

"You can come out with us to run some errands," Mr. Gomez said, giving his wife a look.

"I don't get around much," Carlos said. "When I die I hope they don't bury this damned chair with me, no?"

"You can go fishing with us some time. You like fishing?"

"Fishing?" The old man Carlos said. "What they have around

here to fish in?"

"Oh, we have fishing here in the big city. We've got the Arkansas and the Minnequa reservoir. Not what you're used to in South Fork but it's something."

"I never fished in South Fork. Only work," the old man said. "I can't get around like I used to. They got rattlesnakes out there?"

"You seem to be a pretty tough guy," Mrs. Gomez said. "You're not afraid of no rattlesnakes, are you?"

Carlos straightened up and looked at Mrs. Gomez and her womanly shape and painted lips. "You can take me anywhere," Carlos said.

"You can come with us sometime if you wish?" Gomez said.

"Yes, sir," the old man responded.

"Say, that reminds me, Carlos," Mrs. Gomez said, rising up from her seat and her coffee mug. "Maybe I got something you might want for your wife."

She went into the bedroom and returned with a knitted blanket in hand. "Could you use this to keep warm?"

"Oh, thank you kindly," the old man responded.

"I work with my hands and knit way more than we can use and I thought your legs might get cold—"

"I got no Goddamn legs to get cold but I thank you just the same," the old man said with a solemn voice that took Mr. and Mrs. Gomez by surprise.

"I gotta be getting," the old man repeated as he placed the blanket on his lap.

"Oh, stay a little while," Mrs. Gomez said. "You just came and I wanted to show you more photos of my family and work out a time for us to all head out fishing."

"Yeah, Carlos," Mr. Gomez said. "We want to hear more stories about South Fork and the cabins you've built."

The old man was suddenly taken by a deep spell of coughing and spasming phlegm up into his sleeve and then into his handkerchief.

—

"I DON'T SUPPOSE you'd like to take me over to the State to get me some drinks," the old man Carlos told Mr. Gomez one day as they met in the alley.

Felipa had warned Mr. Gomez about taking Carlos out, but even though Mr. Gomez had only known Carlos for a short time, he held the man's wishes with great respect.

The Chevy lurched forward, and Mr. Gomez clambered out to lift the old man from his wheeled chair into the passenger seat. It was then that Mr. Gomez found the old man's bottle and then his pistola.

"Lookit!" Mr. Gomez said. "Lookit what the old man's been doing."

The old man's hand waved him away from the door and then to fold the chair.

"Come on, Carlos," Mr. Gomez said.

"What?"

"You carrying? I can't take you with a gun in your belt." And then the man dragged the wheeled chair behind the seats. Walking across the ride Mr. Gomez thought about how to disarm his passenger.

"I don't even have cartridges for the thing," the old man promised. "I need it for protection. For show, you know? This Goddamn town ain't safe."

"Carlos!"

"An old man was killed in his home. Just last month. I heard it on the radio. And just last week they killed a man walking home with groceries."

"Well, keep your bottle hidden because if they see that down at the State then we'll both be out on our asses."

They were both arguing inside when the old man pulled the gun and handed it over to Mr. Gomez.

"When I was your age, Gomez," the old man Carlos sneered.

"No man could take my roll of dollar bills or my pistola. I would kick their ass in the sunshine."

"Yes, sir," Mr. Gomez said. "Yes, sir. I believe that."

The old man's voice rose. "No man could've done that! Not a man in this world could've done what you just done!"

"You're right! Carlos!" Mr. Gomez said. "I know you're right!"

"You couldn't of touched me!" Carlos continued.

The man Mr. Gomez held his breath and then pulled from the curb. "Would you like to go or argue? You tell me."

"Let's see about this Senate Bar you've been telling me!"

They drove out to Main Street and then went out to the farthest stretch of the bar away from the door, and after a minute Mr. Gomez brought the old man a double rum and RC Cola and two Coors drafts. Hunching over onto the table the old man pulled his drink and laughed suddenly. "I found a real man," Carlos repeated and then he slapped Mr. Gomez on the shoulder. The old man took the drinks to his lips slowly and steadily and clamped his eyelids shut, shaking his head after he sipped. "By God!" the old man said. "I think I can drink more now—"

"What's that you say?" Mr. Gomez said.

"I said with no legs I think I can drink more, no?"

Later behind the payphone the old man Carlos made his way to the toilet and found a narrow doorway. The wheeled chair fit just snug enough into the doorway to become stuck, and it made the old man Carlos boiling mad. The tragedy of the drunken moment burned at his forehead and cheeks.

The bar grew quiet and no one said a word. A bee-hived woman at the phone looked down at him and smiled bleakly with a tight mouth and wanted to help, but she had no idea how to sidestep the anger and the man's slurred cursing. She moved aside when Mr. Gomez came to assist and then she ignored the old man. Mr. Gomez continued with the half-jocular tone he had begun with, and he wasn't mad or exasperated as much he was worried.

It was then that the old man pissed himself in the bathroom doorway, his arms and hands steady as stone as he tried to push his way through the door and as Mr. Gomez shimmied the wheeled chair back and forward and then left and right.

"See what you done," Carlos said. "Goddamn!"

Gomez watched the man's lap fill with piss, and then leak down his seat down to the wooden floor and out from under his wheels.

"Carlos!" Mr. Gomez said and then his mouth opened with embarrassment. A dark shadow of hurt and then terror came over the old man.

"Goddamn it," the old man said. "I ain't much of a man no more, Gomez."

Gomez stopped and turned and for a moment they faced each other. "Don't talk like that, Carlos. Don't say such things."

"HE'S GETTING AROUND better, no?" Felipa asked Mr. Gomez days later as he was working in the alley fixing a break in the rusty chain-link fence. "His spirits are better since you've been sitting with him and talking to him, no?"

"I can't say. I don't know about anything like that."

"I just wondered," Felipa said. She ran her hands onto her apron, cleaning the moisture she found on the fence line and then on some of her garden tools. The picture of her husband was so painful she cried over it but only outside and sometimes in the early mornings while the old man had lumbered into the kitchen for morning coffee and toast.

Mr. Gomez turned his eyes on Felipa, eyes as sober as first light would allow, and when he spoke it was with a pathetic kind of ignorance about the old man and his ways.

"What do you think?" Felipa asked.

"He's eating and drinking with his Compadres is all I know," Mr. Gomez managed out of his embarrassment and nervousness for speaking to his neighbor.

"I think he's got a lot better since we moved out here. That's what I think but them doctors tell me different."

"Seems strong to me—"

"In his head, is what they say. Tell me to prepare. What do you think about that?"

Mr. Gomez was suddenly aware Felipa was much younger than the old man Carlos. Maybe by forty years, he figured in his mind. At least thirty, he reconsidered. "I wouldn't say that," he finally managed.

"That's the damned trouble," she said. "I thought he'd be better here away from the valley and closer to his people. Closer to his children. I thought he'd be well enough in the Fall for at least a bus trip."

Mr. Gomez sensed she wanted to hear something, but he had no idea what that something was. He unbuckled the straps to his pocket and pulled the first cigarillo of the morning. Mr. Gomez shook his head. "One thing for certain, Señora," Gomez said. "It just takes a long time. I had an uncle who lost an arm in the mill, and it took him a long time. And well, his trouble wasn't half of what this man has."

Felipa looked at Gomez' face and searched for kindness but when she opened her mouth to respond, Gomez's eyes drew down with a sudden sadness.

"My Tio Ronaldo passed so I guess that ain't the best thing to bring up to you," Gomez said.

"Maybe we shouldn't of moved out here in the first place," Felipa said. "It just seems to have tangled everything up. The daughter and little girl don't even visit." She watched her neighbor shake his head, and then bend to pull out some weeds near the concrete foundation of the fence.

"Family can be tricky. I don't know what to tell you."

Felipa then handed Gomez an envelope with five dollars folded inside. She had taken the time to write Gomez on the front of it and even the address. "I want you to take this money for the gas," Felipa said. "I want you to know how much it means to us that you have him with you so much."

"What's this?"

"Like I said. Money for the gas. Please take it!"

"No," Gomez said sternly and then he nervously wiped at his neck and then he dropped his ashes straight onto the grass. "No money."

"Please take it. For me," Felipa said with a finality to her voice. "God knows that cheap ass viejo will never offer it."

FOR A WHILE the streets were empty and calm as the cross-eyed Jeri drove Lena out to Carlos'. Then the unpaved road swung right and a painted sign on a stake read "the bricks."

Jeri laughed out loud and howled, "Hit the bricks, Pal! Ha!"

They had come from their apartment on Routte Avenue. But ahead the road felt barely travelled and led on past empty dirt lots and rutted trails. From the brief clearing onto Prairie Avenue, the maple trees were colored autumn.

Jeri slowed down, his foot on the clutch. "Which one of these roads are we here for?"

"Straight on," Lena said. "I'll know when I see it."

"Goddamn unpaved side streets are hell on my tires."

He eased the car off the dirt track onto pavement, and Lena leaned with Bruna close to her breast, and the two watched blue skies and the vanilla clouds cascading, carrying over branches and above the institutional rooftops.

Lena said, "Can't you wait to smoke?"

She got a whiff of Jeri's cigarillo and then rolled her head against the seat to look at him, his dark, round face and combed-over hair. His square hairy hands gripped the wheel, and the day was slowly slipping away from what Lena at first thought as wonderful. She shivered with a new sense of fear and ambivalence.

In the narrow streets of the neighborhood and the freshly paved roads, white flashes of birch trees passed by. The car slowly rolled up and down unfamiliar streets, and Lena caught the smell of what she thought was exhaust and then burning tires. On the other side of the street, they met a scene of broken down junkers and garbage cans.

Lena sighed and stared, but she couldn't read the numbers or the street signs. The specific numbers were lost in the streets of her memory. "It doesn't seem to be any of these," she said.

The street climbed and then dirtied, and gravel chattered underneath the tires. Someone had piled cinder blocks towards the center of the street and Jeri had to swerve around. Then, at the end of the last street and before the last turn on the last cul-de-sac, a German shepherd charged out, heavy voiced, and a man sweeping out a gutter stared silent and then straightened as the Ford rounded and then came to a stop. When they were almost past, Lena saw a woman in the doorway of the last screen door that reminded her of Felipa. "You sure you want me to drop you?" Jeri said. "I can come in and at least distract them for you if that's what you think I can do."

"Go on and take Bruna," Lena said. "I have to see about their situation first."

"I don't know why we even have to come down here—"

"Because he's my father, Jeri," Lena said. "And he'll always be my father and I have to see about him from time to time."

LENA WAS STANDING in Felipa's kitchen and her pot boiled over and rattled every once in a while, spilling hot water onto the burners, and the crackling sound of steam filled the room. Her kitchen stood the size of a small bathroom alongside a bathroom the size of a closet and alongside a closet the size of a cabinet. Felipa kept her coffee mugs underneath the table in old milk crates. When she pulled one mug from the crate and handed it over to Carlos sitting in his broken down and rusted wheelchair, the old man immediately blew into the mug to free it of dust and imagined spider webs before filling it with the black liquid.

Later, when Gomez returned and pulled the man up, Lena helped the old man into a fresh t-shirt and into a clean pair of pants, the excess material cut down and unkempt safely pinned underneath. When she had him settled Felipa could breathe and think of herself. She could head into the bathroom after ironing her own dress and fixing her own hair. She could spend those stolen moments in the bathroom and put on her make-up, her red lipstick and rouge with her only necklace and hair pins. It was only then that Carlos could smoke and talk to his daughter about Bruna and Jeri. They spoke in the largest room of their institutional housing, the quiet of the bedroom while Lena sat on the edge of their bed and talked to her father. He asked his daughter to open the window so he could smoke his nasty smelling pipe and release the dark smoke from his nostrils.

"She wants me dead, hija," Carlos whispered. "Like all women in my life she wants me dead."

"Why would you say that, Papa? No one wants you dead."

"Did you bring me anything to drink, hija? I sit here and wait for weeks for you to come and visit me and I just need something to drink."

"Papa."

"My birthday was last month and nothing from you, girl."

"I'll bring your daughter to see you, Papa. I'll bring Bruna."

"I don't have a daughter. I don't have anyone around here. Do you see anyone around here?"

"She's almost five and I have her every weekend in the church so you would be proud, Papa."

In the silence of the room Lena took a breath and stared a moment, grunted and then went into the kitchen. She stood at the counter and cleaned coffee grounds from the sink bottom.

She drew another mug and then poured her father a last cup of coffee.

Felipa made sounds from the bathroom and then entered the kitchen to laugh out loud at Lena. "Your father only drinks from his bottle after his morning coffee. He counts on me to take the bus out for whatever he drinks. Or he pays the neighbor to pick up his drinks. You ought to have him, Lena," Felipa said.

"I have Bruna. And Jeri. He can come visit but—"

"Last week he put eggs to boil on the stove and then fell asleep and nearly burned down the whole damn house, Lena."

"I didn't know."

"He needs to be watched. So you should have su papa with you." Felipa stood stiffly and angrily as she filled her purse with her cigarettes and her wallet.

"I can help you with money. I can help you if you need my help."

"When we lived in San Luis, we had Compadres. Here, all we have is you and you never come around."

"I said I can give you money," Lena repeated.

"I work and I can't take care of him."

"Poor old man," Lena whispered into the air after the coffee was drained and after she watched Felipa and the thick-bellied neighbor Gomez once again manage the old man into the bathroom and as the door shut behind.

"Poor man, shit," Felipa said, pushing the old man's chair into a corner and beginning her morning chores of dishes and then sweeping. She acted as if Carlos' daughter was not there. She pretended to be alone as she worked. She said, "I'm the one who does all the work. You should say poor, poor, Felipa. No one around here ever says that."

jail

Carlos remembered seeing himself in a mirror while he crawled towards the Whitehorse Bar and Grill's beer tap. With his elbows up on the bar, his hands around the cool metal of a rail, he saw the woman behind the counter dial the phone, and then later, he remembered striking her forehead with his own before falling onto the floor. He remembered the patrons in the bar squealing and then roaring and then the Deputy dragging him. He remembered losing his Stetson and then soiling himself in the Deputy's Crown Vic.

He remembered spitting and screaming into the heat of the glass as he watched buildings flying by. The light of the day was draining away, and streetlights crackled to life as they drove. He kept the Deputy waiting minutes before he exited the car and then lost his breath as he fell. The concrete scraped at his hands and elbows before they left him on the cell floor.

Deputy Munoz had a white, smooth face with a prominent nose and Carlos commented on how the thing looked like a woman's and how only someone who hates his people could work for the County Sheriff's office. It was nearly an hour before he could answer their questions about his name and the location of his billfold. The new arrivals around him laughed and watched him with amusement, half out of distaste and half out of endearment.

"What the hell do you want from me?" old man Carlos barked. He terrorized them and sat as a cowboy ready to burst at any move or word. “What the hell are you after?” he repeated.

“I’m asking you, Carlos,” Munoz said, “Where do you live? Who brought you out to the Whitehorse this evening? Where do you live?”

Without answering and from a tough slouch, he said, “This place is for my death.”

“For heaven’s sake,” Munoz said. “Please!” Then a Deputy came with paperwork, and he ordered Carlos to be quiet and respectful.

“Lord in heaven,” Carlos continued shakily before the vomiting spells. He refused more orders and slipped from each man’s grasp.

“Hold him!” Munoz ordered and then two more deputies came in.

“This old man can fight,” another wailed as they struggled with his hands and his thighs. The very look on Carlos’ face was one of sickness and viciousness.

“How about it!” Munoz said. “How about settling down so we can get your paperwork.”

The old man barked, “Cabrónes! Pinche bastards all of yous!”

“YOUR PAPA NEEDS YOU,” Felipa cried, after dialing Lena’s digits. “How about paying his fines,” she demanded.

“What are you talking about?”

“Lena, hija,” Felipa said. “They have him down at the county sheriff and they need money for his fines.”

“What has he done?” Lena asked the woman.

“Not too complicated to figure out, no?” Felipa said after first staying silent and nearly ashamed. Her nostrils tightened, her lips thrust out in force as she spoke and then listened.

“Goddamn it, Felipa,” Lena said. “I have work and I have Bruna—”

“Drunk and disorderly and they need their money, hija.”

"What do you expect me to do?"

"Just as I say, mujer!" Felipa said. She had not wavered since her first words. She expected respect for her husband and for the first time felt pushed into a corner.

"It'll cost me money I don't have—"

"He needs you, girl."

Lena breathed a simple agreement: "I'll see what I have."

CARLOS CAME OUT of the cell silent in his thoughts with blood-soaked teeth and shirt collar. His head was down, his Stetson was in his lap revealing his grey curls and receding hairline. When they took his elbows and removed the cuffs from his hands, Carlos looked alertly around the room and found his oldest daughter's eyes. As he passed the front counter and as he watched the deputy in charge of money changing, he moved along quickly and quietly before nearly falling off his seat.

After two minutes, three more officers came into the front space of the office carrying another drunk, with the two on the outside supporting the man on the inside. After turning the man over, the officers headed back fast in the direction they had come for yet another man. And for a second only Carlos and Lena and the money changing officer inhabited the front area of the office.

"Your mother phoned, no?" Carlos said through bloody teeth and snot. "I should've hoped they called your mother."

"She's not my mother, Papa," Lena answered. "And what happened to your teeth?" Lena's eyes burned with concern, her face thrust forward towards her father and then she wiped at his face with a handkerchief from her purse and for long seconds the two sat in silence.

"Nothing," Carlos said at last.

"I guess that's what you get for drinking and ending up in this place, Jefe."

"Do you think you should get me out of here before they all come at me again?"

"I'd sympathize more with you if you weren't as mean as a damned dog to me, Jefe," Lena answered and then looked at her father in horror. In her eyes the old man had given in and to her astonishment his stained shirt and pants smelled sharply. "Look at you, Jefe," Lena repeated. "How could they leave you like this?"

When Lena returned to Lucy Venudo's Buick, they were in a deep silence that left Carlos sheepish and guilty. He looked at the car and then at the two women: "Where's your husband?"

No sooner had Felipa seated the old man and tied his wheeled chair into the trunk than she looked at the man sharply and the two quarreled as Lucy drove. All the old signs of belligerence returned as the old man questioned the women.

"A woman needs a man around," Carlos said to both women. "Hey, you! Mujer! You got a man around here."

The fat and quivering Lucy, aiming to see who had called her out, saw an old, bloodied man with a grinning face and bristly white whiskers, white eyebrows and a cocked hat on his head and could only answer, "Yes, Jefe! I got a man!"

"Am I mistaken or are you supposed to be with Jeri," Carlos repeated. "Or did you drive him off like the last one—"

"Denver," Lena said. "Arapahoe County. He left for work in the city. I told you—"

"Well, I left the country myself to live in the city and maybe that man has a plan. A man has to have a plan," he repeated as he buried his head low, leaning his weight heavily on the metal door and the cold glass and looking around downtown Huerfano carefully. "This sad town. Lots of people coming and going. That steel mill never holds them, no?"

Lucy was giving the man her full attention, and Lena was sitting and holding her purse tightly. The old man straightened up easily, loose shouldered, and finally Lena barked at him to sit and relax.

"Buy you a drink?" Carlos asked to no one in particular, and Lena bent towards him as she spun around. The old man grinned amicably.

"No, Papa," Lena said. "I got to go see about your Goddamned teeth and then I got to take you home." She raised a polite hand as she spoke to each point as she spoke. "So we ain't got time for no drinks. No money neither."

"Oh, this one's damned trouble," Lucy said, smiling as she watched the old man in her rearview.

Somehow in daydreams Lena never thought this would be her latest reunion with her father, and she was immediately pleased she hadn't brought Bruna or Felipa along.

"So what happened to your teeth, Papa?" Lena finally allowed herself to ask.

"Eh?" the old man managed, preoccupied with his Stetson and the crease and the proper fit, but it kept getting hung up on the headliner.

"I said your teeth? What happened to your teeth?"

"Yeah," the old man said. "I got bad teeth."

"It makes you look old."

"I am old—"

"Older, she means," Lucy said.

The old man took a few seconds and searched for the redhead's eyes in the rearview. "I'm lucky to have any kind of teeth, I imagine."

"What are you gonna do about them?"

"About what?"

"The teeth?" Lucy said.

"Yeah, your teeth," Lena repeated and then reached over for the old man's cheek and gums, realizing she hadn't seen the old man in years much less touched his raggedy face. She lifted the lip and forcefully inspected the gums. "What are you gonna do about your bloody teeth?"

"Since when do you give a shit about my teeth?"

"Oh, never mind," Lena snapped.

"I got no money for teeth," the old man said.

"Mmm," Lena answered. "I know a place where you can get them plastic ones."

"Plastic."

"You know. Dentures."

"Shit," the old man repeated.

"Better than having a mouth filled with dead teeth. Bloody teeth."

"I'll go if you take me, hija," Carlos finally said, and it was almost a whisper.

"I don't care what the hell you were thinking," Felipa barked. "But I swear I'm gonna tie you up in the bed, old man. Is that what you want is for me to tie you up in the room like a God-damned animal."

"Shut up, mujer," Carlos countered. "Like I'm a Goddamned dog."

Lena's eyes felt weak with tears as she watched it all and the couple marched and rolled inside.

INSIDE LENA STOOD as Felipa removed the man's pants and the two carried the old man into the bedroom. Felipa brought in a pan of water and some soap and the two women washed the man's legs. Carlos' snores filled the house and then Felipa gently rolled the man onto his side and replaced both his bandages.

"You do this every day?" Lena asked.

"Every morning and night," Felipa slowed to answer. "Gotta keep it clean."

"I had no idea—"

"What?"

"That he was so helpless like this."

"What the hell did you think?"

"I don't know," she said.

Later she watched Felipa clothe Carlos in pajamas and then feed him soup and some warm tortillas, and she watched some of the bits slide down the man's neck in ragged lumps.

"I ain't saying it's been easy," Felipa said. "But he's been good to me. He's a drunk and a prickly piece of shit sometimes but he's my husband and I do what I can."

the patrón's home

Before Lino and Carlos had their audience with the Patrón and the Patrón's boy, Lino gave the advice, "The llano moves as the oceans."

"You've never seen the ocean."

"I've been to Massachusetts and seen the ancient and grey Atlantic, Carlos. You're not the world's only traveler. I've travelled in books. I've studied Chinese mythology and Greek philosophy. There is always a hidden power, an opposition at you pushing. Causing emotion. What did you know of Germans on war overseas before the Army? And what did you know about the Patrón and the llano here in New Mexico before Colmor and the Cutoff, Carlos?"

IN THE PATRÓN'S COURTYARD *Lino commanded Carlos to remove his hat. The Patrón wore a cigar on his lips and was sitting under a tree in the shade of a late afternoon already with a plate of fried meat and tortilla. He held a large buck knife with its long blade slicing at a tomato.*

"My family has been in Colmor since 1870, founded the damn town. It was all my Grandfather," the Patrón Waddingham began. "After la gripe took my Grandmother and my mother, I thought we'd lose this land. But the government came in and extended our claim. Well, extended the bank's claim. I was born for this land and work. Los Malos come in and steal it out from under me. They

chop up the meat in the fields like monsters. Like sinners."

The Patrón's boy, Arthur, walked right out to Carlos' horse and pulled the government pistol from the saddle bags to admire the weapon as Carlos and Lino stood and watched.

"Do you know Eddie Duran, Carlos?" the Patrón asked. "A good man. Hard worker. He used to work the Broken Arrow ranch near Wagon Mound. His family died from la gripe and he lost it all," the Patrón explained as he munched on a juicy tomato. "I hear you as good with animals as he was. He was always telling me about the purity of animals. I'm sure you liked Eddie. He once told me that animals make him feel closer to God. Eddie was a Catholic. Animals were his living, but he lost his place and came to work for me, so they were my living. That's what I told him. I said, Eddie they are my living and not yours. They are my animals. My horses. The ranch horses you work, those are my horses and my living. My son's livelihood. Eddie was stealing from me wasn't he, Lino?" the Patrón said.

"Yes, Patrón," Lino said. The soft and defeated tone and fear in him and his voice made Carlos nervous.

"And you know what we do with cattle thieves, Lino?" the Patrón said.

"I like your pistola," the younger Waddingham said. "Let me buy it off you."

"Son," the Patrón Waddingham said, moving over to his boy and slapping at the boy's drunken face. "This has to stay controlled. He's a soldier and a veteran of the war; he isn't going to let it go so easy." The old man held his son's face for a quick second and threw his unfinished tomato. "How is it that you have this weapon? They say the government takes them back from you. The pinche government takes everything."

"It was my cousin's," Carlos said. "I'm taking it back to his people. His father. It was my Tio's gun. They didn't have guns for us to train with so my cousin's father bought it for him."

"You have bullets in you?" Arthur asked. Carlos shook his head.

"And why no gun for you? Where was your father?" the Patrón asked.

"My father had no money and doesn't believe in guns or killing."

"Oh, I see. Your father is a good man, no? A good Catholic, I imagine. And where is your cousin."

"Buried in San Luis, Colorado."

"And why haven't you returned the weapon?"

"I've not made it home. I've been working."

"Just pay him some money and let me have the gun, Papa," the young Arthur said impatiently.

Just then the young Arthur Waddingham pulled the lever and drew the chamber open and pulled a cartridge from his pocket and dropped the metal into the gun. Lino paid no attention, but Carlos was ready to drop to the ground as he was trained.

"Hand it over, Arthur," Lino finally said.

"Don't ever speak to me common, Lino," Arthur said. He had nearly blood-red hair and the thinnest, most bitter looking eyes. Just then he turned and shot the head from a chicken in the yard with his own wheel gun. Pow! Then he pulled the hammer back and fired Carlos' weapon to explode the chicken's body. The ground was black and white with feathers and blood-stained dirt.

"Closer to God," Arthur said. "Here, you can have the thing back."

A FEW MORNINGS AFTER *Arthur killed the chicken with Carlos' gun, a horse rode up to the bunkhouse. Carlos watched the old man Waddingham with his large head and cover and severe limp hobble with his cane to the doorway.*

"A man needs friends," Old Man Waddingham said. "My boy has his heart set on your government weapon, so I've come to call."

Lino had already explained that the Patrón Waddingham wasn't interested in the gun. "It's not your gun so much as you,

Carlos."

"Why does he want to buy me? I already work for him, Lino."

"Working for him don't mean you're loyal. If you sell the gun, you might as well be giving him all you own. It's a test. I hate to tell you, Carlos, but he can come get the gun anytime, in the night while you sleep or while you are out with the fences. What he wants is your obedience and he knows he can't get that unless you hand it to him."

All this was going through Carlos' head as the old man Waddingham stood in the doorway to the bunkhouse.

"Come on back to the house and we can negotiate the price for the buy," the old man said.

Carlos looked at his feet and was silent.

"Mara is a steady woman, no?" the old man said. "She's like a daughter to me. A fascinating woman. She's younger than my boy—"

Carlos thought it odd Waddingham referred to his thirty-year-old son as "my boy".

"She plays piano. She ever tell you that? Learned it in church. I don't got no piano, but I told her if she came out to my house once a week I would order one from Wagon Mound. I got a guy who could order me any damned thing I want."

"I don't have the gun no more," Carlos lied.

"What's that?"

"I took it out with me to where the train tracks meet the land, meet the ditch, near the cutoff. I threw the damned thing. I field-stripped it and threw it out. Don't have it no more. I took it all apart and threw the spring and the everything out to the llano. The land can have it. I have no plans to head home anytime soon anyway."

The word around the bunkhouse is that the Patrón had been born in 1855 and his father died when he was an infant, and when he was five years old, he was living off the land, living off horses and horse work, training and selling horses and then building his empire after moving on to cattle. He inherited the land, but the cattle and the animals came from his tooth and nail work. That's how Lino described it, tooth and nail. They say every adobe building in Colmor, the church and the schoolhouse came from his own hands or his money and interest in some way or another. They say he was the holdout for the Governor before statehood.

"I could buy the weapon," the old man continued. "It's not about that. I got a guy who can get me a gas-powered model T down here anytime, Carlos. And a tank to hold the gasoline in. Pull it all down to my property. So it ain't about the weapon."

Carlos stood with his mouth open at a loss as to what to say or how to react to the words. It was the same way when a buck sergeant or captain screamed incomprehensible orders. He hoped Lino would step in to distract the man.

"What we want is a weapon with a story. A weapon that's been to war. I want a gun that's been to Europe and returned. A piece that put bullets home in those Germans. That's the prize for my boy…I got a whole damned armory down at the house, Carlos. But your story is what I am looking for."

"I've been better and I've been worse," Carlos said. "That's my story. And it will only be mine."

"I ALREADY TOLD HIM a lie but it's going to come true," Carlos later said to Lino. "I'm going down to the cutoff and bury that damned weapon. Take it apart so no one can have it or do no more with it. Benito won't mind. He wasn't much for soldiering anyway, not matter what he would say. He just wanted to get out of his father's home. Get out of the state."

"Good," Lino said. "You lie to a liar. You cheat to a cheater. Now you finally doing something right."

—

THE FOLLOWING WEEK the courting continued with the Patrón inviting Carlos over for a cup of tea with rum. The Patrón wanted to talk more about the war in Europe and the weapon Carlos had returned with. He had many questions for Carlos while they walked through the Patrón's back pasture. Really, he had brought Carlos in to trim the hooves of his prized filly. The Patrón asked his questions while his workman labored under the afternoon sun.

The horse that day was of medium build with beautiful full eyes and there was no doubt of this horse's prized ancestry. This was no work horse and was maybe the most expensive horse Carlos had ever attended. The two were out so long Carlos began to get comfortable, though he never referred to his relationship with the Patrón as a friendship; Lino wouldn't allow it. "You attend to his horse and you drink his booze but that don't make you brothers," Lino had said. The Patrón's boy was unsocial, taciturn, and absorbed in himself, Carlos observed.

"They tell me, Carlos, you don't want to stay here in Colmor but you haven't went home," said the Patrón.

"Who told you that?"

"I have a small empty house here near my stables. I need a good man to work with my horses. I see the way you take care with the animals."

"Horses are a burden," Carlos said. "We used to say this in the Army. To care for a horse means to take the expense and the burden. Animals eat before we eat, we used to say. Saw a damned amount of horses dead out there, too. Never seen so many dead horses so didn't get much experience in the field with them after training."

"They killed horses out there much?"

"Killed everything. Some horses hurt, so you could only put them out of their pain. When we had the cartridges. If not, we just left them to die."

Later Carlos repaired a loose window on the back house and installed a wood stove. All while the Patrón watched and asked questions.

"My boy can't do a damned lick of work like this. He was raised in leisure. Always had someone cooking for him and cleaning for him. That boy would sit in the kitchen and starve before he'd feed himself a hard-fried egg. He's inside most of the day and I can't get him to rise unless I demand it."

Carlos pulled his pouch of tabacco and nervously rolled a cigarette.

"That's his horse you shoed and trimmed. Hell, he can barely place a saddle. But he can shoot and kill and ride. Not much for working, but he can ride. Damned near couldn't live with myself to have a boy that can't ride. His mother's a Pueblo Indian woman. I tell him she's from Boston, Massachusetts. That's a lie."

Carlos struck a match clumsily. He had the sense he was learning a heavy weight of secrets.

"He never knew the woman," Waddingham continued. "You ever heard the story of the white woman kidnapped and killed by Indians? They say that's the founding story of Taos. Have Lino talk to you about that one some time."

"I never heard that story."

"Indian killed her so she wouldn't corrupt the Pueblo."

Later Lino told Carlos the story was of a woman escaping a knife to kill herself, to sacrifice herself. "Every Indian has a sacrificial cave story," Lino later explained. 'The Patrón's wife took her own life in those back pastures is the story...They say the Patrón's boy still sleeps in the mama's bed. They say he hates the Patrón for what he done to the mother."

"You mean they say the Patrón killed his wife?"

"Probably killed her. Better than have her leave him and take the boy with her. Just stories. Say, next time you out there, ask him. Say it just like this: 'Hey, Patrón! Did you kill your wife or no?'"

—

THE WORD WAS the Patrón's son, Waddingham's son, and his man from Wagon Mound brought a radio box down. They brought the box and a new, lighter Winchester rifle—the old man always had every new model of rifle brought in—a crate of cartridges, and a new mare all in the same trip. Also, the man brought in new patterned material for Mara that Arthur wanted as a surprise.

Lino said the radio began in the Mesilla Valley. He said he heard about it in a Las Cruces barbershop one time back when he worked at a university.

"When the hell did you work for a university and when the hell were you in a barbershop?" Carlos said.

"I said I worked at a university, not for a university. And why so hard for you to believe? I am a learned man of philosophy and I have knowledge from all great philosophers. I worked in the garden, and I worked at a cafeteria. They let me spend time in the library, too, Carlos, for your information. I still have books from campus."

"That's about right," Carlos said. "Stolen books, I'm sure."

"A man must steal his knowledge in this world, yes?" Lino said. "And I can tell you they had a man there named Goddard and he was like a God to them. He took a mail order box, and he built a box that projected his voice to other boxes as far as a thousand miles."

"He built a radio?"

"Yes, a radio box. This man in Las Cruces, this Goddard, calls it 'broadcasting', Carlos," Lino explained. "Like spreading seeds in planting, Carlos. Music from a Victrola, music on the air."

"I seen them in the war. They call down death and destruction."

"This one plays music," Lino said. "An air concert, the papers said. Music on the air. A wireless concert."

The word around the ranch was that the Patrón Waddingham's son ordered the box for ten dollars from Wagon Mound, and he was to have concerts in the courtyard at the big house.

"They call it KDKA and I seen one and heard one with my own ears, Carlos," Lino said. "Beautiful Beethoven and Mozart right in the air, Carlos. A true experience. I have truly lived, Carlos."

"You heard music from a radio and not a record player," Carlos said. "Is that what you saying?"

"No, that's not what I am saying," Lino said. "What I am saying is that in Arthur's mind, he would be dancing with Mara in the courtyard to his wireless concert like he learned about in the Boy Scout Handbook, a wireless battery-powered radio, all to impress Mara. The Patrón called it a talking machine. He had a few records too, Hands across the Sea banjo music. And what he called tin pan alley music but mostly he had reputable music, Beethoven, Mozart, and Chopin. God's music. He paid one dollar for each record."

"Lino always knows about the costs—the figures and the bottom line," Carlos said.

"Man's got to know his coin," Lino said. "This was when the old man learned that Mara could play piano, but he knew no one who owned a piano and knew no one who could get a piano, until he met his man from Wagon Mound, of course. The piano was always on its way. It became a promise the Patrón never delivered on."

"Why the hell are you telling me all this, Lino?"

"Jesus, don't be so impatient, Carlos. Well, the old man came around one afternoon and found Mara with his boy, Arthur. It seems the Patrón Waddingham and the boy Arthur both had their heart set on the girl, Mara."

"Both?"

"Yes, that's what I am telling you, Carlos. And both had made their promises and the old man took his hatchet to the radio and nearly took it to the boy, but Mara got in the way."

"Do you know this for a fact, Lino? Or is this more of your chisme. You know I don't like people talking about what's peoples'

own private business."

Lino said, "I'm telling you because you're going to lose that one. Mark what I say."

Carlos laughed while at his chores, "I can't lose what I never had. Just days ago you were telling me how the Patrón owns everything on the property. Owns her body and her whoring—"

"But don't own her soul," Lino said. "Hell, no one owns a woman's soul."

1967

lena's man

"You're such a strong man," the women at the Donahue would say once Lena's man Jeri entered and bought them drinks. He combed his hair in the bathroom there and spoke to every woman in the bar. Sitting across from a pink neon that read

Food

Alcohol

Tobacco

he would reply, "Well, I should hope so." He moved to where the women sat and stood over them drinking his beer and urging them to speak more to him.

Sometimes in his work clothes and sometimes in just a plain t-shirt, the sleeves folded over his biceps or up over his shoulders, he spent the evenings drinking.

One night Jeri met Robert Martinez down at Hogan's Bar with a large, young woman that Jeri could not take his eyes off. Her hair was jet black and her large cheeks were rubbed with pink make-up, and sitting next to her Jeri felt warm and aroused. The three of them drank together, Robert once-in-a-while kissing the young woman and motioning for Jeri to give them some privacy. Robert's flat, brown face kept motioning to Jeri but the young woman was more attracted to Jeri and so Robert was hurt and threatened. Robert and Jeri were old friends from Army days and a short stint working in the steel mill. Robert asked about Lena, talked loudly and openly about Bruna, whom he referred to as Jeri's familia.

"For Christ sakes, cabrón," Jeri begged, and then turned to his new lady.

LATER THAT MONTH Jeri made his First Holy Communion out at the apartment. The priests let him do it right out of county jail. Father Dwyer came out to the apartment along with Monsignor Holland. Lena cooked a huge dinner. Jeri and the men sat on the front stoop of the building while two nuns along with Lena and Bruna did the dishes and drank coffee in the kitchen. Jeri showed the men his car and told them of his plans to fix up Lena's Buick rather than purchase a new one. "Just needs work to the body," he told them. The whole ceremony took less than the time to eat and drink. Father Dwyer never asked about Lena and Bruna or the marriage situation, that was just how the church worked in the old neighborhood. When it was all through, Jeri felt like a new man while he drank wine and smoked his cigarettes, all while Lena and Bruna went to bed.

"IT TOOK ME A WHILE to realize it," Jeri lectured to Lena, "but you gotta know I had the best mother and father anyone could've asked for." On Saturday mornings Jeri stayed home and slowly drank his coffee and nursed that crudo feeling. Jeri knew the bars and hangouts around the Army Depot the way most men of the old neighborhood knew the garages or the junkyards.

"Then what happened to you?" Lena said.

Jeri dumped spoon after spoon of sugar into the black mess in his mug and answered, "Watch it, mujer."

"There is no strong man without family behind him."

The thought went unanswered, and Lena continued to cook for her girl and clean the table around Jeri. Lena never cared for morning coffee or for morning chatter that added up to nothing. She cared for her work and for her daughter. "Shut up about all that," she finally answered.

"All you need, I mean," Jeri continued. "All a man needs is family."

Lena could not help but laugh and threw her estropajo into the dish-filled sink with a flourish.

Jeri looked at his watch and then yawned. "It says in the paper here they are hiring on gimps down at the steel mill. Maybe su viejo can go down and wheel around and clean up for the union. What do you think, baby?" Jeri put to the young Brunacita. "You think su Grandpa can finally bring in some money so we don't have to support him? You think the old man has it in him to work?"

"My father was a carpenter," Lena snapped finally. "Twenty-five years ago, the man would've run circles around a fool like you. Now have yourself some more coffee before this all blows up on you, Jeri."

"Really?" Jeri said. "And what does he have to show for it."

"Don't start with me—"

"I'm just asking what the man has to show for his years of work. Nada tostada, mujer. Nothing."

STILL IN WORK COVERALLS, with sun on his face and shoulders, Lena's Jeri stood hesitating on the sidewalk, holding a can of paint and paintbrush. His knees were stiff from working and his feet were aching. Today, despite the fatigue, he would paint his newly purchased one hundred fifty-dollar Studebaker ready to be free again.

Windows were open all up and down Routte Street and there was a rush of traffic with faces sure to be catching him slap the brown paint up and down the hood and then the doors. Every other stroke of the brush he would stop and listen to the sounds of the neighborhood that did not seem warm or familiar. Though he had spent the years with Lena in her duplex he had never felt comfortable in the town Lena dragged him too. Though he had work and he had money and now a Studebaker from his travelling to this town, he wanted no familiarity with the place.

"Then what are you doing here?" Lena told him at breakfast. "Why do you stay with me if you hate me and Bruna so much."

"I have no hate for you or the girl."

"Then what are you talking about." Lena finished the discussion.

"Jesus Christ, Lena. I just want a Goddamn car."

"You have no license, cabrón. You have no license. What possessed you—"

"I know I have no license. But I have money for this car and I've already committed to Mr. Hernandez."

"What possessed you to buy that old man's car? Call him and tell him no. We need that money. We have a car."

"You have a car, Lena. You have the car and I have nothing—"

"You'll leave me. I know you, Jeri."

"Ah, mujer."

"You'll leave and I'll have nothing here."

"Just because a man buys a Goddamn car doesn't mean he's leaving, mujer," Jeri said and that was how Jeri left it.

DAYS LATER, as he painted the passenger door and then the sideboards, Jeri breathed easier for a change. What was it in her head that made her think he'd run off? What was there in this damn town to draw him back if he was to leave? He stepped out of a neighborhood kid's path along the sidewalk. No children? No money? He had the pool hall and the Compadres from Monte who had found work in the steel mill. He had the gambling at Shanghai Lounge in Walsenburg and the slots in the back room. He had his Tia Roberta though she was miles away in Denver but now he had a Studebaker with brown paint slapped onto the metal.

He had Fernando Baca who also worked at the Army Depot and drank with him and gambled alongside him. He had his nudie magazines and the girls down at the Alibi Lounge. He would probably find Fernando and the girls down there now with their beer and cold cut sandwiches, or moving around the pool table, whistling and listening to jukebox favorites, practicing shots and telling stories. At this time of late afternoon there might be a few spaces available at the counter for dinner and maybe even a cop or maybe two collecting their money or a tribute of beer to keep the bar room open.

Here he only had harsh sky and sunlight and the work of changing the color of his new Studebaker and the bottle he kept in his lunch pail. He had the eyes of his Lena on him out the duplex's window and her judgment. Her voice sat in his head: Who paints a car with house paint, Jeri? What fool of a man paints his car in front of the house with a bucket of house paint?

JERI AND LENA'S DUPLEX was an old house cut into rooms with a single dormer window, and the one shower room was shared by each tenant. Each side had their own kitchen with a breakfast nook near the window where they all ate together. Beyond the alley and the houses were the furnace stacks of the steel mill and the streams of headlight coming into the night shifts just above the bluffs of south Huerfano.

The yard was next to Bessemer School's basketball court and the family hardly used it. Directly across from the alley was the brunette Lucy Venudo's place and the house of Lena's oldest Compadre Vicky Martinez, and even though the gate was hidden and protected from view Bruna found her way to Vicky's house every afternoon. At night Bruna waited for Lena and Jeri to return home from work. The insects of early summer were loud and Bruna faced their bites and the wings of moths. The children were all home with aunts and with Comadres as the women like Lena and Lucy were out with their men out on Union Avenue drinking and dancing after long shifts.

Sometimes Bruna stood in her dressing gown if the hour grew late, and despite Vicky's protest, she sat and waited for her Lena. More than a hundred yards west was the empty ball fields of Bessemer Park, and across the fields and insect-haunted playgrounds Bruna imagined she could hear the children playing from each duplex stretched to the horizon. The girl listened carefully for her Mama and Jeri to return. By standing up on Vicky's stoop she could nearly see Jeri's Studebaker pull in and then her Mama's red hair emerge in the glow of the streetlamp at the end of the drive.

The families were lucky to have the work apart from the farms and fields of San Luis. Lena and Vicky both said this. Altogether the houses were a good place for a family, in spite of the overgrowth of weeds and trees creating an immense narrow alley. So many less lucky ones were crammed into parents' homes and sharing beds and rooms, but out here in the city beyond Monte Vista and San Luis there were friends and there were Comadres like Vicky and there were freedoms. "I go to sleep counting my blessings," Lena sang out loud whenever she returned home from work and found her daughter moody or tired. "You hear me, girl?" Lena insisted. "We are very lucky."

JERI FOUND FERNANDO BACA sweeping peanut shells and lint from the tile floor out at Fernando's Tavern, and Fernando's Compadre, Navi Lucero, was complaining over the empty cigarette machine.

"Well, son of a biscuit," Fernando Baca said and jumped off of his stool.

Next to him Navi stood up to verify the excitement. "Say,

Jeri," Navi said. "Long time no Goddamn see, Jeri."

"Yeah, Jeri," Fernando continued. "The hell you been?"

Jeri dropped his car keys onto the counter of the wide oak bar and lit a cigarillo. For a minute the place jumped with excitement over Jeri and his car.

Fernando was the first to grab the keys and inspect them and smile. "I don't believe it, mano," Fernando said. He handled the keys as if they were foreign objects. "When the hell did this all happen?"

"I know that car," Navi said.

"When did this happen?" Fernando repeated. "Why can't you call me? You got a telephone on the wall, no? That's what they use them for. To call people and tell them how the hell you are—"

"That's Hernandez' car," Navi continued, nodding towards the car parked across the lane. "Don't remember it brown, though."

"How much you pay?" Fernando said.

"Yeah. How much?" Navi said.

"Two bills," Jeri said, more to himself than to the men behind the counter.

"I'll be Goddamned," Fernando continued. "I thought you'd be the last man in the state to have a ride. Much less old man Hernandez' Studebaker."

"I never thought anyone would buy that thing," Navi said.

Knowing Navi to be a stingy, suspicious little man, Jeri continued to smoke and didn't even respond or look in the man's direction. He just smiled and leaned over and helped himself to a glass and a draft right from the tap.

"I'd take an old Nash or Chevy before that thing," Navi continued to no one in particular, sitting down to his seat in front of the cigarette machine.

"It's empty, cabrón," Fernando shouted. "How long you gonna fuck with that thing. Hey, give the man a smoke, Jeri?"

"I want my own pack," Navi said.

"This is my last," Jeri announced. And with his first drink of draft he raised his head to the metal ceiling and took a mighty drag, the dark smoke spilling from his nostrils.

"Come clean now, Jeri," Fernando said. "You really buy that car?"

"What am I liar?"

"No, Compadre," Fernando said apologetically. "I just know you don't drive so good, no?"

"I thought you said he had no license?" Navi said. "Hey, looks like you painted her, too."

"Oh shit," Fernando said. "You paint her?"

"I just got done," Jeri said after he dropped his glass down to the counter and then pulled his comb from his pocket and pushed all his wet hair from his brow in one quick move.

Navi walloped Fernando and convulsed with laughter as he pointed out into the space between himself and the parked Studebaker. "Looks like shit. I hate to tell you."

"No way," Fernando said.

"Yes way," Navi said pointing this time more intently.

"Holy shit," Fernando said. "Yah. I can see the streaks of brown. What the hell did you paint it with?"

"I had some brown paint," Jeri said proudly.

"House paint, cabrón," Fernando said. "What the hell?"

Across the counter Navi grabbed the keys and cradled them. "Poor little Studebaker."

"Ain't that some shit though," Fernando said. "There ain't a browner car around the neighborhood. I can promise you that—"

"Looks like a piece of shit," Navi said.

"Fuck you, Navi," Jeri said.

"A big brown rolling piece of shit—"

"Hey," Fernando interrupted. "Give my Compadre some respect."

"Come on, Fernando. You can't tell me it looks good?"

"It's got a new color and what fuckin business of it is yours," Jeri said, ending it. He drained his beer and then drew himself another one. Several other men came in and he saw a few more stopping at the entrance to stare at his car and the makeshift paintjob. Then there were three tables going and Navi had to hustle to fill drink orders and some sandwich orders. The smoke-filled air was alive with movement and laughter. Still more people dropped in, and each commented on the shit-stained Studebaker parked up onto the concrete.

After a few minutes Fernando and Jeri walked out to the Studebaker to stare and talk. The sun was down by that time and the lights above the entrance were just coming up bright again and the men could see the hood and the streaks of paint clearer.

"Pretty good business here, no?" Jeri said.

"Yah," Fernando said. "Money's coming in here and there. You know how it is. Slow and then a rush after the mill shifts."

"But I mean you making out good here, no?"

"I can pay the rent. If that's what you asking?"

"A man can be proud when his work is his own."

"Yeah, I guess—"

"I mean I could only wish and dream to be in a place like this."

"What, you gonna open a place?"

"Not in Huerfano," Jeri assured. "Denver. Or in the Springs up north. Maybe near the army base would be a good place, no?"

Fernando could only nod vaguely.

"I mean the GI's need to drink and eat, you know."

"You got a good job with benefits. Government work at the Army Depot. And a kid?"

"Lena has a kid. I ain't got no kid. Jesus, Fernando. I was just gonna take you into the room there and whip your ass at pool. And here you go getting all high and mighty with me."

"Just saying, mano."

"Yeah, yeah. Just sayin—"

"You gotta woman and a kid in the house and you want to leave to Denver?"

"Jesus. It's for the kid. I mean the money is rolling in here and I thought I could you know duplicate it and shit out there. That's all."

"Yeah," Fernando repeated, slamming his open-handed slap to Jeri's shoulder. "All I'm saying is you got a family."

And much later after Jeri drained three drafts and Fernando had already turned the open sign around and made his last call, he watched Fernando mop the counter with a slight strain and then reluctantly fill final orders. "Just like back home," the man repeated as he worked slowly and then counted the nickels and random change the neighborhood folks had paid for beer. This jealousy of the business and Fernando's work only made Jeri want to sit and drink past closing. Fernando was quick to lecture the drunken Jeri, "Quit this hell of a life and get home to your wife and kid."

false teeth

Lena and Lucy Venuda had the old man Carlos down at Bessemer Dental Care. The old man was quite calm for the fifteen minutes in the waiting room, but when the doctor finally had him in the chair and the impression made, Carlos trembled with a stream of soundless words. Bruna entered and set up a chair next to the old man and held his leathered hand.

"They say you have pario … or perio … perio … dontal or dental disease or some other thing," Lena said. "Can't understand what they say."

"Que disease?" the old man replied.

"See here, Carlos," the large-faced Doctor said. He held the dead tooth out, but the old man made no move to come near it. "Too many of these dead!"

"I think he just wants this all done with," Lena said and gave the dentist a sign to keep on working.

Later, the gums became bloody and the dentist wiped his fingers. "We've got a ways to go here, sir," the Doctor said and his voice echoed from around the room and was so impersonal and dry.

Lena was so angered with the man. "Can you give him something for pain!" she said. "Something at all!"

And when she was just at the point of shouting the dentist away, she was told the procedure was all over, and the dentist gave the old man a shot in the gums to deaden the pain.

She threw a sympathetic look into the old man's face and then settled down into her chair. And after they brought the quickly made dentures, they told the old man to wait twenty-four hours to set his new teeth in place, but the old man was so vain he could not go a minute without his teeth. So he set them onto his swollen gums, and this made him lie in pain all night, pouring the strongest whiskey onto his bleeding gums.

THAT FOLLOWING WEEK Lena came by to check on Felipa and the old man. Sometimes she took walks with him around the block and through the lanes of the projects. It steadied him to hear her voice. She told him of Bruna's schooling and her typing class, and the young girl's work for the Father down at St Francis. She told him about how just the other day she heard that Bruna would be taking a trip with the Father to Kansas to tour a convent and how all Bruna speaks of was her love of the church and the work down there.

Sometimes Bruna came down and sat beside Carlos. When she did, the talks opened to music and news the girl learned in school and down at church. The lips moved and it was difficult for the girl to hear the old man, and sometimes there was no conversation between the two. Bruna would comment on the chill in the air or might point out a hummingbird working over Felipa's flower beds, but she usually expected no replies. And Bruna always took it as a good sign that her presence seemed to calm the man's breathing, even if he had no words for the girl.

One afternoon she came quietly onto the porch and found Carlos with healed gums and rocking like a child. He was not talking but humming a tuneless little song to himself.

It was early August and dense heat lay over the yard and out to the alley and it was Carlos who spoke first. He looked over at Bruna brightly and said, "Felipa named you Bruna."

"Yes," Bruna said.

"Felipa's Grandmother was named Bruna," Carlos said. "She

was the skinniest damned woman. You met her, no?"

"No, sir," Bruna said quietly.

Carlos hummed and then for ten minutes he attempted to roll a cigarette until he finally needed a match.

"Let me get it," she said, rising and moving towards the kitchen. "I'll ask Felipa—"

"Don't ask, hija," Carlos said. He appraised the girl's movements through drawers and baskets carefully as she searched. "She doesn't want me smoking. Says I'll burn the damned place up. Hides the lighters from me too," he whispered to himself.

Felipa was in the living room, her face sweaty and she looked up limply, brightened by the young girl's face. "What are you here for, hija?"

"Carlos wanted a match."

"Aw, hija. Carlos ain't supposed to be smoking." She rose promptly and dropped her magazine and then her mouth tightened and trembled.

"How come?" Bruna answered.

"His gums for one thing. And he can't handle the matches? He drops them and loses them and last month nearly set the whole damn house on fire—"

"But I'll watch him, Felipa—"

"I don't care who watches him! He ain't supposed to be smoking!"

"My mama says he's had a hard life and should have whatever he wants," Bruna said with a hard look. Three days later when Felipa was at work, Bruna brought the old man salt and then store-bought cigarettes.

ONE SUNDAY AFTERNOON Felipa came home and found Carlos gone. Felipa walked out through the neighborhood, across a narrow-paved road and then caught the bus to St Francis Church. She crossed Northern Avenue and then walked over to the edge of the festival grounds to scan for Lena. "Carlos' gone," she said when she finally found her.

After a long moment Lena said, "How long?"

"I was at work. I walked in and he was gone. Sometime since this morning."

"We'd have seen him coming down here," Lena said. She looked across the festival grounds. "I have to work here for the church. Can you and Bruna go and look?"

Bruna came at once from her ticket booth duty and said with a rush of affection: "What should we do?"

"That Goddamn old man has abandoned me!" Felipa said to the two women, making it much more dramatic and tense.

Bruna and Felipa agreed to walk across the street and then down Northern to the State Bar and Grill and then they glanced into the mirror over at Don and Pat's Hideaway. They disturbed some steelworkers arguing and then Bruna stayed behind as Felipa wandered around the next bar down Northern and then the next.

At the Longmont Inn they stood at the front door afraid to enter and look down in from the window and down the long bar. They stood at the neighboring parking lot, staring along the narrow alley and then above empty lots.

"How far could've he gotten with that chair of his," Felipa wondered aloud. "Did you see him in any of those windows, hija?"

"He wasn't there and I looked all over."

After they returned to St Francis and the festival, Felipa stood holding her hands and nearly chewing at her upper lip.

"He never left on you like this before?" Lena asked as she went back to the work of handing out tickets and collecting more dollar bills.

"Only to drink with the neighbor but he don't do that no more," Felipa answered. "This is the first time he went off on his own."

"I'll call my friend Lucy and maybe we can drive around," Lena said.

LATER, IN THE CORNER of the festival there was a commotion and then yelling and a small fight broke out. Lena squinted into the crowd, into the thrashing and rattling, and saw Carlos pulling at a man's green t-shirt.

Bruna's voice filled the ticket booth and the crowd around them: "Mama, there he is!"

As they approached, they saw the argument and heard the old man's voice scolding the young man, "Fucking faggot you never respected me or any fucking working man so get the fuck away from me or I'll fuckin drop you where you stand."

"For the love of your God, Carlos!" Felipa said, rushing behind. She slapped the man's t-shirt from Carlos' hands and half lifted the wheeled chair into a new direction. Lena grabbed the old man as Felipa steered him out of the crowd. Carlos' clothes were greasy and filled with dust and hay. There was blood on his lip and his false teeth were missing.

"Bruna!" Felipa yelled. "Get your father out of here! Please!"

Lena hung on to Carlos' arm till the sound of the people died down. "I don't suppose you can tell me what the hell you are doing down here by yourself?"

Carlos sniffed. "A man needs a drink and food and has to get air," he said. "A man cannot only do what he's told by women all the Goddamn time. I know I'm living on Goddamn charity, but you don't have to tie me up and make me feel it all the Goddamn time!"

Lena let go of Carlos' arm.

"I don't have to hear this," she said to Felipa.

"For Christ's sake, Carlos," Felipa said. "You damned old fool! We're not against you! We all love you—"

Before Felipa could move Carlos had his shirt pulled from Lena's hands and then snatched his beer bottle. Then he clenched it tightly to his lips and spilled the bottle and then turned his head as Felipa tried to yank it from his grip: "Goddamn it, mujer!"

And as Felipa steered Carlos to the edge of the festival and away from the ears and eyes of the crowd of Catholics, she whispered as if to a child, "I'll walk you to the damn old folks home myself, Carlos. If I have to."

Lena's own nerves were on edge, and she was trembling.

"I tell you, Lena," Felipa said. "I can't leave this old man of yours alone for a second. I can't live or work or sleep—"

Carlos smiled, "Where did my bottle run off to? It'll find its way to me. Damn man tried to steal it—"

THAT EVENING after they all sat for dinner Bruna waited on the porch as Felipa and Lena talked of the San Luis Valley. She looked over the tiny yard and as the night came on and the summer streetlights buzzed across the alley, she heard Carlos snoring from his little room.

She overheard Lena and Felipa talking and then planning and then much later arguing over Carlos and the money to put into "some kind of home."

"Just who is supposed to pay?" she heard from Felipa.

Then later she heard from her mama, "You've got us cornered now don't you, Felipa!"

"I've never asked for anything from you!"

"And when have I ever asked for anything from you for my Bruna?"

They sat arguing and then settling to disagree and then Bruna heard them negotiate and then stumble.

"You know he has to be sent away from here!" Lena said.

"You've really got us cornered now," Felipa said.

"Well, who? I guess all you have is us to help you! I don't see your people coming to drive him or help you with him! I don't see your sister or her husband coming to lend you a hand. So who else will help you?"

Inside, the two women broke up their argument and snapped off the light. For a minute or two they stood in the kitchen door, both staring at Bruna, her neck and her short hair.

"I guess we'll get," Lena said as signal to Bruna.

"You can stay here in the living room," Felipa answered.

"You ain't got room for us. We'll walk home. I ain't ashamed to walk home. I'll look in on you tomorrow," Lena said.

AS THEY WALKED DOWN Prairie Avenue Bruna asked: "Where's Carlos going? Where's he going away to?"

"Don't know."

"Is he leaving us? He can't leave us."

"We have to do something with him, Bruna. What if he wanders to the 4th Street bridge or what if he's hit by a truck or something?"

"He can't live with us?"

"Lucy's father lived alone for as long as he could and then he walked himself in front of a damned bus! You have school and I have work and Felipa isn't about to move in with us!"

"How will they pay, Mama?"

Lena thought of this talk, plenty of times. But they were finally steady and making money and paying off bills without Jeri, and Lena thought it unfair to bring Felipa and Carlos into their home and their lives more than this. "Where was your old man when we needed him? When he had legs. Never sent you or me a dime and now you want to change everything."

"It's just like you're sending him to prison or something. Just to protect the routine we've got—"

Lena stopped and then leaned into her daughter's face. "Carlos and Felipa have been strangers to us. Haven't sent us a dime or haven't sent you one card and now you want them as live-in family or something."

"We'd be sending him away to some place to die after I've just met him. You forced me to go see them, Mama. And now you want to send him away to die—"

"He sent me away and then he sent you away," Lena explained. "And we'll do the best we can to help but I ain't cut out to be no nurse for no old man who didn't give a shit about me."

"He told me I was named for Felipa's Grandmother—"

"I don't care what he tells you. I got work and you have school and that's it, you hear me? You hear? He's Felipa's now. He's all hers. And sometimes you have to do something like this out of kindness to him. It's hard. I know it's hard. I cry for him too but sometimes you have to do something like this because that's all you can do—"

"Mama—"

"So, I don't want to hear nothing more about it now. You hear me, Bruna? You hear me?"

"Yes, Mama."

"I mean it—"

"Yes, Mama. I hear you."

"You loved Jeri so damned much and all he did for you and what happened with that. Nothing."

"Okay, Mama."

"I raised you. Not Jeri or your damn Carlos. You hear me. It's me and you and nobody else has anything for you. You hear? Didn't I do everything for you?"

"I know you did, Mama—" Bruna's knees trembled a little as she spoke.

"You don't know your father Carlos like I know him. You'll never know what he put my poor Mama through. You'll never know—"

Bruna hesitated and then asked what she'd been dying to ask since the first day she spent with Carlos and Felipa in their little house in the projects and in their little fenced yard facing nothing but alley and other projects. "Carlos told me he wasn't my father," Bruna said quietly and almost naively. "Says Felipa laid with men and wasn't sure if he was my father or if some other man was."

"I don't know nothing about that, Bruna," Lena insisted but first she stopped and stared into her daughter's still eyes. "Who told you that?"

"I told you. Carlos told me."

That night in bed Bruna dreamed of Carlos standing in his bedroom staring out towards her and Lena as they argued. She imagined the man had legs to take him into the duplex and then down the hallway toward Lena's bedroom. Her thoughts hurried with fear driving them, and she cried when she woke. She called for her mother through the cracked door to her bedroom.

church

It was absurd to be out and about with Lino out in his Sunday suit coat and blanket, but Lino wanted to follow Carlos to church. To see his Catholicism in action. Lino was always talking about action with beliefs. "Hey, Catholicism," he would say to Carlos. "Your beliefs are nothing if not put into action."

The church in Colmor was no more than an adobe room with a single high arch and that held no church bell. Father Dwyer had been assigned and found no metal worker available to fix the rusted metal the Catholics of Colmor called a bell. The ranchers had left it out in the elements after a storm brought it down and it stayed at the back of the room and behind Sunday services. Lino wasn't a Catholic but he was curious. He admired Carlos' religion and wanted to follow. The ranch hands and respectable women from Colmor found the sight of a Pueblo Indian dressed up in a suitcoat wrapped in a blanket concerning, but Lino got into the pew and found his seat and immediately blessed everyone around him: "Blessed be the Catholics."

"Try and quiet yourself," Carlos said before smiling and laughing out loud.

Father Dwyer hadn't made it ten feet from the aisle when Lino very loudly and awkwardly dropped the silver and turquoise ring he had acquired in a card game in Santa Fe. The Indians there played with what they sold and traded in the center square, or so went Lino's story.

"The stone has the power and will come back to me," Lino said

as he threw his body to the dusty floor searching. "Wait and see. It'll come back to me." It was at this time Lino decided to very loudly and awkwardly reveal to Carlos how he always hoped Carlos would marry Mara and use the turquoise ring. "This is my most valuable possession besides this suit coat, and I had wanted it for your future, Carlos."

Carlos sat still and red faced as the Father and the pink round faces around him shushed and sat shocked.

"She's a whore but a beauty and the whole town has had her, all the men in here. Mr. Edwards the blacksmith over there and the doctor Blake and probably even the Father, though I can't hold evidence to that. I'm just saying, Carlos," Lino said. "She seems to know every man of importance in Colmor and in this church that I can see right now. Mr. Howard there and the Sheriff Hunter. It's like all of Mara's acquaintances all in one place. Honorable men and magistrates. It's a great privilege for me to be among them all now. The only one who hasn't been with her is the one who loves her and that's you, Carlos."

The crowd began to talk and then whisper furiously at this point, talking turned to yelling and then pushing and copious amounts of strong arming until Carlos and Lino were out on the dust and hardened ground behind the church. Nearly 30 people at the church that Sunday and Lino had insulted nearly every one either by his talking or his crawling or his very presence.

"You had me bring you to start all of this, didn't you, Lino? You knew what you were doing. Probably threw the ring out on the floor to start all this."

"Damnit," Lino said. "This church is a hangout for all the sinners and procrastinators, don't you see that? And I really did lose my damn ring. And that's the truth. It's the only thing worth anything except my soul."

On the ride home, the good people of the county as he called them came to his memory and Carlos laughed out loud at the look of them.

"I didn't mean to embarrass us or you," Lino finally said.

"Hell, you don't get embarrassed, Lino," Carlos answered.

THE NIGHT BEFORE *they gunned Lino down, before they shot and strung him up, Carlos stared up into the cobwebs of the bunkhouse before sleeping and dreaming on Lino's thoughts about life and religion. Carlos had spent the week riding fences which normally only older hands worked, and so he returned late at night, packing out his own meals. He couldn't remember specifics from the last few conversations with Lino, his only friend at the Cutoff. The dreams, though, were of Lino's thoughts on Catholicism and religion from Europe, as he called it.*

"They brought it to you and it ain't from here," Lino had said as final words on Carlos and his religion. "They brought it to you but the people here the Utes and the Navajo and the Tewa Pueblo Indians here believe in four worlds. And Gods that travel in between the worlds. I hope to travel them myself when I'm finally gone and freed from this world. Like climbing steps up a pyramid or a stairwell in a cathedral, like the damned pyramids in Egypt. Seen it in the Bible and in those schoolbooks back in school. But the Indians can't tell me about the next world that's coming. Have to figure that one out for myself."

THEY HAD LINO'S BODY *up on the table waiting for the doctor to come in the 15 miles from Wagon Mound. Carlos had seen the same scene from his Army days. The body left alone because no one had the knowledge or the courage to do anything for him. The word was that the Patrón's men came for him as they did the previous month to bathe the old Indian.*

He's dead and gone and we will never speak again, flashed through Carlos' mind. He had felt the same with the news of Benito's death.

The word was that Lino was a traitor. The Patrón found that the man had been giving away yearling cows to Los Malos, the kids from the village to feed their families, and those cows were not his to sell. Most of the Pueblo Indians of the village knew about it and saw it as business but the Patrón and the son saw it differently. Folks used to say a man named Ketchum, caught by the southern railroad detectives for robbery, was the only man hanged in the history of the county of Colmor, but the Indians and hands knew he was just the only white man killed. Indians had escaped the law but not death. The Indians accused were just shot or hanged as a matter of business. The word was Lino ran from the men when he saw the blades meant for his hair. He may have hit a few of the men who came for him.

Carlos worried and hoped about this next world for Lino, Indian hell or heaven as he saw it. Carlos resisted visiting the body and most of the hands avoided the bunkhouse, sleeping out with the horses and the cattle. The body had been cleaned and Lino's forehead was caked with corn meal which was the Pueblo tradition. Carlos noticed the buckshot scars.

The buck sergeant back at Camp Cody had told Carlos that when one has made a decision to kill a person, it would not do to go about it in a long, drawn-out way. This was during bayonet training and sparring. That was why Carlos had the idea to ride Lino's horse to the Patrón's house and have his revenge. Lino's body was taken on the dog cart back to Taos, and he was to be buried after the Tewa Pueblo ceremonials and forty days of fasting and immuration with the Elders.

Carlos gathered his belongings for that as well, the idea being to kill a man and then travel to a ceremonial ritual. That idea filled his thoughts for hours before he finally travelled to the Catholic Church in Colmor, the same church he had been kicked out of weeks before with Lino. The camp and the town were bustling for the summer round up, and it was as if Lino's death didn't matter at all, as if the death of the man made no difference to the people in Colmor and the ranch hands, just one more empty bed in the bunkhouse to be filled. Carlos had these same thoughts in France when he heard word of his cousin's death, and the war went on without hesitation. This world kept on breathing. The Catholic priest Father Dwyer didn't recognize Carlos since Carlos had stopped shaving and taking care with his appearance, and after reminding him to take off his hat, the Father reminded Carlos to bless himself and to make the sign of the cross upon entrance. "It's a reminder of the baptismal promises," Father Dwyer said and at that Carlos laughed. He thought of how the whole thing was a waste to Lino. "Why not take it from church and carry it with you all the time," Lino had said. "The same man who hates me and throws me from the church wants me to promise my soul away."

DAYS LATER *Carlos would ride the 90 miles to Taos and to the Kiva of the Elders and feel the contrast of the two hundred or so folks, women inside and men outside, some of them recognizing that Carlos wore Lino's serape. Lino said the serape had taken him days and days to complete and it had no mouth, the weave was unbroken. "No serape like this in New Mexico for sale," Lino had said. "This is a thing of beauty, and it is for use. Don't put it away, Carlos. Use it."*

CARLOS IN THE CHURCH *at Colmor sat with his Bible and prayed and stared up at the hanging Jesus, the estandarte. For a minute he found tears for Lino and his brooding and heaviness, and he read the words from his Bible, places in the book his mother had marked and that had meant something to him. He read and read and sat until he reached some of the pages Lino had ripped free. He wanted to continue reading and comforting himself, so he pulled a Bible from the pew in front of him. A silver ring had been wedged into the pages, a turquoise and silver ring. Carlos recog-*

nized it as Lino's lost ring. The Bible had the same passage ripped so it must have been Lino's ring and Lino's doing or another of the Tewa Pueblo Indians who frequented the church. Pueblo Indians who after years of living and working near Colmor had become Catholics. Lino had called them apples to Carlos' surprise, "Red on the outside, Carlos, and white on the inside."

He had said this the time he was drunk and joked with Carlos about the time New Mexico would be taken back by the Indians. "There's a volcano forming north of here," Lino continued with his lecture. "It grows swiftly from the land sprouting, a solitary one near Huerfano County, and they call it the Huerfano, the orphan because it sits alone. There are many like that one in Northern New Mexico, Carlos. Soon the land itself will erupt and spew out all the Spanish and Anglos from an old volcano erupting fire and brimstone and lava right here in Colmor like in your Bible, Carlos."

"Don't talk like one of the viejos," the oldest hand had yelled out to Lino. "Words got more power than you think."

Carlos thought on this memory of Lino and placed the ring on his finger. He thought of how Lino had dreamed Carlos would place the ring on Mara's finger. Lino believed marriage would save a man like Carlos. Save him from himself, save him from his past actions and words. The ring had come back to Carlos the way Lino had believed it would. The ring mysteriously lost for months was now back on his finger.

As he was distracted in thought, Mara sat down next to Carlos as his eyes closed to pray. He held the power of that memory and the power of this coincidence.

"I heard you were running away," Mara whispered, staring down at Lino's ring on Carlos' finger. "I hoped maybe you would have some words for me before."

Soon she had her baby girl on her lap, the girl in dirty shirt and shorts and bare feet. "I've looked after all living things in my life," Carlos said. He was nearly delirious.

"Dogs and horses. Vegetable gardens and orchards. Lettuce fields in Colorado. Always thought of myself as patient and calm. But this business with the Patrón and Lino."

"Magdalino was like a father to me," she said, and it was the first time Carlos had ever heard anyone call Lino by his full name. "Respectful and patient like you. He was always impervious. I like that word, Carlos. Impervious. Lino taught that word to me. He cleared the way for me. He had food for me when I was down. Hell, I am in Colmor because of him."

Mara's daughter, Lena, was nervous and fidgety. "I bet she'd like to climb up into those rafters high into the darkness in here and see what it is like up there." Mara stood up and consoled the girl. Mara was always in thin skirts and flimsy moccasins. "The whole town is wondering if the friend of Lino is going to kill the Patrón."

"What's that you say?"

"I been in a lot of homes. I was taken in by Lino from time to time when I didn't have half of what I have now. I ever tell you?"

Carlos shook his head.

"I was in the picture show in Wagon Mound. I was being asked out of the aisles by the usher and the manager there, and I was pretending I was deaf."

"Deaf?"

"I sat and pretended I had no idea what they were saying. Everyone around us had their tickets and their people and I was just sitting. Only been to the pictures there one other time in my life but I wanted to be there. This was right before I moved here, and Lino got me the job working. I wrote my father 183 letters when I first got to Colmor. Some of them short notes. Lino is the one who wrote them or me. He had paper and pencil and helped me with the words."

Carlos slipped off the silver and turquoise ring and slipped it into Mara's hand.

"Lino wanted this for you."

Mara smiled and clenched her fist. "The whole damned town believes you're going to kill the Patrón."

"What's that you say?"

"I say the whole town says you're going to kill the Patrón. The Patrón himself is probably thinking it. At his house eating a big old dinner, already got a new cook and he's probably sitting with his son and dogs and wondering when you're coming."

"Did your father ever write you back?"

"One time."

"Only one?"

"Wrote me to tell us he didn't have a whore of a daughter. Didn't have no grandbaby. Didn't appreciate me calling my girl the name of his mother. Lino had me saying I was impervious. So, I'm leaving too. I have a bag and I'm leaving. No money and nowhere to go but I'm trying home. My father has to take me back. Or maybe my Grandmother will have me back."

Carlos nodded and leaned back.

"Go kill a man, Carlos. I never said that before to anyone but go kill a man. And the son too if you can. You know how the Patrón's son pulls his weapon. You seen the holes in Lino like I seen them. That was the Patrón's son, and you know it. So, if you don't do it, I'm going to take my daughter and do the damned thing myself."

"Lino always believed in another world where there was no killing and no death."

"Well, it ain't this world, Carlos. A soldier knows that. I know that."

Mara pulled Carlos' side arm, the government pistol, from a bag she held. The Springfield he had taken apart and thrown out into the llano. The one he swore away after meeting with the Patrón and the Patrón's son.

"Los Malos found it and gave it to me. Traded it to me."

"Traded for what?"

"You know," Mara said. "You know. Now take it and kill a man."

sweetheart

One afternoon after school Jeri found himself home well before Lena, and he found Bruna daydreaming and with the weight of the sun on her arms and neck. Jeri said he knew of a house where they had puppies to give away.

All around her the air was hot and thick and there were locusts and birds flying and chirping and the distant chime of five o'clock from St Francis church. Cars down the streets hummed and grew in their whine and strains of brakes as they slapped past.

"I got a friend down here, girly," Jeri said to Bruna. "I got a friend here who's got a whole yard filled with Boxers."

"I thought you said puppies, Jeri."

"Boxer is a kind of a dog," Jeri said. "You never heard of a Boxer dog before?"

"Are they cute puppies, Jeri? Are they cute?"

"Hell, girly. All puppies is cute. You know that."

For a few blocks longer Bruna thought of names for the puppy she would soon find to match the kittens her Mama had already brought for her. She heard the traffic and felt the itch of the bugs to her legs and arms as she moved and loyally followed Jeri. She blinked and thought groggily but was single minded.

Then it struck her that her Mama might not want a dog in her nice clean house and she remarked to Jeri. She lifted the curls from her neck and she asked again and again.

"No," Jeri insisted. "Su mama don't care. I'm getting you a

puppy and she's gonna love it."

An extraordinarily happy look came over Bruna's face, and though Jeri seemed half out of breath as he walked, he noticed the girl's contentment. Bruna's brow lifted and her mouth widened and smiled, and her eyes jumped from the traffic to the street and to Jeri.

"How much," Jeri said to Old Woman Cavuto and the stream of Boxer puppies that rushed her metal gate.

"It's not the money," the woman said through her hairy lip. "I want to know you can care for them. You know I don't want to hear the city picks them up once they get too big for your house."

"Nobody's more worried about that than me," Jeri said. "What do you think, Bruna? Can you be mommy and daddy for the baby here?"

"I can be mommy but not the daddy."

"You know what I mean, Bruna."

"Look at this one Jeri," Bruna screamed. "This one looks sick and small."

"That one's the runt," Old Woman Cavuto explained.

"What's a runt? Is he sick? Hey, Jeri. Is he sick?"

Still with a terrified and anxious look, Old Woman Cavuto explained how some babies are weaker and need more attention and care.

"Oh, no," Bruna said.

"How much?" Jeri asked.

"I'll call him Sweetheart, Jeri. You like that name, Sweetheart?"

"That's a damn fine name, Bruna. How much, lady?"

They came home, with a Boxer puppy and a rope for a leash, and they were halfway up the stop before Lena screamed and carried on. Jeri walked like a prisoner amongst police who had just approached him for questioning. His darkly smooth hair was shining, and he had his head nearly down before Lena began in on him.

"Jesus Christ, Jeri," Lena snapped. "Don't we got enough animals around here or don't you think we have enough mouths to feed."

"Leave it be," Jeri said. "She loves it. Looks how she loves it."

"We got cats and rabbits in the yard and now we have another damn animal. Do you even think of this shit before you do it? Do you even think?"

"What?"

"I'm home all day with the house filled with animals and now I gotta put up with a Goddamn dog."

Jeri lifted his shoulders again. "I wanted to make the girly happy, Bruna."

"Of course, and then you are gone, and I have to pick up the thing's shit all day. All by myself."

"Everything isn't bad news for you, cabróna."

In the yard after dinner the atmosphere of the house was weighted and awkward. Bruna had the feeling that somehow, without anyway understanding, the whole house had arrived at the decision of ignoring the puppy and Bruna or the whole situation. The adults sat in the kitchen and smoked and drank their beers and coffee and never said a word to one another or to Bruna about Sweetheart. It was still too hot outside for sitting and in the house Jeri and Lena were too aware of each other to be happy. The dark smoke of their cigarettes eased out the screen door and out the window over the sink. She wondered how such a sweet puppy could cause so many problems so she held the smooth-haired dog tightly and watched it shit and piss throughout the yard. Later she watched the contempt in Lena's eyes as she came outside to smoke and judge the little girl and the dog. Later Bruna watched her mama shovel up the dog's mess and dispose of it over the fence and into the alley as she cursed and puffed at her cigarette.

That night the sky was dark and immense and impressive to

Bruna and the shadows of the yard stretched up and down the fence line and her mother seems larger and more alive than other days.

"Anyone think of who was gonna clean up after such a dog, eh? Tell me. Eh?"

Bruna shook her head and shrugged in a sadly obedient way.

"Goddamn it!" Lena said. "What you name her, girl?"

Bruna smiled and then whispered, "Sweetheart."

"He's a boy," Lena said.

"Yes, Mama."

"You named a boy dog Sweetheart. Sounds like craziness to name a boy dog Sweetheart. And that dog is gonna grow into a monster."

"They say he's a runt, mama. Not too big."

"That dog is a large breed of a dog and will grow to be as huge as a house and we ain't got but this tiny little yard. Who's gonna walk him when he's big as the house? You?"

"I walk him around, mama," Bruna said.

After dinner Lena went outside to tie Sweetheart to the Spruce tree near the alley.

SINCE SWEETHEART HAD COME to the house, strange compulsions moved Lena to watch Jeri more closely. Bruna found herself reciting the names of all the bars Jeri stayed after his work at the Army Depot. And while Bruna was with Vicky, she watched all of them from across the parking lot. The highway traffic poured north as Lena circled the Senate and then the Hideaway. Bruna looked curiously as the men walked into the place. She searched for Jeri's bald head and bulky frame. On her left as she circled Fernando's Place, Lena found a little eating shack where men sat and ate long johns and coffee, and she remembered years before Jeri brought her and Bruna when he still cared to spend dinner as if they were a family. The mere look of it with

Coke signs and beer ads saddened her and filled her nostrils with the peculiar smells of the steel mill, and the culture of men who ate and drank for hours after work, refusing to come home.

She parked and watched the men closely as they ate, and the metal rasping of car horns and traffic rose louder as she scanned for Jeri. She thought she was exactly as her mother was, waiting for men to return home to be fathers, to return home to their women and daughters.

Next, she was pushing Vicky's doorbell and parking her car around the block to stalk her own house across the alley.

"What the hell do you want to do that for?" Vicky said as she heard Lena's plan.

"I gotta know what he does when I'm not around."

Vicky stood there in her short sleeves in her housecoat and asked Lena if she was drunk or just acting drunk, to which Lena never answered. Vicky smirked and took Lena's purse and hangers filled with the two houses' laundry and pressing work.

"Just watch Bruna for a few more hours, Vicky. Can you do that for me?"

Bruna was up off the couch where she read her magazines and schoolwork. She came forward with questions and the leash of her dog. The girl looked pretty and rested but eager to speak to her mother and follow. Lena was blinking and drowsy and hurried out the door. She was feigning sobriety and begged the daughter to be still and good for just a little longer.

"But I want to take Sweetheart home, mama," Bruna yelled.

Lena's hand pulled her around.

"Stay inside," she said, "until I come back. I'm taking a walk."

"I'm going with you."

"No, Bruna. Stay inside with Vicky."

Bruna was standing at the screen door carrying a little smile that turned to a smirk as Lena walked around the house and across the alley. The girl's eyes followed from the door and then from the kitchen and then from the screen door as she followed her mother's path.

"Stay inside, Bruna," Lena mouthed as she walked quickly. One hand stayed on her hip as she walked and the other carried her freshly lit cigarette she'd been balancing and puffing since leaving her car. She was more and more bothered as she eyed Jeri's car in the garage. The profanity in her throat came forward as she questioned Jeri's motive for staying home by himself and not picking up Bruna as soon as he arrived.

She was staring and tipping her head sideways to catch a better view of the door and then at the car parked in the garage. She had made her way around the concrete path alongside the house before she heard Bruna's voice behind her steps. "Goddamn it, Bruna," Lena snapped in a whispered voice. "Go to Vicky's and I'll pick you up soon. Goddamn it, don't nobody listen to what I say no more."

"But I want to go home, Mama—"

"Do as I say. You hear?" And with that she felt an obscure shame, as she was certain the neighbors had heard her argument over the side fence as she marooned Bruna for her work of catching Jeri.

"But mama—"

For an instant Lena was furious, so furious she shook and hollered at her young daughter. "Goddamn it, Bruna, I ain't joking with you. Get to Vicky's now."

Bruna's eyes were inspecting her mama closely and sadly before she walked back to Vicky and her smelly kitchen.

"I tell you for sure, Bruna," Lena said. "If you come walking over here."

And it struck Lena as she spied into her own windows that this might be the lowest moment of the sad relationship. It wasn't that Jeri had refused to marry and it wasn't that Jeri couldn't stop drinking or that he had lost their money drinking and gambling, and it wasn't even the idea that she had caught him before. It was the idea she had turned against her own daughter.

It was the laughing and giggling that she first heard that made her eyes close and ache. She felt half sick and close to vomiting. Even while she heard the laughter and as she concentrated at the bedroom window, she wasn't quite sure if it was all conscious anymore or some great evil pushing her to put her face close to the glass.

"You piece of shit man," Lena thought and then she hollered and wailed. At first her lips were quiet and delicate and then the softness slipped. She pulled her shoe from her foot and slammed at the glass with a crack and then with both hands slamming and cracking at the broken glass. When the glass was removed, shards of it were slicing at her forearms, and as she had the curtains pulled to the side, she found Jeri from the waist down naked with a black-haired girl from the east side pulling and searching for her clothes strewn over the floor and hallway.

"Tell her to come here, Jeri! Tell her to come here! I'm gonna kill this bitch in my house, Jeri."

Jeri's eyes were round and innocent.

"You were at work, Lena," he said. It was all that Jeri could manage.

With a quick look the woman was dressed and down the hall, and then Jeri had the front door blocked to Lena and her screams.

"I hear your Goddamn cabróna in my bathroom, Jeri. I hear. You fuck of a man—" Lena's lips twitched, and she lurched forward on the porch onto the front screen unaware she was bleeding and missing a shoe. "I hope she's worth your life, Jeri," Lena screamed. The porch thudded with her shoe and her bare foot. She stood gravely as Jeri introduced Lena to his girl with polite indifference.

Jeri stood gnawing on the end of a beer bottle, swigging and smoking obviously as drunk as Lena. "Stay away from her," Jeri said. "If you ever do this again you crazy bitch I'm leavin your ass alone."

The girl put her hand out to Lena before the two got into Jeri's car. Lena knew there was no use in screaming and carrying on though she did anyway, taking her second shoe from her foot and cracking it down on the windshield. She held Jeri's eyes as she slammed the heel down again and again.

"You crazy bitch," Jeri murmured out the window with a tight voice.

"If you're not home tonight I swear I'll cut up all your God-damn clothes. You hear me. If you're not home tonight I swear I'll do it. You fuck of man."

The Studebaker screeched off and Lena looked on, considering chasing after. Her eyes and ears held a sudden fuzziness and burning, and her arms were pained. On her delicate reddened fingers there was a flicker of red blood and a glint of glass.

dilemma

Bruna Montoya was 16 years old that summer of '67 and had never driven a car a day in her life when her mother asked her to drive Jeri the thirteen blocks from the White Horse Bar and Grill to their home on Routt Avenue.

Jeri had a '53 Studebaker Coupe in those days, jet black with a two-tone paint job that didn't come standard from the factory. Little Jimmy Mestas had taken it upon himself to give the car a canary yellow stripe to the bottom half. That made the little car look fast and Jeri knew that made his car special. He had cherished the car ever since the day his '50 Chevy Belair came up with a cracked block and he traded it in for the Studebaker. Under normal circumstances he would have never trusted that car to the young Bruna. He loved that car and the tire pressure it sat on.

For a girl who had never driven a bicycle before, Jeri might as well have asked her to steer the city bus home. And as she sat in the driver's seat outside of the "beer joint" in question, and that is exactly what Bruna's mother had called it that afternoon as she begged Bruna to walk down in search of Jeri, Bruna shook and felt the sweat run down her front lip and down from her armpits staining her bright blue sweater vest.

Initially Bruna resisted but Jeri and Bruna's mother were not speaking to one another and Bruna's mother had wanted nothing to do with the White Horse Bar and didn't care to catch Jeri with his crew of friends down at the place. Bruna had known enough to translate "friends" into "girlfriends". And that afternoon as Bruna's mother took a chicken from the coop out behind the apartment and twisted the head with a quick snap and squawk, Bruna knew she would be in for trouble.

"I want you to go down there," Bruna's mother cried out the front door and Bruna nodded, "and tell that S.O.B. to get his ass home."

"Okay, mama," she said.

Now Jeri had been drunk for days. Bruna knew everyone knew about Jeri. Everyone also knew that Bruna's mama was the one to call the bartender down at the White Horse, so Jeri angrily jammed the keys down into Bruna's palms and then he looked up and down the block.

"I been here for hours. Calling and calling. Where the hell have you been?" Jeri yelled.

He placed a cigarette between his lips and proceeded to search for his matches. He found a nickel on the ground and lost his balance placing the coin in his pocket and almost fell before Bruna caught him with both hands. The two almost chopped each other to the ground. For the first time the two embraced, clasping hands and holding one another for balance. For a minute he seized the keys from her, but he soon replaced them into her small hands. Jeri had never looked so tired or old to Bruna as he did that moment on Santa Fe Avenue.

"I can't drive, Jeri," Bruna said.

"You can drive," he said. "You can drive. You can drive."

They reclined into the red interior and Bruna gripped the steering wheel. Her lips that afternoon were coated with a light pink lip-gloss from the Woolworth's that she was nervously licking and biting at. Her small, delicate hands ached as she clenched and gripped the metal gear shift.

"Get the clutch down to the floor," Jeri instructed. "Get it down to the floor. And don't make an ass of yourself. Don't make an ass of yourself."

Bruna stared out over the traffic moving north and her thoughts and muscle control faltered. She had studied Jeri's driving in the past, sitting in between her mama and Jeri on countless trips out west to Colorado, out to Monte Vista, and the Montoya's family lettuce farm. Her arms suddenly felt heavy and tired as the engine kicked over and the car vibrated with energy.

"Well come on," Jeri said. "Come on. Come on. Come on."

The car rolled and Jeri had his hands on the steering wheel and the gear shift. The gears strained and moaned as she let the clutch out and the car lurched and then died. When the car finally got going, Bruna's eyes were locked on the road and she never once moved her head. Jeri was screaming and raising his arms. Jeri did not allow Bruna to change lanes or shift out of 2nd gear. That was his instruction. Fear and frustration built in Bruna's eyes and neck as she became hyperaware of road signs and colors. The car passed 4th Street Bridge and then downtown near Union Avenue. Each street sign and street corner passed with waves of worry and Jeri's screams.

"Brake," Jeri yelled. "Brake. Brake. Go. Go."

Sweat poured from Bruna's hands and forehead, moistening the curls over her ears.

"Keep away from the curb," Jeri yelled. "The curb. The curb. Keep away from the curb. Brake. Brake. Brake. Go. Shift."

"All right," Bruna said with the confidence of eight blocks behind her. "Don't get mad."

Jeri raised an almost reassuring hand and nearly smiled.

"You know Father Dwyer drinks," Bruna said. She mostly said it to calm herself down. She mostly said it to calm Jeri down.

"What you say?" Jeri asked.

"I say Father Dwyer drinks," she repeated. "I seen him."

"What's the church come to," Jeri said. At this he slumped into the door and leaned his forehead against the passenger-side window.

Out in the street Bruna's eyes dulled with the ache in her

hands from the metal steering wheel. For a few blocks, while Jeri closed his eyes, she was free of the sense of impending batters and bruises to Jeri's car. For a second she was excited by the speed of the car and the control of the engine as she stepped lightly on the gas. For a few blocks she felt whole. Few cars were on the roads and few distractions were on the sidewalks as she passed Centennial and then Lincoln Street. Near the Chief Theatre she slowed down to read the marquee. She studied the strange title of the film: Dr Zhivago. Soon her eyes strained in the afternoon sunlight and the dark shadows hiding out between the rectangular buildings of Junction Street and then farther out to Colorado Avenue. Bruna sat up squinting just before hitting the parked Mercury.

Her curly hair was in disarray as Jeri jumped up and screamed Bruna's name over and over. The two cars grated together and another wave of confusion and fear spread over her as she lost control of the coupe and was thrown off course into oncoming traffic.

For a second, she closed her eyes and let go of the steering wheel.

Before the Studebaker hit the curb of the far side of Colorado Avenue and the front end popped into the air and jumped up into a small yard and the chain link fence that guarded the grass, a buzzing of depression and despair came into Bruna's head. She looked at Jeri's closed eyes and aching face and she clenched her crucifix. She knew that the family was absolutely lost.

the law

Les Dow was the Sheriff of nearby Eddy County, and he had a spread near Sofia, New Mexico. Carlos rode out the morning after Lino's death. Carlos believed in the rule of law, so he rode out to ask the man for counsel. Lino had said the man's boy was on his way to becoming the first attorney general of New Mexico after law school. Lino studied the man Dow in the papers. He was on old law man, and they say he knew Tom Mix and had the film star at his ranch in the summers to help with the realism of the pictures. The man's ranch in Sofia was a young operation in comparison to the Patrón Waddingham's. After the man bought out smaller outfits like Eddie Duran's, several thousand acres now belonged to the soon to be retired sheriff. Dow was surprised to see Carlos wearing Lino's serape when he rode up covered in road dust and llano brush.

Dow's face was darker from the sun and his head was nearly ghost white. He had a long bushy moustache, and his rounded ears were set apart from his head like railroad signs markers when Carlos rode into his world. He had a thin black cigar in his fingers as he spoke.

Dow nearly gave the same speech the old man Patrón Waddingham had given. "Colmor was tents before Waddingham, single saloon, livery stable and a three-roomed hotel." The man took a puff from his cigar and then he stared up into the dark blue sky. "You rode sixty miles all the way out here to tell me about a dead Indian and a dead Mexican," the man said.

"Yes, sir. I came to report murders."

Dow's men sensed something in Carlos and then walked up from the animals. Carlos noticed how closely the crew of men resembled the Patrón Waddingham's men. In fact, Dow had a clean white shirt just like the Patrón.

"The man out there is like me. He's got problems of industry, draught, market prices and values going up and down. Deep snow in the winters. Most men have gone out of business, cleared out, but not Waddingham. He's got me thinking about fenced pastures, windmills and the digging of wells because new laws have outlawed free grazing. Then he has a payroll. You know that?" Dow said. "You know I rode with the man crossing the Canadian River bringing horses over from Oklahoma. Wagons stuck in the mud, but the man never lost his wits. He's a damned good cattle man. Tough boss. People don't follow orders and the boss has to act. Or it affects payroll." To Dow the question of two lives was a simple as that. "Now I got animals to brand," he said, finishing it. And with those words his men heeled a calf and dragged the animal closer to the fire. "Got a doctor coming out to vaccinate them. Another damned expense for a cattle man."

"But sir," Carlos said. He was shocked and angered and then he returned his cover to his head. He had taken it off while Dow spoke out of respect and weakness. He turned to mount his mare.

"Don't worry," Dow said finally to Carlos. "A man dies and another one is hired on to take his place. That's the business. You'll get your pay if that's what you are worried about or if you're worth a damn as a hand. Or you can come here and talk to my manager if you need work."

Dow pulled his work glove and threw down his cigar to give Carlos a limp handshake, and then went back to his day's entertainment.

—

THE AFTERNOON CARLOS RETURNED from Olfie, they had Lino upright and in a box with the sign saying cattle cheat as they had done with Eddie. The man was grey and looked shriveled and empty. Carlos' cousin Benito was never a believer but the sight of a dead body for the first time made the man see differently. "Maybe now I can understand the idea of having a soul," Benito had said to Carlos. When Benito passed, Carlos never saw the man. They were separated by orders and Carlos had heard through telegram.

Carlos went into the storeroom and collapsed on the feed bags and the bags of frijoles and grain and collapsed into tears.

"When they come, they come early," Lino had always warned. "No help for you in the morning light."

Carlos had five cartridges left; one he had fired by accident on the llano before Taos and Lino's morada. The spring was loose, and he knew it was only a matter of time before a jam or misfire. Who knows how long the cartridges had been with the gun? The gun had been delivered to Carlos by the government agency in charge of collecting and shipping Benito's body back from France. Carlos mailed all personal items back to Benito's people in San Luis but he kept the gun. Benito's Bible, his leather pouch filled with letters and a partial diary he mailed off. The necklace locket filled with pictures of his mother and father gifted to him before leaving for Camp Cody he had also mailed off. But, of course, he kept the gun and cartridges.

Carlos slept maybe a few hours off and on holding the weapon, and every sound and every bit of noise was Arthur's companeros coming to slit his throat.

There would be four of them for sure: Paul and Ray Padilla and Jose Diaz, Ray Padilla being the most violent, the one with the largest frame and forearms and the widest back, though the man had no work ethic. Ray was a low IQ soldier for Arthur; that's how Lino had put it. He always advised Carlos to stay far from the industry Arthur had going for himself. Four men for sure and maybe at least one shotgun, seeing that Lino had buckshot scars to his neck and shoulders.

"Dead in my boots," he thought. And before he finally fell asleep, he fieldstripped his weapon and cleaned the dust and mess the best he could. He cleaned the cartridges and oiled the gun to at least pretty it up and smooth up the action. He found his work knife but never bothered to sharpen it. Arthur's men carried Bowie knives, but Carlos' knife was for work and not death.

And with these thoughts his hands shook; he had wanted no more of this life for himself, this life of killing and hunting. He nearly laughed out loud to think of the mindless men coming for him.

Lino had once said, "The people here don't care about justice or ethics of conduct, Carlos, so get that out of your head. As long as there is work and money circulating and flowing that's all anyone cares about isn't going to be cause for concern. The elders back in Taos see it differently but you're 15 miles from Taos and at least 60 miles from the nearest law. Out here it's just the Patrón and his companeros and they are mindless and heartless, so you have to deal with that reality, Carlos." And in that night of no sleep and dread Carlos hoped for a better world for Lino, more peaceful at least.

party

Martha Lujan always arrived first after her meter maid shift with her bottles of rum and her six-packs of RC colas and her own set of glasses. The overweight and uniformed brunette patted at Bruna's young rosy cheeks when she swaggered in.

"I bet a curvy thing like you has many suitors, no?" Martha asked.

"I belong to God," Bruna answered, stealing the answer from Father Dwyer's lectures.

Then Dita entered next with her son Robbie, the annoying boy with the lisp and lazy eye. Dita had the only electric blender of the crew for daiquiris and other mixed concoctions. It was a steel monster and filled the house with an angry ice crunching growl.

"I can't hear myself think with that thing," Bruna thought and sighed.

At least at a bar Bruna could escape all these people but it was all in her house and in her life.

"You're not too old for me to lay out," Lena snapped. Martha and Dita laughed while Robby pestered Bruna with his bag of marbles and his shoe box filled with playing cards.

"Leave her be," Dita ordered while the boy whined.

The men would follow: Mariano from down the block with a bag of ice, the man they all called Marijuano as a joke but also because of the product he sold around the neighborhood. Then

Phil Vigil who always dressed in a suit and tie. "Real suave," Lena said to Bruna.

"The man looks like a lizard," Bruna declared to her mother whenever they walked the blocks downtown and then walked past Burgerman's Shop for Men where Vigil made his money. In another time and place Bruna worried it would have been Phil living with Lena instead of Jeri, since Phil was over the house so much as Bruna was growing up. Phil had money or at least the appearance.

"From his clients," Lena bragged on his behalf. "He works for it. And the car is a product of his work, Bruna. See what work can do."

But Bruna only saw him flirt with old ladies, wives and young girls buying dress shirts and pants for fathers and husbands at home. She hated his slick ways. "Of course, he works for his own, cabróna," the women all barked at her.

The only man Bruna wanted around and the only man she took pleasure in missing and seeing after weeks away was Tio Leo. He always arrived late and drunk and he lumbered his awkward hipster self through the door, always in sunglasses and dress pants with wing tips. He smelled of beer and his cheap cigarillos, but Bruna managed to love him.

"How are you, Tio?" Bruna yelped as he entered, surprising the others around the house. Though he was a drunk and spat when he talked and slurred his responses, she always hugged him and carried on. "You're so fat but happy, no?" Bruna joked as she kissed the man's bald head. She pinched at his ponsa and inspected his belt. "You never eat so how do you stay so round, Tio."

When Bruna was 12, Lena and the boyfriend Jeri had driven all over town searching for Leo. They hit the bars and then the houses off of Union Avenue and then the apartments off of Junction Street. "Where the Goddamn addicts all live," Jeri said as he steered. "See how your Tio lives." Then if Lena was nervous or paranoid, they'd hit the city jail and then miles out of town to the county jail and then finally St Mary Corwin. This happened so much in Bruna's life she grew up believing this to be what family was about. She never blamed Leo, though, the way she blamed her mother and of course Jeri. "I drink but he's a Goddamn junky," Jeri barked as they drove and as they worried on the man. "He has junky friends and Goddamn junky ways."

"He's not a dog to throw out," Lena returned.

Bruna remembered the strangeness of the word and the feeling of the old man she loved and missed. They had found him in a motel room with one of his many girlfriends or else they found his truckito in the parking lot and searched for the door and the room where he slept alone and wasted from nights and nights of the needle. They ran him through the bath and the shower and found him clothes to sleep in and took him in and even gave him Bruna's bed. She always had worry for his health. At this get-together he was only beer buzzed and swaying to music from Lena's hi-fi.

DRINKING AND DANCING was how the group spent the hour after dinner and after Bruna finished her homework sprawled out on the couch with her bag of potato chips and her RC Cola can with a straw.

"Put some rum in that RC Cola," Phil joked with her and the crew laughed as they told their stories and as they huddled around Lena's dinner table and hole of a kitchen.

"Where's your typewriter, Bruna," Lena yelled. "Phil wants to borrow your typewriter for some letters."

"But Mama," Bruna argued.

"Bruna," Lena yelled. "Phil needs it for one night. Don't be so stingy with your possessions. I let you into my home and I'm not stingy with my bed and my food, Bruna. Now don't embarrass me with my friends around."

"Your friends are lowlifes, Mama," Bruna said. The slap resonated through the house and Mariano was the first to give his drunken laugh and then Phil. Soon, the entire crew laughed and wandered out as poor Bruna cried and dragged her typewriter from its hiding spot in her Mama's closet. Lena was immediately sorry, and her chin moved apologetically. Her friends were around, though, and so she had to laugh to play it off.

"Leave her be," Dita said as she directed Robbie to the bathroom and Martha agreed.

"Hey Martha," Phil said as he drained his rum and RC Cola.

"Don't say 'Hey' to me," Martha returned. "You don't know me."

"You a meter maid, no?" Phil said. Phil had his coat off and his tie undone and was leaning over Lena's dinner table to ask questions. "Why you working, Martha? Why you working so hard?"

"What you talking about?" Dita asked.

"I'm not talking to you, Dita. I'm talking to Martha. I am just asking why you working? I know you have a husband and I want to know why you working?"

"A woman shouldn't work?" Dita asked.

"All the women in this house work for a living," Lena added, gesturing with her glass of beer. "Ain't no man taking care of me. I work for my drinks."

"Yeah," Martha Lujan finally answered. "I work for the county and I give tickets to rollers like you."

Bruna sat and stared with her warm cheeks. She always imagined Phil as aggressive towards Martha because he loved her.

"I ain't the kind of woman to stay home while my old man works. Your wife is home barefoot and pregnant with your baby and worthless but to lay down and scream," Martha said.

"Damn, woman," Phil said. "I was just clowning with you. No need to take that all personal and shit. Don't have to show your venom to me. We all friends here."

—

BRUNA ESCAPED OUT THE BACK DOOR and walked for three blocks, and then she circled just short of Northern Avenue and the liquor stores and neon signs of the all-night laundromat. "People don't know how I can walk," Bruna once told Martha. "They all ask me, how can you walk to school and to the bus stop and all the way to Union Avenue over the 4th Street bridge? They all want to know if I need a ride but I like to walk. I like to think and remember. I like the time alone. Away from my Mama and the memories of Jeri and the rest of the low life crew and extended family Lena has thrown at me."

Some nights she walked to the VFW and watched the old folks dance and drink and then she sipped from the empties they left as they whipped around the dance floor the size of a welcome mat. Sometimes she sneaked cigarettes from her Mama or bummed them from the old men who were more than happy to talk to the youthful girl and her lemon-smelling hair and dress. Sometimes they held her hand and asked her to dance but she always pulled away to the street and her walk. Sometimes she headed past her closed school and then to Abriendo where the houses were larger and not apartments or duplexes and she wondered at the large picture windows and the driveways filled with cars and the green lawns and ivy-covered walls. Sometimes she stopped at the city park and wandered to the manmade pond. "I'm not afraid to be here after dark," she whispered to herself as the headlights whipped past.

WHILE BRUNA WALKED, Phil Vigil sneaked into her bedroom, into her closet, and bent over inspecting her shoes and clothes. He hadn't liked the way he smelled, and at first thought of taking a shower as the crew quieted down. He had the dizzying impulse to walk into the young girl's room and smell her through her clothes, her sweaters and her dresses. He took off his shirt and pants and stood for a minute in his underwear while he chose. It would have to be the skirt. He'd seen her in this skirt. The cotton wraparound kind with green, red and yellow flowers. Then he searched for a bra. He knew the danger of standing only a room away from Tio Leo and Lena's sleeping snores. He simply couldn't resist. After a sea of rum and Cokes, the feelings came to the surface. Martha's mixed concoctions and Mariano's cheap herb, brick-packed and barely cured, surged through him. "You'll never do it," Mariano had said. "Lena would have your damn verga if she caught you ten feet from the girl."

"I see her every week," Phil repeated as he drank and smoked and as the dark smoke filled his lungs. "Her little waist and ass. I see her."

"Reminds me of this girl I hired to work at my store. People said she fucked old guys like me for clothes and for food. She was Mexican I think," Mariano said.

He pulled Bruna's only larger sweater from the mess of her bedroom floor and adjusted it all in the mirror. He found a look of himself he could stand and then he smiled into the mirror and the darkness of the room. Satisfied, he then searched for shoes and stockings, which to his anger were all too tight or small and made his toes crack as he forced them into a pump and then a pair of patent leather flats, the flats Bruna usually wore to church. He sat at the desk where Bruna typed her homework and her letters to Jeri and her imaginary letters to her father. He looked through her books and her steno pads. He felt excited. He lit a cigarillo as he thought of her makeup and her perfume. He tried on a necklace. Bruna came to his mind as he put his head to her desk and stationery.

The music played sadly and mindlessly from the living room as Bruna entered her home and navigated the drunken bodies. She helped her Tio to his feet and then to his resting place on the couch. She turned down the hi-fi and clicked off the television. She cleaned up the bottles and glasses before attending to her drunken mother. She pulled the sleeping mother to the easy chair that Bruna always remembered as Jeri's. Then she helped Martha to the cab she called for and then helped Dita while carrying the sleeping Robbie to the same cab. The engine idled in the middle of the quiet street and the sound came in through the open front door and the night's cold burned the air. For a moment Bruna considered these questions: Where are you, Daddy? Are you missing or are you hiding?

Phil had a spot of wet in the front of his pants as he placed his clothes over Bruna's skirt. He had to pull the sweater over his head and place his dress shirt over Bruna's bra and necklace before doing his tie and placing his sports coat over. He finished by straightening the knot and his collar. He poured cool water from the bathroom faucet over his face and neck, the water spilling over his collar and staining the shoulders. The trouble and ache of the last few minutes sobered him. Now was the time for other things. Now was the time to find his way to the front door with his hidden prizes under his clothes and now was the time to hide Bruna's sweater now that the music and noise from the living room had quieted.

As Phil waited for his senses to return on the porch besides Lena's and Bruna's building, he stared down to his Cadillac and the dirty side skirts. He felt bliss standing inside of Bruna's skirt and underwear. Mariano's weed wore off and he focused more clearly on the tree tops down the street and on the subtle shades of wood smoke lifting from the houses and apartments. On the porch, the lights went out and then Bruna came to close and lock the front door when Phil smiled guiltily through a sliced screen door and then asked the young Bruna what he could do to help her close down her home for the night. He said, "Hey, girly. Can I tell you how much I admire your mother?"

"You can tell me," Bruna answered, "but it won't do you no good with her. She don't listen to me. Especially when it comes to married folks."

"Divorced folks," Phil said. "She knows I been divorced a while. She knows."

"Oh yeah?" Bruna said, seriously surprised and interested. "You pretty confident now then, no?" And maybe it was the cigarette Phil offered young Bruna or maybe the way he spoke to Bruna with regard. And maybe it was the cigarette Phil offered young Bruna or maybe the way he spoke to her with regard. Maybe it was a trick to get her onto the porch that she felt, but when he handed her his cigarillo and then his lighter, Bruna finally opened her door to Phil and slid out into the chilly night over onto the porch and then onto the concrete stoop. And still she checked over her shoulder for signs of her mama's watchful eyes and then tamped her cigarillo as she always saw the debutantes and actresses on the television do.

"Not supposed to smoke but Mama's out on the couch," Bruna admitted.

"Out?" Phil asked.

"Passed out," Bruna said.

"Then what su mama don't know, huh," Phil said. "I'm sure you smoke at school anyway. I see the kids across the school heading home and smoking. I'm sure I've seen you smoke too."

"You seen me?" Bruna asked. "Oh my god you seen me."

"I seen you," Phil said. "You with the pep squad and I go see my nephew playing b-ball."

"Oh yeah," Bruna said.

"Goes to South High," Phil said.

"You got one of them preppy kids out at South, huh?" Bruna said.

"Open school. Anyone can go to South High. Anyone can go to South, so I see you Central High kids afterwards smoking. I seen you but I just funning you, Bruna. I know su mama works hard and Jeri left you in a bad place and you don't have to hide nothing from me. I know you."

"It's crazy how people hate on each other around here, you know?" Bruna said. She lit the cigarillo and then took puffs inhaling and fighting off coughs and wheezes.

"Damn, girly," Phil said. "Slow down and enjoy. You got time."

Later Phil asked Bruna about a drive in his Cadillac. He pointed across the road and told her about how his car had broken down over the last few weeks several times and how it ate up most of his savings. Bruna still tried to smoke as if she were sophisticated while she stared out at the dark vehicle across the street. She imagined herself in the passenger seat ditching her friends at the bus stop waiting to get downtown to their jobs and down to the school. She thought of her mother on the corner every morning waiting for the bus before 7 a.m. with her sack lunch in hand morning after morning rushing to catch the bus with her exact change as the Cadillac passed. She imagined the cool air through her hair and afternoons filled with cigarillos and mixed drinks.

"Your mama doesn't even have a license no more, does she?" Phil asked. Bruna smoked and nodded sadly. "You guys probably walking all over town, no? Waiting for the buses in this town. I remember you and Jeri out driving a few times," Phil said.

"I drove him a few times," Bruna said. "Crashed his Studebaker too."

"No way," Phil said. "I think I heard about that. Told me he cracked it himself. He told me he cracked it up."

"No," Bruna repeated. "We had to say he was driving because of the insurance."

"No shit," Phil repeated and laughed.

"But I like your Cadillac," Bruna said.

"See the yellow paint?" Phil asked. "That don't come from the factory. No. I got a Compadre who does body work and one day I bring up how I want a yellow stripe to my Caddy. And he does it. Just takes care of it. No other ride like this one in the state for a couple of months and then they start coming from the factory like this. Just started happening. Can you believe that shit," Phil said. "And so I get upset and he laughs. Tells me I'm the man with the vision every time I see him. Always funning with me over it, you know. I told your mother that story, Bruna. You know that?" Phil said.

"What she say?" Bruna answered.

"She just nodded and then doesn't say a thing. She ain't easily amused, no? But good way to be, right?" Phil asked.

"I ain't nothing like my mother," Bruna said.

"What you mean, girly," Phil said.

"I'll never be hanging on some man for everything. I'm getting my driver's license and I ain't gonna rely on some man just because he lied and told me he loves me. No man gonna run my life."

And then they both stood in a sad and unnerving silence before Phil asked for his coat from the house and Bruna headed inside to hand it over.

MAKING HER WAY to her bus stop the next morning Bruna accepted her day's work and thoughts dutifully.

"Your mama all crudo and shit," Phil screamed through the passenger window of his canary yellow Cadillac.

Bruna's face was expressionless. She held her schoolbooks tightly across her chest.

"It's me Phil. I talked to you last night on the porch. You member. I told you I like su mama, member?"

"She's in bed," Bruna mumbled in the strength of the morning light. "She's not working today."

"Got a little drunk last night, no? Su mama can drink, boy. Let me get you a ride to school."

Bruna felt her heart pace and well up for a count of ten. Her face burned.

"I can take you for something to eat if you want," Phil said.

For a few minutes he convinced her. Bruna forgot about school and about her mama's hard words. She dropped herself inside and they stopped and talked.

"There's a good girl. I'm helping you. Oh, and hey I found this in your house last night and I put it in my pocket." Phil pulled Bruna's necklace from his slacks pocket and then he placed it in the girl's hand.

"Mama said you were a thief," Bruna said. She looked at her hands. They were almost shaking and so were her knees. She glowered at the man across from her. "You don't have any business taking what ain't yours," Bruna said. "That locket has a picture of my daddy and of my mama inside."

"I didn't know," Phil said. "I feel horrible. I thought it was your mama's. I swear I did, girly. I wouldn't of taken it if I knew—"

"Mama said you were a thief. Said there are thieves all around and you have to hold to you what is yours—"

"I said I was sorry, girly."

"Don't call me girly. I ain't your girl. Nobody in my house is your girl."

"I saved it," Phil said. "I saved it from being stepped on in the house last night. I put it in my pocket and forgot about it. I was drinking and you know we were all drinking. I thought I was saving it."

"What! It was in my room. All my jewelry was in my room." She felt the tears hot in her eyes.

"Come on, let me give you a ride, girly."

"I gotta go to school. I can't miss."

He looked at the girl's face and shouted, "I should have kept the Goddamn thing." He stopped and caught his breath as the young Bruna quickly stepped out of the Cadillac. And suddenly Phil was laughing. "Look at you, girly. You're so Goddamn mad and all I did was return something to you." He watched the girl jump from the car and slam the car door. "Well break the Goddamn thing while you're at it," Phil shouted. "You stupid cunt of a girl."

Bruna watched the car pass, and later that night Bruna explained to her Mama while she fried up their dinner. The mother's smile was quiet and gentle. "I guess you think you pretty strong now, huh? Man never did know when to admit when he was wrong."

retreat

A carload of nuns and priests departed from Huerfano County in a summer rainstorm. They rode past the steel mill, past the county hospital and past onion and chile farms; past irrigation ditches and cornfields, past horse ranches and cattle ranches. In the back, resting between Sister Arlene and Neddie Cabello, both wearing their best Sunday skirts and hats, sat Bruna. Father Dwyer was driving. Beside him in the passenger seat sat Father Holland, a tall, thin man who was the priest from the old neighborhood.

"We have the whole peaceful trip to look forward to," said Father Holland. "What do you think?"

"I'd say I have to agree."

"We have a car full of youth and faith. You know what I'd like to do some day? I'd like to drive this country and take these girls to every university and parish. Show them California and Oregon. East coast as well. They would appreciate that, I think. When these girls become nuns, I'd like to make that drive."

While the two men talked on and on, Bruna and Neddie nodded, laughed, dozed and jerked awake. In Colorado Springs they had a dinner of burgers, fries and RC Colas.

"This guy doesn't stop talking," whispered Bruna, sitting across from Neddie in the booth. "You know what I mean, cabróna? How you feeling?"

"Hardly wait to get to where we're gonna get," said Neddie. Neddie was a year younger than Bruna but they had been friends all through Sunday school and high school. They played on the same softball team and tetherball team. Though not as attractive as Bruna, and though she wore thick dark glasses that were sometimes taped after being damaged at the Woolworth's Diner where she worked, Neddie had long legs and an awkward lean look to her that the boys took to.

"You may have to keep talking to the guy this whole trip, so don't knock yourself out too quick, you know?" Bruna said.

"I won't. I'll pace myself," Neddie answered.

"Yeah, you'll want to pace yourself. Your priest, Holland, has been around so he knows all the tricks. And he's a boozer, you know how people talk about him."

Rain kept falling and fog was blowing over the road when they reached Highway 24 and also when they finally reached the Kansas border, near the edge of a sheep ranch, at least fifteen miles from the nearest gas station. Del Monte Greens was near Salinas, Kansas, and served two functions: priests spent time there in solitude and in retreat after seminary, and nuns spent time there before going to their permanent assignments.

Bruna, leaning slightly forward with fatigue, coat unbuttoned, sweater open at the throat, hat back and arms stiff down beside her, led Neddie and the Sister on the way in to the main dormitory and meeting hall. In new shoes her mother bought her special for this trip, Neddie followed, moving nervously around the tentative conversations with new acquaintances and roommates. Both girls stood intimidated in front of Sister Arlene and her many clones. Lightheaded from the drive and hours on the road, Bruna listlessly took off her coat and sweater and lay down on the small twin bed. She shifted about while Neddie looked out the small window they shared and placed her turquoise suitcase on the small bureau of drawers. With care, she opened her case and slowly pulled out her clothes and placed them in drawers. The clothes reminded her of home, and since she planned on becoming homesick, she held the sweaters and the one pressed white blouse tightly in her fingers.

There were many contrasts between the two girls. Neddie's parents had lived in Huerfano their whole lives and they watched Neddie closely. Bruna's parents weren't as strict; they drank and went out pretty regularly. Neddie was a size 6 and rather tall. Bruna was a size 4. For Neddie, this had been her first trip out of Huerfano County and out of Colorado. Bruna had shuffled with her mother and Jeri out to the West Coast on at least two occasions. Neddie pulled her white gloves from her hands, rubbing her hands nervously as she prepared for bed. She crossed the room to Bruna, who was now sitting in her blouse and panties on the edge of the bed, her red hair in a high mound on the top of her head.

"I hope we didn't make a mistake coming," Neddie confided. "Don't tell anybody this but I was worrying about this trip all month. I went out last night for a few drinks."

"I was out too. Don't make no difference."

"Who were you with, Bruna?"

"It don't matter if you drink or if you been out, is all I'm saying. You got two hands to pray with, that's all that matters. That's what my mother says," Bruna asserted.

"Who, Bruna? Tell me."

Bruna smiled: "Relles Ortiz."

"Relles Ortiz! You got to want to get out of the house bad to go out with him," Neddie said.

"He's sweet. His brother, too."

"Relles is older," Neddie said. "And he'd be all over you in a second."

"Not too much older. We went out for some food."

"I heard about those boys he runs with. I heard about him."

"Heard what?"

"Well, I heard he took Martha Lucero out to Milton Pacheco's apartment and did the deed."

"What?"

"The deed," Neddie said, bouncing up and down on the bed to illustrate.

"Well, he never took me down there, Neddie. And I hope he never does."

"Hoping never done nothing," Neddie said. "That's what my father says. And you can't be here, you know, out with the Fathers and Sister Arlene if you're out at Milton Pacheco's. I'll tell you that."

"Well, what about the drinking?" Bruna asked.

"What about it?"

"Can you be out here if you be out drinking all the time?" Bruna said. "Because I think you'd be pretty guilty yourself."

"Guilt ain't got nothing to do with it," Neddie answered. "It's all in your head."

A few hours before lights out, another girl came to occupy the third bed in the dorm room. Her name was Manuela Rosales. Neddie was uneasy because Manuela was hardened and didn't wear any gloves. She was Mexican and came in from Española, New Mexico, in a brilliant red sweater. She jogged into the room and slowed to a prance as she emptied her clothes from her duffel bag into the drawers. The year before, at fourteen, Manuela had lied about her age and jumped on board a bus and come to visit her family in Española. She had been working at the Santuaro Church cooking and taking odd jobs until she was of age to make this retreat with Father Allen. Tonight she was excited to be out of New Mexico and yet scared to be around pocho girls like Neddie and Bruna. She wanted to know so much about her new roommates. She asked the girls if they lived in houses or duplexes or apartments. Neddie was ashamed that she lived in her own house with her father and mother and all of her siblings. Ashamed that she had a change of clothes in her suitcase for every day of the week and that she was the only one of the girls to have met her biological father.

"Know what makes a good Catholic?" Manuela asked quietly

after lights out.

"What's that?" Bruna and Neddie asked.

"You got to want to believe," Manuela said. She pulled a small transistor radio from her purse and extended the antenna. She channeled for Mexican music, and the sounds of accordion and mournful wailing played softly to each girl's inner ear. Manuela smiled. "Know what I say? Why else would we come out here and go without talking for a week?"

Before the three finally closed their eyes and gave in to sleep, the girls clasped their hands tightly and they all prayed to make it through the month.

When first light came, they were hit with Catholic solitude, Bible study and lectures without one word allowed between them. Their young female minds were rubbed, patted and kneaded. The decision to join the religious life as a nun, or sister, requires much prayer and counsel, they were advised. They were harangued, reprimanded, and asked not to horseplay while the Fathers and nuns were speaking. They were asked not to listen to anything, no TV, no radio, not even to one another or anything else at all, except for their lessons and their own prayers.

hospital

Felipa called Lena's home at 7 a.m. and asked nearly begging for Bruna to accompany her down to the Denver hospital room where Felipa's mother Gregoria rested. Felipa had said to Lena, "Please ask Bruna. The old man can't come so I need the girl."

At first Bruna said no and climbed back into her bed and refused. Lena came into the room after her ritual of coffee and buttered toast with cinnamon and pulled the covers back from Bruna's head.

She said things like, She's an old woman and she's in trouble. She's your mother, Bruna. And she's your grandmother out there in Denver and she's your people. I'm your people and Carlos is your people and in all your life all you have is your people. They might be no good, but they are all you have.

"The cards I am dealt?" Bruna asked.

"Oh, for Christ's sake that man Jeri teaching you poker is the death of me. It ain't about no cards or money or sitting and smoking your life away with cards and tables of cabrónes that only want your money or your bankroll your dollar bills. This is about a dying woman and she's yours, Bruna."

Bruna threw some clothes on and some makeup and a hairbrush into an oversized purse and put on her most comfortable pedal pushers and Keds and walked out to the bus stop. Felipa turned up in a cab.

"Well, I got you a ticket and we better be starting out," Felipa said.

The ride to Denver was three hours, longer with the stops. In Colorado Springs and then later Monument the two shared a longneck bottle of Coke and Felipa complained when Bruna wanted hers with peanuts. "Where's your money for food?" Felipa asked.

"Lena lets me have my own," she complained.

"With no money we have to share," Felipa said. Then Felipa leaned forward in the shade of the Monument stop. "We ain't made of money," Felipa said. "You have to think of the trip back. Ain't no vacation neither. This trip's for my mother."

THERE WERE SO MANY STORIES Felipa neglected to tell her daughter Bruna on their only trip together. So many stories she kept inside. Stories about her cleaning jobs from way back, her cleaning jobs for rich folks over on the northside of town. Her pay was always cash. That's how people referred to her jobs, "Under the table."

There were stories of her bringing her own cleaning supplies. Her own food because the judge's wife, Felipa complained, didn't cook or have too many groceries and only ate cans of soup with no crackers. She didn't mind travelling the bus with her lunch packed up into a large purse but hated carrying her bucket and rags. Felipa was paid about a hundred dollars a month. She was 34 years old at the time and had a sick husband at home and the judge's wife was 65 or so and her husband, Judge MacKinnon, was always working and never around during the day.

Judge Mac was the third or so household Felipa worked for. First, there was the Doctor's wife and then the grade school teacher. Then the owner of a local restaurant. And all of them paid her "under the table"—no social security or W2 documents filed. Always Felipa brought her own equipment—a bucket filled with rags and a bottle of spray cleaner of some sort and some detergent. “I know how to clean,” she would always say. “Never learned to drive but I learned to clean.”

Another story Felipa never told was how once she cleaned up after a party at the Doctor’s house where she told a group of men how to clean up a clogged sink. The men stood and stared as she worked. Another story had her convincing the nice Doctor’s wife to have her spend more hours cleaning. “The woman didn’t want me to clean,” Felipa later complained to Carlos. “I had to beg her to clean up the bathroom or the toilet or the counters in the kitchen. She just wanted to talk. Talk talk talk. I would try and tell her I have work to do. I hate the idea folks would come over and say What do you pay that woman of yours?”

Another story she never shared had Felipa walking in a snowstorm to shovel the Doctor’s wife’s driveway before coming in to chat and vacuum. “Such nice views and such great big picture windows,” she would tell Carlos about the houses.

And another story had her in the local college president’s bathtub trying to clean the monster of a tub in a very large and decadent bathroom. The bathroom she thought was larger than her and her husband Carlos’ bedroom and the bedrooms in the condo larger than Felipa’s entire house. She was sore for weeks after that job.

She was most comfortable cleaning, she would tell folks.

“I ain’t the type and I have no schooling so what can you do,” she would say. She enjoyed making her own hours, having time for her own sick husband. “Folks won’t hire a 45-year-old waitress,” she used to say. “But they will hire a 45-year-old woman to clean the bathroom. A vieja maid.”

Folks believed Felipa could’ve been a designer or an interior decorator because she had an eye for fabric and textures, in other people’s houses, anyway. She read Better Homes and Gardens and so many style and fashion magazines. But she had Carlos and because he wasn’t working due to his poor health, she worked these jobs for money and to get ahead. “Your Lena got me my first job cleaning houses—and she drove me," Felipa once revealed, but not to her daughter. "A rich lady up on the north side of town. She drove me and I remember Carlos never wanted me working. I had already tried being a waitress, but we needed the income. I remember the lady owned a hardware store or something like that but she had no cleaning supplies. No mop. No sponges. Nothing. Not even a broom. I remember thinking, You own a hardware store and don't have a thing to clean with? I lost the job, though, because she never gave respect. And I have Carlos, so can't always come in when they say, you know? I remember the woman called me up and yelled at me because I couldn't work the hours she wanted me to. She yelled something awful. I had no one to watch Carlos or no car and so what could I do?"

One time when Felipa was at the market, folks saw a woman Felipa worked for down one of the aisles in County Market grocery store. The woman was explaining to Felipa how to clean one of her light fixtures, explaining how to clean each individual light bulb. Where she had the ladder and where she kept the bulbs. Felipa had a notebook with a pen and was getting down the notes as a journalist or a writer might. "The better I work the more of a chance they will hire me back," Felipa would never reveal to her daughter.

THE LAST FEW MILES the two sat in silence as they made the transfers to the hospital on Colorado Blvd. As they made their way from the entrance to the main elevators, Felipa admitted her fear of elevators and confined spaces. "But it's four floors to the room, they said," Bruna said.

"I had this dream a man in a tattered red sweater and jeans came knocking and pounding on my door," Felipa said as they made their way up the stairs. She wanted nothing to do with any elevators. "He knocked and knocked, and Carlos was nowhere to be found so I had to get up and walk to the door and answer in only my housecoat. I was so frightened and startled to be in the home alone and so I slowly made my way to the door and the banging became louder and louder and it was this man. I said, '*Who are you?*' to the stranger and the man pushed the door open and I couldn't hold it closed. '*Do you know Gregoria?*' the man said, and I couldn't hold the door and had to let the man into the house. And I could sense more men behind him, and they all pushed their way in. I said, '*Yes, Gregoria was my mother.*' '*She is afflicted,*' the voice said, '*she is dying.*' And when I woke to the room Carlos was up and in his chair with his hand on my knee and said I was screaming and the vecinos would all hear and think I was being murdered or killed."

At first Bruna laughed but caught herself. Felipa said, "So I called some phone numbers I had. The cousin Hady in Arvada and then Josie in Colorado Springs, and they said Gregoria was in the hospital and sick with the cancer and I should go to see her and be there. It was close, they said. At first I was steaming angry because I felt they robbed me of final days with my mother but I took my money and bought two bus tickets since the neighbors or your Lena couldn't drive me. I want you to know your Grandmother and so does Lena. We've talked and talked on it and decided you must come with me."

Bruna held a great lump in her throat and choked down a few tears and coughed deeply before taking Felipa's hand as she slowly walked up the stairs. It was the first time Bruna got a close look at Carlos' mother's ring, gold with sky-blue jewels. It looked simple and plain, like costume jewelry. Not at all as Lena had described it. She thought of Lena's jealousy. "That is my mother's ring," Lena had once told Bruna with contempt. "Carlos gave my mother's ring – no, took it from my dead mother's hand to pawn and then he finally gave it to Felipa." It was the first time Bruna had read true pain and scorn from Lena's face over Carlos.

Felipa continued, "I decided because of the time here we must meet the family. I have been, how they say, 'estranged,'" she said solemnly. "They had nothing for me and left me with Carlos. Rarely got letters on notice of my time in the family so I've had to fight for this and so I wanted you to know this."

FELIPA EXPLAINED, "I'm rounder than I've ever been at any point in my life. You're young, Bruna, and don't know. But when a woman gets round and of a certain age, she can't step too quick or move too quick and the men make her invisible." Bruna had to wait for Felipa as she held on to the handrail and her large purse and struggled with every step.

"Lena says to keep moving," Bruna said. "Doesn't matter how old you are just have to keep on moving and moving."

"Your mama thinks she's pretty smart, no?" Felipa said and it was the first time Felipa had acknowledged to Bruna out loud and to her face that Lena was her mama.

"Why did you send me away?" Bruna finally asked. She had waited her whole life practically for this moment on the grey and antiseptic smelling stairwell and these steps where Felipa was trapped and had to answer.

"I sent you a letter, girl," Felipa said.

"I know you did, but I want to talk it out and hear your words. I'm here and want to hear you."

Felipa stopped and her breathing became harder and harder, and she wiped sweat from her brow with one of Carlos' handkerchiefs, wiping down her forehead and cheeks. Bruna noticed Felipa had no makeup, nothing on her cheeks or lips. She had hair on her upper lip and sideburns growing down her face and out of control, Bruna observed. Bruna had lipstick and spit curls and had everything Lena had taught her about presentation, about how a woman must look at all times. Lena went to the beauty parlor and gave her lessons in how to wear wigs and to wear her outfits to be as attractive as possible, but Felipa wore a large black sweater and over a pair of large black pants as for a funeral. The difference between Lena and Felipa could not have been clearer to Bruna than it was in this moment.

"Everything I had for you, girl, was in those letters. Carlos was my husband and what could I do," Felipa repeated. Bruna would hear different versions of this story in letters and in phone calls whenever she connected with Felipa over the course of her life or connected with Felipa's side of the family. "She was so young," they would say. Or they would say, "In those days the woman followed the man." Or they would say, "It was all for the best, girl."

WHEN BRUNA AND FELIPA REACHED the third floor and caught their breath and took their turns in the restroom and drinking fountains, Gregoria caught a glimpse of Felipa, her youngest daughter, and she called out to the room, "Oh when the people think you're dying they come running with their children. They all want to see you when you're dying but when you're alive and kicking they are nowhere to be found."

To this Felipa began to cry and call out for her mama while Bruna stayed back and recognized the absurdity to the entire situation. She made herself small and kept her hands behind herself and stared mostly at her pedal pushers and Keds and then out the window and towards the Denver late afternoon skyline.

Bruna observed her grandmother's deep silver hair and her large nostrils and heavy breathing, the boils on her exposed neck and the oxygen tubes weaving from tanks to her nose. After what seemed like hours the two women Felipa and Gregoria stopped crying and holding on to one another's hands to introduce.

"I never ever said the word retarded to anyone around you," Gregoria later admitted to Felipa. "Your father left me, and I had no money and no way to care for you."

And then Felipa cried and cried and admitted to being a wretched daughter always crying and wailing and carrying on, always out running around and never paying attention in school or church. Felipa admitted to sinful ways and a working life after her story in the Denver Ridge Home for girls. She admitted to all her faults and held onto her rosary, something Bruna only knew her mother to do.

And then to Bruna's pain and embarrassment Felipa introduced Bruna as her lovely daughter, daughter of Carlos and product of her marriage and changed ways, evidence in the flesh that Felipa could make better decisions and she'd grown since Gregoria last saw her.

"Come here, girl," Gregoria ordered, giving Bruna an ancient hand. "I have to see my Felipa's daughter."

In the hour that followed Bruna learned Gregoria had cancer, and the word brought hushed voices and whispers. The word made her believe Gregoria had very little time. Only now it seemed Felipa and Gregoria were making amends, holding one another's hands.

"I could go for something sweet to eat," Gregoria said. And with this Bruna made her way down to the elevator and then to the cafeteria with an imposing sign stating the fact that it was closed and listing the hours. She knocked with conviction though she expected nothing and then moved on. A toothless man named Larry, bald and with a pointy and pronounced nose, had been washing trays and mopping with buckets of degreaser when he heard the knock. He believed it to be the nursing staff looking for missing keys. He was surprised to find a waif of a girl with short hair and delicate features, and he was smitten immediately. He was convinced to find some brownies he had from his wife in his lunch pail.

Bruna shook his hand and put her hand on his shyly and smiled. She said it was for her family, for her dying grandmother. "There's no milk," Larry said, or rather no access to the fridge after a certain hour. "They got a deadbolt on it."

Bruna thanked him kindly and made her way back up. She made no effort to conceal or hide the chocolate goodies and made no effort to keep them from the nurses or any of the staff. It was nearly the end of visiting hours, but because Felipa and Bruna were listed as family at the nursing station and because of Gregoria's condition no one would be pushing them out. Bruna placed the plate in front of the woman right on her stomach and Gregoria's eyes brightened if only for them. She paused and then pushed the chocolate and cake of the dessert into her mouth. Felipa helped the woman and pulled her own handkerchief again, Carlos' handkerchief, to help clean the corners of her mouth and chin.

BRUNA SAT BACK DOWN and for another hour listened to Felipa and Gregoria. The two caught up on one another's lives, Felipa's life in the San Luis Valley and Gregoria's in Colorado Springs and then Denver. Gregoria remarried after finding a beautiful man. That was just how she said it: "A beautiful man named Salazar."

The woman spoke in Spanish and again Bruna only caught small stretches of story. Gregoria met Salazar and married the man and moved in with him all within the span of a month. "I couldn't do it on my own," she said. She was in touch with the oldest daughter but not her younger boys. Gregoria cried and cried and begged forgiveness from her youngest daughter Felipa. What could Felipa do but relent and hug the woman and kiss the woman's forehead and laugh at the drama of her life.

Soon Bruna did the same. She said it was her Catholic duty and nature to forgive and care for her birth mother. What a sight to the nurses and orderlies who came in to care and check on Gregoria's status. Then the old woman gave the daughter and granddaughter some of her advice from a long and hard-lived life. She grew up in the Taos Valley of New Mexico and married the hardest of men, a man who served in the military and the man who became Felipa's father. The woman Gregoria hadn't heard from him since the first week following Felipa being dropped off at the city of the sick mental hospital in Denver. She said the man controlled her life and her actions. Felipa was too young to see or realize but her father controlled the mother's time as well as her money.

When Gregoria worked the restaurants and diners near Aurora, Colorado outside of Denver, he would take her pay and control all finances. He gave her a small allowance which was never enough for groceries or food for the kids. She left the kids home alone for so long during the day and she was so far from her home and her people in New Mexico. One story had her fighting over groceries. The man gave her so little, the house had nothing for the family, for the kids, for when visitors came. On one occasion the man yelled at what she had for his mother and for his father when they decided to visit. They were farmers and traders from Del Norte.

Gregoria said, "I had nothing to give. 'Mujer, my people are coming and you must have something the people will need to eat.'"

Gregoria was so distraught and ashamed she went out to the garden and the yard where her potatoes and her cucumbers had failed to grow, and she pulled rocks and leaves and placed them in the basket that was her blouse pulled loosely down to carry the load. She brought them into the kitchen and boiled them and set them out on plates seasoned with chiles and salt and pepper.

She told Felipa, "He wanted food but gave me nothing, so I placed those rocks and leaves out on the table. A nice spread of rocks and dirt. The people came over and were horrified. I just stood there and served. I smiled. I had it all on plates and with a smile until the people politely left and went out for burgers at the Dairy Queen. That bastard of a man, your father, he screamed and hollered and carried on until the neighbors were aware of the tussle and the fighting. He tossed out those plates, don't you remember? No? I thought you would remember. That was the beginning of him cutting out. Running around with women and his good timing friends until he lost his job and his ride and then soon the house." She finished the long story by asking Felipa, "And what kind of a man do you have in Carlos? Tell me all of this man from San Luis. Why is he not here with you?"

BRUNA SAT BACK DOWN after walking up and down the halls. Her stomach growled and it was while down the hall she heard the tussle, the nurses and Felipa wrangling over the brownie or rather the empty plate with chocolate stains and crumbs. She heard the nurse, the ghost of a nurse dressed head to toe in white, say, "This woman has diabetes and is to have no sweets or sugar of any kind. What is your name and what is your relationship to this woman?"

Felipa became silent and couldn't speak. Gregoria closed her eyes and shook her head in denial as when she was a child caught with her hand in the pot with the sugar her parents kept in New Mexico when they were baking holiday treats and pies. Bruna stood at the door listening and then waiting for a chance to speak before sitting and building the courage.

"That plate was mine," she said to the nurse in her most adult and confident voice. "I went down and a very nice man asked me if I was hungry and I was so I took his brownies from the cafeteria. He said it was out of kindness."

"What was his name?" said the nurse.

"Please, he was just being kind and meant no harm or ill will, he just thought it was for me and maybe my grandmother and my mother," Bruna said. She caught herself saying "mother" and felt light and queasy. Then she nearly cried herself over all of this.

"The brownie was for me, and I meant no harm with it," Felipa followed, defending the girl.

"And so what if my mother has a bite?" Felipa said. "She deserves every comfort as she is in this bed permanent." Nurse Tabitha, the gringa woman all in white, became quiet and still, sensing her loss, and made her way down the room, out of the room and down the hall. The women remaining, Bruna, Gregoria and Felipa, stayed quiet and shared a smile and a laugh.

On the bus heading home back to Huerfano County before a late dinner of packaged chicken salad sandwiches from the bus stop, the two shared a soda out of the same can. In Colorado Springs Bruna and Felipa sat silent in the idling Greenline Bus. They were tired and closed their eyes nearly at the same time and tried to converse to stay awake but the talk was disturbed with traffic sounds and passengers loading luggage and making noise dropping bags and suitcases.

The bus arrived in Huerfano at 330 a.m. The bus depot on Main Street was quiet and lowly lit and the women began the slow walk to the pay phone.

"I have some money for the taxi," Felipa said. "And I think you should go home with me and check in on Carlos."

"No," Bruna said.

"Maybe spend more time and more nights with me and Carlos," Felipa continued, without listening or even looking at Bruna's face.

"No," Bruna said quietly.

"We have an extra room, and you can look out for Carlos. You two get along so well sometimes and I forget sometimes how much he likes to talk about the old days and the way things were when he was young, you know," Felipa continued.

"My Mama is waiting for me and will worry on me, and I don't want that for her. I want my mama's home. My own bed and my own life on Routte."

"But your Lena is always moving," Felipa said. "She always finds herself put out and looking for apartments or rooms to rent. What me and Carlos have is permanent. You can come in and help with the old man. He feels something for you and you're good for him and he's good for you," Felipa said. "The old man Carlos needs you. And he's your father. He's your blood."

"Lena is my mama," Bruna repeated. "She's my Mama and my father. And my sister."

"You don't even make sense," Felipa said.

"She'll worry. I'll have to get home."

In a moment Felipa was hurt and turned her back on Bruna after giving the girl a handful of dollar bills. Felipa left the girl at the corner. Thirteen blocks and the 6th Street bridge separated her from her bed and her room down on Routte Avenue. Bruna dropped the dime into the pay phone and rocked herself at the booth until Lena's voice crackled over the line. Bruna said, "Mama, I'm ready to come home."

calling to account

Carlos began the morning work of breakfast for the crew, as he had done with Lino. It was mostly habit. He put on a pot of beans with a spoonful of lard and then a pot for coffee and then he set his pan de campo down into Lino's Dutch ovens. He made sure to grease the metal down the way he had been taught. The kitchen pots and pans seemed quiet and lifeless with no Lino.

After coffee and some buttered bread, he lay prone at the back of the bunkhouse, betting odds Arthur's men would approach from the west. Some of the Tewa Pueblo Indians walked by with their washing and when they caught sight of Carlos and his Springfield pistola they scrambled away over the barbwire fences and down to the creek beds. Ray Padilla was the first to ride in—the lazy-eyed brother of Paul Padilla. Carlos knew him as the biggest and most mindless of all the Patrón's men. He crossed himself, touching his forehead and his chest and then the right and left shoulders. Then he sent the first bullet home to Ray Padilla's heart through his barrel chest. The man slumped over and fell from his mount in a heap. There was no sign of Arthur or his father.

With only four cartridges left he hoped to scare the pigeon-toed Jose Diaz and Ray's brother by slamming three shots into the air. The men quickly dropped their ropes and their Colt wheel guns and ran off. "Doesn't take much to scare a coward," the buck sergeant had burned into Carlos before the ship to Europe. "Most men want nothing to do with hurting or killing so we have to train that out of you," the buck sergeant had said. Carlos imagined the ropes they dropped were what they used on Lino and Eddie.

"Poor old Ray," Arthur called out. He shared his saddle with Mara on the three-year-old gelding Carlos had shoed and trimmed. Carlos cursed himself for being surprised and called out so easily. Arthur had on his crisp white shirt and his shiny long barreled shotgun resting across his saddle's pommel. He held it between Mara and Carlos as they galloped up from behind Carlos.

"All I wanted was a gun with story," Arthur said. "Poor old Ray has a mama and a daddy back in Colmor. Poor old Ray." He seemed to be genuinely hurt for the friend on the ground. "Not too smart but a hell of a good friend to me."

Mara looked sickly with glass eyes and her cheeks bruised pink. "He didn't know what horrible things he was doing," the girl said to Arthur.

"Hell, no one knows what I do. You know my father doesn't know half of what goes on. He signs the payroll and has his name on all the deeds and the paperwork. He knows the bankers and the politicians. He shakes hands and makes the deals. But it's all on paper. I'm the future of this ranch and the old man speaks on the old ways with his companeros. Like I said, he don't know half of what's going on here."

"Is that the shotgun that killed Lino?" Carlos called out.

"I don't know what you say. I don't know what you're saying, Carlos. I hunt with this rifle. This was my father's rifle. He wanted me to have your gun from Europe. Now go to your man, sweetheart," Arthur whispered to Mara, forcing the girl down. As she dismounted, she nearly fell onto her backside. She had on a nightgown, and she was barefoot. "Poor thing can't go the way she used to when she was a girl," Arthur said.

Mara stepped back from the mount and Carlos knew by the red and blue to her cheeks the Patrón's boy had put a night's worth of hurt on her.

"You know Mara was 13 years old when my old man brought her out to the Cutoff. She's been working for us a long time. Lon-

ger than Lino or Eddie. Lino ever tell you? I know he was one for gossip. I know because Mara knows. She tells me. Ain't nothing she keeps from me. She knows loyalty. Not like Lino or Eddie. Stealing from the property. It's a shame really."

"You sent them boys in here first," Carlos said. "You sent them in here as bait or to test to see what I would do. You sent them in here and you knew I was waiting..."

"You hurt Ray pretty good. Looks dead from here. Look here, Mara," Arthur said. "Ray didn't know what hit him. Poor old Ray. Look, Mara, he's as dead as you can get."

Carlos raised his dead cousin's weapon and fired his final cartridge, the metal exploding and jamming the cylinder into place. Arthur flinched and then smiled. Then he raised the shotgun and had it right on Carlos. "Dead in my boots," Carlos thought to himself in an instant. He would've shot and killed Carlos dead if not for Mara, if she hadn't grabbed the reigns of that gelding and pulling the man nearly down to the ground. She grabbed and slapped wildly and held the rifle along with Arthur. Mara had turned the rifle around on Arthur as the man and horse spun and nearly fell.

"You can't shoot me, Mara," Arthur said. "You'll break your shoulder with the shot."

"I can shoot," Mara said.

As Carlos approached the shotgun exploded with metal, and Arthur fell backwards with the blast. He choked and gagged with blood and nearly laughed at it all.

Most of the hired-on Pueblo Indians had made their way back from the creek and watched the whole incident from the bunkhouse and nearby pens where they were kneeling and watching. The Patrón was one of them and witnessed the whole incident. He had ridden in and limped his way down after hearing gunfire. He was nervous and cautious, so he followed his Indian workers. He stood among them and witnessed his only son shot and killed by the young Mara.

The Patrón pulled his Stetson and stared on and never spoke a word. He just walked over to hush Mara. Arthur just sat slumped over while his father pulled a nickel-plated revolver. It was instinct. He walked over to Carlos from the corral and was nearly crying himself. "My son! My boy!" he cried out.

Carlos stood with a jammed weapon and once again closed his eyes and listened to the Patrón's bullets in the air gliding and tracing around him. He waited patiently for the metal to come home to his chest or neck. He nearly wanted it as he silently whispered his Hail Mary's. Lino's people say Carlos was crossing himself and praying when Mara struck the Patrón down with the second cartridge of Arthur's long barrel. "You bastard of a man," Mara screamed before Carlos had her down the creek and up onto Lino's mount.

IN A WHILE *Carlos pulled Lino from his open casket and wrapped his stiff body with blankets. Mara said her prayers and cried out loud as he worked. Carlos put his hand to Lino's chest and crossed himself. Then he went on to the work of covering and burying Arthur and Ray Padilla. "Leave them to rot," Mara said as Carlos continued. "That's what they would have for you."*

neto's girl

"I got the banana," Neto Ortiz called out to Bruna, "if you got the splits." Around them güero teenagers were propped against their cars and licking at vanilla cones outside the Jones Avenue Dairy Queen. Neto tried not to feel ashamed of the dirt in his fingers or the sweat stains down his shirt, the broken sink that was his face.

He had seen the young Montoya girl many times around the neighborhood, and once at the St Francis Festival at the Stations of the Cross. He noticed her ears were pierced but without earrings.

"You're as stupid-assed as your brother," Bruna said, struggling with the straw in her milkshake. "Your brother around here?"

Neto shook his head and gave the ground a smile.

"He still have his Ford?" she asked.

Neto glanced at a poster of two dancing ice cream bars and then at Bruna's honey-lotioned legs. "What are you, like a cheerleader or something?"

"Pep squad," Bruna answered, and she bent her knees slightly when she spoke the words. "You know I was writing your brother overseas, Neto? He never wrote me, though."

"Your mother a widow?" He couldn't resist ignoring the brother's name, and as soon as he asked, he immediately regretted the words.

Bruna lowered her eyes and squirmed in slow motion.

"I heard that somewhere," Neto said. "I heard it. Maybe I heard it at church or in the rectory. People talk. Around, you know."

"Watch what you say, Neto, because I don't want no one talking bad about me or my Mama."

"I ain't talking bad about you."

When her tears came down, Neto was moved by a sudden sympathy. He chucked his milkshake to the ground and spit. "I could crack my head open."

"What?"

"I feel like beating my head," Neto admitted. "I mean I think the whole thing is sad and I don't know what to say to it, you know. I don't know what to say to any of it."

"You don't have to say nothing," Bruna said.

He stood at a sudden attention and declared to the parking lot: "Well, I won't let anybody talk shit about you anymore. You can count on me. I ain't that kind of Catholic anymore."

"Well, I know you are my friend, Neto," Bruna said. She smiled.

Near the posted wall that read

Pawn

Loans

Guns

he thought he might try to put his arm around her. Bruna would have none of that.

IN THE SHADOWS of her people's three-room, second floor apartment on Routte Avenue, Bruna's view was garbage cans and the yard near the alley. Over the sty that was her people's kitchen sink, she rinsed and stacked plates and lifted the drapes with soapy fingers.

Lena got up from the kitchen table and called to anyone that would listen, "I waited all Goddamned night for this good for nothing cabrón."

"Fuck, mujer." He was hungover and tired, now heading for bed. "Shut your fat mouth."

Lena wore her housecoat, no bottoms and no socks. She pinched at the end of her clove cigarette and yelled from the front door, "I want every woman in this goddamned neighborhood to know what a drunk bastard of a man you are."

"You better be careful," the sixteen-year-old Bruna warned, finishing up her chores.

"Careful of that cabrón?" Lena retorted. She was more and more convinced of his unexceptional qualities and his drinking ways, his tendency to stay out all night.

"Stop doing that. He's liable to kill you."

"I want him to hurt me, the bastard, so I have the proof. He's the one that better be careful. The way he talks to me. Like a Goddamned dog," Lena said before heading to the bus stop for work. "I want him out of here."

Jeri had phoned the apartment the night before from the VFW or the Arcadia or wherever he happened to be; most bars were on Union Avenue in those days. If Bruna answered he would hang up and keep calling until Lena answered.

"I love you," he had drunkenly said. "I want no one but you. I am the only legit man you know, woman."

THOSE TROUBLES LOST SIGNIFICANCE with the arrival of a brand-new Royal typewriter that Bruna was to share with her cousin Connie. Bruna forgave Jeri his crimes or at least forgot about them in the tap-tap-tap of her practicing. The sound of those faded black-and-gray metal-capped keys was how she imagined the sound of work and sophistication. Mainly she pulled the typewriter from its pasteboard case to type up her prayers onto index cards, and later after Jeri bought her a box of typing paper, she typed up stories and letters for the church. It was not redemption or praise she wanted but a skill that could lead to work and a way out of her mother's world.

The next month Bruna received a score of sixty words per minute and 96% accuracy in transcription of dictation at Central High, an accomplishment she attributed to the gifted Royal. She walked out to St Francis and showed Father Dwyer and Father Holland and suggested maybe she could work in the rectory office.

At dinner she jiggled her legs with excitement, and in the middle of conversation she smiled and revealed her love of typing and her accomplishment at school, and how she would become a secretary.

"You're the smartest girl," Jeri complimented.

"Or the most nervous," Lena answered. "Look how you're chewing."

"That's how you get the most out of life," Jeri winked.

Bruna gazed at the horrible couple for long moments as if to gain some understanding or realization. "I don't want work typing," she declared. "I want to work in the church. I'm resolute."

"Oy lo. Muy chingón," Lena said. "Do you hear her? 'Resolute', she says."

"It means I am serious."

"Get out of here with you 'resoluteness'. And come when I call you to wash dishes."

BRUNA RODE IN Relles Ortiz's '56 Ford and asked, "Do you have any idea what it's like to live with that man Jeri?"

"How do you mean?"

"I mean he's been to jail but he does go to church. And he buys me things. I mean he doesn't mean to hurt my Mama and I know he don't want to."

Relles glanced at her while steering. Bruna's hairdo and face were near perfect to him and that sometimes left him dumbstruck and unsure of what to say. This was one of those times.

"I mean I don't want to believe anyone could be that way to anyone," Bruna explained. "He's fought with Mama plenty of times, but I don't want to believe someone could be that way."

"Someone will bail him out," said Relles.

"I knew he wasn't my real father. Since I was young. A little baby, really. I knew he wasn't my father or any real blood relation. Sure, I called him daddy. I did and I shouldn't have. Mama says not to put anything past him. I don't want to believe, you know?"

Relles stared at the windshield and the dead bugs.

"He won't really let her talk on the phone to people. To family or her friends from work. And he'd get so mad at her for talking to Mr. Medina. He works with Mama at the cleaners."

Relles nodded.

"You know Mr. Medina," Bruna continued. "Well, Mama told him this story about this man down at Dundee Cleaners. She told him he perspired right through his shirt and undershirt so much during the summer and through the shifts at the cleaners he would have to shower in the middle of the day. And so Mama tells this to Jeri and he hits her face."

"I know Medina."

"He picked her up and let her have it. I'm ashamed to say that Mama didn't do a thing to deserve it. And she didn't do a thing to stop him neither. She told me that was a part of marriage and I knew right then I would never want to be in one. You know the real shit of it? They ain't married. Never walked down the aisle or nothing."

"It must be love."

"You think that's what love is? Or what family is supposed to be? Watch what you say because I won't stand for insults against the sanctity of marriage. Father Dwyer says that marriage is a special honoring of God. He says it is about a connection between a man and a woman."

With a loud knock he made the brakes squeal in front of Bruna's building. She looked over her shoulder to see if the neighbors or if her Mama were leering. "I've heard about you boys taking girls out to Milton Pacheco's apartment," Bruna said.

"Who told you that?"

"Neddie and the girls around," she said. "No, I was just asking. You mad at me for asking?"

"I'm not mad. I'm worried, that's all."

"Worried about what?"

"Your soul and my soul. You know what they do there?"

Bruna said mockingly, "I know about you. You and Marquita Lucero."

"Well, I'm already done in for," he said. "But you still have a soul to save."

"So why are you worried about my soul?" she said. "We haven't done nothing."

"Well, going out with me means something, don't it?" he said. "People say shit all the time, Bruna."

"What would they say, Relles?"

"Well, what they said about Marquita. See, you even heard about it."

"Yeah, Neddie told me."

"The truth is I never done nothing with her."

"Really?"

"Yeah," he said. "People talk."

"Why would they say shit about you and her? I mean I've heard awful things about you and Milton getting her up there."

"I can't understand why people say the things they want to say," Relles argued. And the sudden honesty filled him with panic. He kissed her mouth with an uneasiness. In that moment she looked so exquisite to him, so lovely and graceful with her white gloves and her glow-in-the-dark Rosary beads in her purse. Her feel, her presence and her voice, the feel of her mouth and tongue felt like it would all be soon over, so he kissed harder and so did she.

THAT MONTH NETO VISITED the fat, bowlegged Delacruz girl while her folks worked in the onion fields past Blende, Colorado. He stole kisses or grabbed on her ass, but mostly it was talk, vague plans of the road to Colorado Springs or Denver.

The girl was a quiet, dark-haired daughter with a large face and a short, round body that drove Neto mad. One night he placed a ring box in her hand. He finished by trying to put his hand down the front of her pants.

"What are you planning, Neto, to fuck me or marry me?" the young girl asked.

He gave no answer. Not quite sure what he should do, he placed her hand stupidly on his crotch and kissed at her with a misplaced force. When the Delacruz girl pulled away and stood up, Neto sagged against the cold metal of the truck and he placed the cheap dime store ring in his pocket.

"My father would shit all over you, Neto."

"I'll tell him I don't care," Neto answered.

"And when he asks you if you have work or a place for us, what will you say?" she asked. "You don't even have work."

"Is that what you think about? I don't think about those things at all."

There was a silence between the two so heavy and cold, the Delacruz girl trembled.

She stood behind the truck and pulled her arms into her sleeves for warmth. "Answer me, Neto. Do you really care about marrying me?" she finally asked. "Or do you just want to fuck me."

ON THE DAY Relles Ortiz and Bruna Montoya came together through the door of The Donahue, a new time of jealous and naïve energy began for the entire crew, especially Neto. He was in a fall, and only his compadre Blacky was working regularly at the steel mill. Cornbread Baca was part time and doing maintenance. Neto's father and family felt impatience and he could hardly look at them, his eyes at the floor when he came home from The Donahue and a night of drinking.

As he walked home, down Northern Avenue and down Spruce, under bare sycamore and pine trees, the entire neighborhood felt drowned with pungent rain and mist. That night in bed, as he rested in his cot, he listened to the wind and the dripping from the eaves down the ancient wood to the cellar door. He thought of all the good things that had abandoned him. All he wouldn't have. There were days of dense humidity that he fought through for the next week as he crept around the neighborhood.

What the fuck they have to do that for? thought Neto.

One day later he went on a drunk and called Jeri; he called from the Donahue's payphone. He had no coins or change, the phone just made the call. He hadn't spoken to the man since the days before he left overseas.

"Oye, Velasquez," he yelled into the receiver. "I got some good news about one of your girls."

"Who the fuck is this?" Velasquez answered.

Neto heard voices from the background in Jeri's house. He imagined it was Bruna.

"She ain't ready for the Lord," Neto said. "What do you think about that?"

"Who is this?" Velasquez said.

"You hear what I say. She ain't ready. And she ain't clean."

"Who?"

"She's knocked up, Velasquez." There was silence on the other end. "You hear what I said, Velasquez? She ain't ready for no Lord."

"Who the hell is this?"

"He fucked her sideways," Neto said through the sobs. Coldly he put the receiver down, kneading the skin around his ears and forehead, concentrating on points across his head, rubbing circles into his eyes. His t-shirt sank into damp armpits. "He fucked her. Relles fucked her and knocked her up real good."

THE PERSON WHO brought green chile and tamales to Neto's father that summer was Bruna's Jeri, whose old brown Studebaker sometimes would overheat in the driveway. He never arrived by appointment or after a phone call. The folks knew of him as one of the San Luis Velasquez brothers who lived on Evans Avenue. "That bastard showed up anytime day or night," Neto's father, Santiago, once complained to Neto.

He would appear at the front door of the house in his hipster apparel, wing tips, dark glasses and long-sleeved guayabera, the pockets heavy with a small notebook and a pouch of Red Man, an eyeglass case and sometimes, if Jeri was ready to play, a small red Hohner accordion case. His long, thin hair, parted at his left ear and combed over a bit, and his awful expressions like "hot enough for ya" and "could fry an egg out here" annoyed Neto's father, to whom he came as a compadre, a fellow man of the steel mill. Everyone knew he could drink and everyone knew he had spent time in jail.

"Some dinner?" Santiago asked him respectfully in Spanish.

"Mr. Ortiz," he said. "This is very important concerning your son and my daughter Bruna."

Jeri sat at the dinner table and lit a second cigarette, placing the first one onto Abuela's lace table cover without seeming to care there was no ashtray.

In a few seconds Santiago was screaming for Neto, screaming his name out towards the kitchen and down to the basement where Neto usually holed up. "Why don't you go get him?" Santiago ordered his wife.

"I didn't mention any particular son," Jeri said.

"Which boy do you mean, compadre?" Santiago said.

Jeri Velasquez shifted in his chair with a groan and sigh. He could remember a careless time between the Ortiz and Velasquez families. I wish I didn't have to be here, Jeri thought. Talking and smoking with old friends after a few swallows of rum helped him keep his wits. He could speak of politics and the steel union with the Abuelo Ortiz, who would not judge or be hurt. Jeri Velasquez wished this to be one of those nights, but the man sensed a storm of jealousy and hurt coming. And when the man learned of his daughter's pregnancy and when he guessed the truth of his compadre's son, he could not help but want to rush to his friend's living room and dining room to question and warn, to hurt the boy in question.

Neto was in the middle of the room before Jeri Velasquez noticed him.

"Where'd you come from?" Velasquez said. "You bring your face over here, boy."

Neto walked over obediently and with a smile, genuinely expecting no wrong from Jeri Velasquez. It was hot and humid that summer night and so Neto's hair was wet and his face sweated because the wood stove was going even in the summer. Neto came through the kitchen to the men's place at the table.

Jeri accepted a drink from one of the women, his Tia Florinda or maybe his Tia Rita. Jeri let the rum touch his lips and he gulped it down in a mix of despair and pleasure. This was his fifth drink since making the decision to confront Neto, and by this point in the evening, he was increasingly warm and sweaty and anxious to speak. He smelled the odor of cooking beans and garlic from the kitchen. He immediately jumped to his feet and took Neto's immense shoulders in his own hands and stared the boy in the face. The nieces and cousins working on the place settings and the women in the kitchen rolling and preparing tortillas soon stopped and came to watch the two men grappling.

Soon Jeri had Neto up against a window and was pulling Neto's mama's drapes and her tin crucifix down from the wall. The man held Neto's white tank top undershirt in his fists, and Neto made no move to resist or fight, out of respect for the older man and his mother's home.

"I know about your phone calls, boy," Jeri kept repeating. Santiago sat still, mostly out of surprise and puzzlement. Santiago had thought Velasquez to be a delicate man with a large round belly and found this new smoldering man to be completely out of order. Neto became aware of Jeri's eyes and the big dark rings of two sleepless nights. Jeri stepped and drove his fist into Neto's chest and face, getting four or five strong blows in before Neto squirmed away. Jeri Velasquez stood embarrassed as the front room of the house filled with family, by this time Relles and my cousin Kiko.

Jeri had nothing to say and kept his glance downcast to his hands and car keys, sensing himself surrounded and growing quickly tired, drunk. Later Jeri would go through a whole mix of emotions as he drove himself to The Hideaway Bar and Grill out on Northern Ave.

JERI WAS DRUNK when he arrived home that warm evening in December. He removed his slacks and the new shirt and his wing tips, his straw hat and socks. With a sweat trickling down his biceps, he pulled on his brown robe while Bruna and Lena cleaned the evening dishes. He threw a piss in the small toilet off the bathtub. He wound the leather belt into a firm bandage around his right fist and tested it with blows against his left palm and the mattress.

When Jeri came down the hallway, between the family photos and Lena's crucifixes, his mind was already on leaving. The ache in him felt unending, he wanted to be done with Lena and her disgraceful daughter, and he had the odd sensation that what was to happen next was inevitable. With an economy of movement, hands down by his side, he followed Bruna to the far side of the kitchen, wanting to hurt her for his pride and for his anger, for his family name that Bruna's mother would never take as her own.

Jeri's first slap received no response, and Bruna took the second on her small elfish nose and her cheek, and her left eye. He leaned there over her as Bruna huddled down on the cold laminated tile, and in a single reflex he slapped down at her legs and buttocks.

"Keep away from her," Lena said. Tears streamed down her face as she pounded and smashed the man's shoulders.

Jeri repeated, "She's the fucking whore of the neighborhood."

Bruna covered up through most of the battle and struggled to cover up her stomach.

"Don't you ever touch that girl! Don't you ever touch that girl, you fuckin' pig!" Lena answered. "You pig of a man!"

Jeri dropped the belt suddenly to grab Lena's struggling arms, the broomstick and chair coming at him. He found himself battered and cut, butted twice and pulled around the room by Lena and the smaller Bruna.

The young girl tugged and pushed after losing her weapon and the older Lena retreated, ducking and kicking at the hulk of a man. Lena found herself on her knees where the kitchen table and dinner plates once stood. "You fuck of a man," she repeated. "I'll kill you!"

WEEKS LATER, Jeri was drinking a beer, sitting in his car when Neto walked up with his crew. Erminia Cruz, Jeri's girlfriend at the time, was pointing the air vents towards her thin face. Jeri had promised her a nice evening out and so he drove her to the Summer Festival at Assumption Parish, the first festival of the summer. They stopped off at the Harbor Inn for some cigarettes and a six pack of Schlitz. She held one of the cans between her lotioned legs as she tried to feel the cool air against her face. Her beers were kicking in when they pulled into one of the last slots.

The rear-view mirror brought Neto's face to Jeri. And because he was drunk, Jeri didn't register anything odd at first. The crew of men approached and joked to Erminia, "A person needs religion for their life and the beer for the world."

"I thought she was family," Neto told him over and over.

Neto's compadre Cornbread came along and pulled the tire iron and smashed at the Studebaker's windows to the surprise of Neto.

Erminia screamed and jumped out of the car carrying her shoes in one hand and her beer in the other. She fell on her tailbone.

"I didn't think anything like that could happen in the parking lot of a church," Erminia said years later. "I trusted everybody then."

Cornbread's blows were deep and uncontrolled and the glass smashed out onto blacktop. The whole thing seemed strange and unprepared, the three men from the steel mill and the single man from the Army Depot tussling in the church's parking lot.

Neto's thoughts were this: his white undershirt was sticking to his chest. The festival was full of people but the whole thing felt empty. Neto kept hitting at Jeri, who was drunk and couldn't fight. Jeri acknowledged Neto and Cornbread with a heads up nod. "What the hell?"

Neto tore Jeri from the car, got the man down on his knees and begging for forgiveness.

"Kill that son-of-a-bitch," Cornbread said.

Blacky ran in and held Jeri's massive arms the best he could. The incredible noise of Jeri's moaning owned the brawl over the music and laughter from the festival. Jeri felt the power of Neto's fist smashing at his face and chest, and dizziness set in.

"Christ Jesus save me," Jeri might've said.

—

DAYS LATER Neto sat in the wooden pews. Neto's entrance broke Bruna's dread that morning as she kneeled on swollen legs and ankles from her night job out at Newberry's Café and Bakery downtown. The weight of shame she held in those baggy sweaters Lena forced her to wear.

"I never seen you here," she told him.

"They say I have to find religion," Neto said.

"Your mother and father?"

Neto nodded.

"Well, people talk too much, Neto," she said. She crossed her arms and leaned into the wood pew, and she rested her arms on her pregnant belly. She put her feet up and stretched her short legs.

"All of the families are a big mess," Bruna said.

"It don't bother me." Neto put his hand on the girl's stomach and Bruna put her hand to the top of his.

wrecks

Most folks don't know about Bruna Montoya and Relles Ortiz' first date out to the old City Park Zoo. When Relles died it was as if the memory had died; no one would speak of it. I've seen old home movies shot on Abuelo's Instamatic camera. My Uncle Neto showed me. We used to sit in the basement and set up the projector to watch the two films Abuelo had labeled "The Mummy" and "Dracula starring Bela Lugosi." We happened to load up a roll of film into the projector, and there was a grainy Bruna and Relles up on the screen, him in his full dress uniform standing next to her, both staring down into the bear pit. Bruna wore a red coat with a fake mink collar and her hair was done up, her features tender and pure and her skin fair-colored, smiling shyly at my father and at the camera.

THE DAY OF RELLES' DEATH my Abuela wouldn't stop screaming. She was in with her laundry and it was one of the few times the woman did not own her temperament. Neto joked she screamed for days before the funeral and before the body was laid in the ground. In my mind this all stood true:

She screamed in Sunday service. She wailed through the night as a steady stream of aunts and cousins and nephews came through the house with their dinner dishes and desserts. She screamed when Father Dwyer came to the house for prayer and for his own personal condolences. Her muscles shook and strained as she cried and the tears fell large from her eyelids and face. At first the family, including Neto, thought they might lose the woman to grief as no amount of consoling kept her quiet. Later she even screamed as she cooked meal after meal for visiting familia and visiting nuns. As the Abuelo sat and smoked and drank his beer and whiskey from shot glasses, the Abuela screamed the way she did that November morning when she gave birth to her oldest son.

The night came and the Abuela went mad and got it into her head to burn up all his belongings. Every scrap of clothes and every object of memory. As her family slept and while her nieces and nephews dreamed, in just her housecoat she grabbed an old lettuce carton filled with her husband's tools and dumped them onto the front porch. She began with clothes and letters. She piled on strips of paper from grade school and middle school, Christmas ornaments and school photos. An old leather book cover made in high school. She found his wallet among Neto's possessions, under his cot while he slept. She pulled the footlocker and duffle bag with her son's uniforms and every object from his army life. She pulled his tools from the garage and his coveralls off the hook on the side of the garage door.

She found the gas can among the chaos of lawn tools, hand tools and rusted machine parts. She held her Rosary beads and poured the liquid into the footlocker and onto photo albums and the duffle bags of clothes and linens. She sprayed the lighter fluid.

Neto woke to black smoke and ran in bare feet and Levi's to the door, thinking the worst for his home. "Cabróna," he called out to her. "What are you doing?"

She didn't respond. She sat and wailed. Neto pulled out the footlocker and the boxes of clothes and bedding. He yelled for the garden hose and for his neighbors to bring shovels of dirt.

The Abuela's housecoat was singed and burned. Her skin was red with blood rushing to the surface and her screams reached down the block.

"They all talked of it in Mass," Neto told me later.

The family seemed to scream for their lost son and war hero, but they all knew the Abuela Ortiz suffered each hour and each day. The whole family suffered. All except for Neto who spoke plainly and coldly about his brother.

I can speak this way about the accident because this is how my Tio Neto has always spoken of it. I can speak this way because I never knew the man. Never spent a day or received a letter from the man, never had one conversation or shared one beer. My relationship existed merely in photos and albums, solitary moments on my knees with the plastic smell of Polaroids and aging plastic sheets covering photos. Mildewed school yearbooks and wedding photos half burned and bruised with smoke. An old driver's license and letters written from a naval station in Guam. Dog tags and one footlocker filled with burnt dress uniforms and old clothes, an old letterman's jacket with paint stains and wallet-sized photos of his Bruna.

THE FIRST I EVER KNEW of my father's death was a newspaper clipping I found in Neto's wallet. My stepbrother Romes and I were stealing money for video games and the dollar movies when we came across the faded clipping with the name Relles Ortiz. "That's your father's name," my stepbrother Romes told me.

"Eighth and Abriendo was where your grandmother placed the descansos," Neto would say but I was too young to understand. "Your old man never drank. Not like that. Not like the family might say. Ain't nothing like it appears, Manito. I can promise you that."

My father had been driving out to work. He was working at the old state hospital in the x-ray lab. They had him running between facilities cleaning out chemicals or some such thing,

Neto would tell me. That was one of about three jobs he was holding on to.

The County Sheriff told me that the official report listed a sanitation truck had pulled out from an alley and the old Chevy broadsided. The driver was dead on impact is how the news articles read.

"You know sometimes the people would say I killed him," Neto said. "They get the fight arrest and the accident mixed up in their heads and say he died because of the fight we had. Can you believe that shit? How fucked up is that. A man killing his brother. People fuck all the stories up."

On that corner I have sat and thought countless times about that afternoon and what he might have thought or seen, a large grey truck coming out of the alley and him with no way to turn. The racing in between jobs with a woman at home and a child about to come into this world. "My poor, poor brother," Neto said. "Found his way out of a war but not the neighborhood."

I HEARD THE RAIN FELL all day and night the day after the funeral and Bruna's hair was covered with plastic when she found her way to the Abuela's basement. She pushed her way through the door.

Neto was sleeping one off when Bruna pulled the string on the bare light bulb and had a seat on the mattress. She rested her hands around her stomach and rubbed the belly that was Relles' child. "I can't make rent, Neto," Bruna said.

"Don't worry about that," Neto said.

"What do you mean?" Bruna stared at the concrete floor and for a long while Neto didn't say a word.

"You didn't come to the funeral, Neto?" she said.

"Been laid up with a cold."

"You weren't here, Neto. I asked your mama and she said you weren't around."

"Went out for work," Neto said. "Man's got to work."

"Your daddy says you haven't worked in weeks. Your mama says she hasn't seen you eat in days. Are you having pains?" She patted Neto's cheeks and put her cool hand to his warm forehead. "You don't feel too warm. Where is the pain? Is it your stomach or your back?"

Finally Neto told her straight: "Lost my brother."

"We all lost him. We're all sick, Neto, but you got to come and grieve with the family. You know? I mean don't you think I'm not sick? You don't think I got to be sick over this too?"

"Needed some days," Neto said. "I don't have a thing to do with you anyhow. You my brother's girl and I have nothing to do with you."

"Listen, Neto," Bruna said. "I got no more work. I can't work at Newberry's. I mean I can't waitress."

"They fire you?"

"I'm pregnant, Neto," Bruna said. "I have to have the baby and need my own place. I can't live with my mama and Jeri no more."

"My mother will take you in," Neto said. "You can live here."

"I need to live on my own," Bruna said. "To show them."

"Show'em what?"

"That I am doing for myself, you know? I'm sick over all of this too." Bruna put her face in her hands and she wept.

BRUNA KEPT THE STUDIO APARTMENT and cooked for Neto, the fake husband who slept on the hardwood floor. He woke in the middle of the night hurting for his brother, breathing hard with guilt and staring at his new surroundings.

One night he sat up in his bed thrashing while the young, naked woman showered and hummed. When he finally woke, he knocked the foldout over and across the room. He staggered over to the window and looked at parked cars. His t-shirt and pants were wet with sweat and his lips hurt from thirst.

On the next night he walked the streets of Abriendo Avenue. There was a coating over his tongue that tasted of mold. He walked into bars and ordered drinks for people and watched them drink with a silent satisfaction. One man he fought with over a stool and on another night a fight with a man went out into the streets, nearly to the front door of Bruna's apartment. The building woke up to the sounds of thumps and screams.

Finally, he stopped working and sat in the dollar movies over at the Chief Theatre. He rode around on busses and slept in the public library. He paid the rent for half the month, then not at all, until the landlord, Mr. Archuleta, had no choice but padlock the door. At Archuleta's apartment he argued and pounded at the walls. The landlord had no choice but to call the cops and so Neto left without Bruna's clothes or photo albums.

THE DAY WAS ENDING when Bruna caught up with Neto. He had been sleeping in the storeroom of The Klamm Shell, sometimes working as a dishwasher. He had just drained two doubles and felt warm and sleepy.

"You living here now?" she said.

Neto struggled to recognize her then turned away to stare at a viejito who kept calling the bartender "nurse" and laughing out loud. Neto said, "I haven't seen you."

"I tried to make you more of a grown up. I tell them all I tried, Neto."

"For Christ's sake."

"You're as dead as your brother, Neto," she said, pushing and slapping at his chest. He wouldn't raise his hands to her. He just sat in his favorite stool and hunched over a fresh glass.

lunch at crewbegg's

It was Thursday afternoon just before the lunch rush from Crewbegg's Department Store across Main Street, and pregnant Bruna felt the temperature in New Berry's Diner to be higher than normal.

"Most girls think they know how to wait on tables," Nan Goolsby told the new gabacha Bruna was assigned to train. Nan was the shift manager and might have hated Bruna because she wore a wedding ring and because her husband Relles kissed her after he dropped her off to work.

"My only reason for saying is because one should always be thinking about the next task," Nan said.

Bruna didn't say a word. I'm knocked up and married, was what Bruna kept thinking. She thought that more and more instead of thinking about Relles Ortiz. And it was rare for her to have these moments of fear, of panic and dread really. But lately they had come more and more since the wedding and then after moving with Relles into a little apartment off of Abriendo Street. She had no idea where her life was going and in the diner with the customers and the smell of greasy fries and hamburgers Bruna felt even worse. Her feet ached and her legs burned with fatigue. It was only three hours into her shift and her legs felt as if they were splitting apart.

"You've got to get organized on an hourly basis," Nan kept telling them. "Then you won't have to walk around the counter so much. It's your own fault, Bruna. It's your own fault. See the new girl gets it," Nan said.

After the lunch rush came, Bruna was assigned to mix soda and water in order to clean the stainless steel around the soda fountain and the booths and then she was assigned to clean the toilets. Nan sat in the booths and talked with the new girl and taught her how to count out change to the customer. They chatted and laughed while Bruna mopped up the entranceway and then the men's restroom.

Pifanio Jaramillo came in and sat himself in the booth nearest the public telephone. He placed a typewriter on the seat beside him as he slipped in. He lit a cigarette and then he swept the salt and peppershaker from the tabletop with his forearm. You're miserable, he thought to himself, even though he wasn't drunk that afternoon. He combed his hair at the part towards his left ear with his hands in the reflection in the picture window. He watched the traffic down Main Street.

Bruna missed him the first trip she made to the supply closet and then she missed him a second time as she came to the restrooms. She missed him a third time before she dumped out her mop water.

"Hey there, girly," Pifanio announced. The expression on his face held no emotion and no hint of what he must have been feeling.

It took a second for Bruna to recognize the man she had only seen in pictures. "I sent letters," Bruna said. "You read' em?" Her tone of voice was serious and identical to the tone she thought of when she thought of strength and certainty, like in the movies.

"I just came in to see you for myself, Bruna."

"You shouldn't have come in here."

"Your mama alright or what?" Pifanio asked.

"She's good. Now leave."

"I want you to give this fifty bucks to your mama, alright. It's money and I want you to give it to your mama."

"We don't need any money from you."

"Take it. It's money and I want your mama to have it," he said. He placed the fifty-dollar bill on the sticky table top.

"How'd you know I was workin here anyway? I could get fired if my boss sees—"

"Your mama told me. Your mama alright or what?"

"I told you, she's good."

Pifanio's thick fingers reached down and pulled the typewriter case up to the table top. He dusted off the ashes and the dust from the typewriter. "I wanted you to have this," Pifanio said. "I asked your mother what you might want as a gift and I wanted you to have it."

Across the diner Nina and the gabacha watched the entire conversation. They just sat and watched.

"I had feelings for your mama, Bruna," Pifanio said. "And I wanted to come in here and give you these things."

Those words tormented him, and he hoped Bruna could feel it coming off of him.

"I'm not much of a father," he said, almost crying. "But I wanted you to have this and I want your mama to know I'm sorry," Pifanio said. "Tell her that for me, Bruna. Will you tell her that for me?"

"She never talked about you," Bruna said.

"I know."

"She loved you and you were no good, Pifanio."

"I know."

"You gave her nothing but grief and trouble."

"I know. I know."

"And I didn't mean to bring you here," Bruna said. She almost cried right there in the diner.

"I know you didn't mean to, girl. I know you didn't mean to."

"We have a family and a whole life together."

"I know there ain't nothing I can say or do, Bruna. Please take this money."

Bruna didn't answer or say a word. She looked at Nan and the gabacha and then she sat down across from Pifanio. She took off her latex gloves and then she caught her breath. She took the fifty-dollar bill and placed it in her apron.

"Want some soft-boiled eggs," Bruna finally said.

After lunch Pifanio walked out and Bruna put her typewriter with her purse in the upstairs office. She folded her coat over it so no one would see it or so no one could steal it. Bruna never spoke to her father again but later Bruna heard Pifanio had died from a heart attack in San Luis. Later she would lie and tell people he had left her money; that was what she told people when she talked about the man they called her father.

1980

the otherworld

Outside of Lino's Taos morada Carlos stood barefoot with the intention to practice the sungazing Lino had once taught. It was near dawn and the air was warming with a crushing wind. He stood in the mess and tucked his shirt into his Levi's, noticing just how thin he had become. Thinned by "the habit of consumption," he thought, as his Abuelita always referred to her own dead husband, Carlos' Grandfather. The air felt harsh and drier in summer, and the time had passed strangely since he had first met Lino. "Brujados," he whispered.

He wiped at his face with his leathered hand and then at his neck. He spent a quick second straightening the brim of his hat. Could I have slept an entire season? Carlos thought. "I'll be God-dammed," he said.

Back inside Lino's home, Lino's widow was on the floor with her best cooking and her best serape waiting for Carlos to wake. Carlos was struck by the similarity of the work and food she had prepared. Lino's memory forced him to sit and brazenly drink mescal from the bottle and glass.

She looked at the cowboy and then leaned in and kissed his forehead, wiping at his hair. "I will serve us a meal, vaquero," the woman whispered, rising and filling a small metal plate with beans and rice, a freshly warmed pan de campo. She approached the cowboy, kneeling before him and grasped the bottle that Carlos held tightly in his hands. She took the bottle and replaced it with the plate. She smiled and beamed as Carlos scooped the warm food into his mouth with the bread. White Bear's voice shook with emotion. "Lino always said spiritual survival can begin with a plate of beans. Maybe why he was a cook, no?"

"I will pay for Lino's horse and be on my way with the woman and the girl," Carlos said, trying to rationalize this wisdom. He was nearly pleading. "I'll do all I can for you. For Mara and the girl is what I am saying."

"But a man must eat," she replied. Then she kneeled in closer and placed her hand to the man's chest as they both huddled on the floor.

"I am so sorry," Carlos said, finally breaking down. The woman's cooking and words had brought Lino's memory. "I'm a sinner."

And while Carlos began to weep and explain the past weeks, the woman wiped at his face and neck and interrupted and continued, "You know, when the Spanish arrived here, they whipped my people when practicing their own religion. The Pueblos throughout the southwest, including those in your San Luis Valley, Carlos, revolted and rose against their Spanish masters. Then my people drove out the Spanish invaders for decades and decades until a new generation arrived to apologize and give new tribute and charity to the elders. The Spanish influence was strong and had already happened, you cannot fight change. Only my clan rejected the new Spaniards along with Christianity, even the mix of Christianity and Indian tradition the Spaniards introduced to ensure peace. The others decided to attack and burn their brothers to the ground. Spanish priests and other clan leaders, brothers and cousins of the clan alike, burned the homes and dragged the people off for torture. My people burned and were burned along with their elders and were buried in unmarked graves covered in rock and granite, so they would not be recognized from the otherworld."

"Why are there such things?"

"There seems to be no end to the horrible offenses we commit upon one another. That world of the past and this world are parallel and exist together. That I have seen. That's all I know."

Carlos wiped at his mouth and eyes and looked at the woman uncertainly. When Carlos calmed and quieted, he sat crying and found himself revealing: "I should've done more for him. Do you hear what I say to you?"

"Mara tells me what you done. She tells me and I tell the Elders."

"You should call me a sinner."

White Bear could only sit and try to console the man and herself. "I was chosen for that man Lino," White Bear later revealed. And with this her smile began to crack and she wept openly. "I was chosen to be his wife. I was chosen as you have been chosen. As my husband was chosen to meet you. And you were chosen for Mara. I must believe. A part of you will always stay here. With us. But you are no prisoner. He will return to me and speak to me, Carlos. Vaquero. Like the old clans and the victims return to me. As they came to you. In stories they reveal their secrets and wrongdoings. In my dreams and my stories. They will come to you. They run off for others but for us they return. They give and they forgive."

"Mujer, I don't understand what you say. Is this a hell for us?"

She continued, finding composure, "This is a place of feeling and regeneration. Do you know this word, cowboy? Regeneration? Like the cycle of the tree and the seed. Who knows when it began?"

Carlos could not understand. He shook his head and wiped at his neck. "I don't want you to be without him," he said simply. "I don't want to be without him. That's what I know."

"The road to Colmor brought you to us is what I am telling you. The chaos brought us to you. And now you have Mara and the girl. The road brought them to you as well. You were drifting when we found you. No one cared where you went and now look at what you have. You will be together someday again with the man as in your dream. Do you remember the story of the dream you brought to us?"

old man to bed

On the first afternoon young Bruna made her way to Carlos' home in the projects it took her two bus trips and then she asked her father the question mostly on Lena's mind.

"Jefe?" Bruna said. She buttoned the old man's flannel.

"Que?" Carlos answered, lifting his eyes.

"Why do you drink so much? You know it's not good for you—"

He was formal and direct: "I'm 76 years old and I have lost my legs to the country and to the San Luis Valley and to land I've never owned, and I can have a Goddamned drink if I need to—"

"Okay," Bruna said. "Okay. You're so damned feisty. Aren't you, old man?"

"What the hell is this 'feisty'?"

"You know? You got a lot of piss and vinegar in you to talk this way?"

"I'll talk anyway I want to—"

"You talk to Lena like this?"

"I talk to any woman any way that I like—"

"Can't to me—"

"Que?"

"I say you can't talk that way to me—"

"Why not?"

"Because I am your daughter and I won't let you talk to me this way—"

"A man does what he wants and when he wants speaks his

mind and no woman tells him different—"

"You ain't no working man. You haven't worked in years, old man."

"I worked enough for the whole damn lot of yous. That Jeri and that mother of yours. I worked enough for the three of yous. Who the hell you think was putting money for you in the mailbox all these years. Sure and hell wasn't Felipa!"

"My mama works pretty hard."

"Yeah, I guess she does," he stopped and thought and then laughed. "Favorite out of all of them is what she is. I loved her more than my own wife."

"Felipa?"

"And Lena's mother. Your Grandmother."

"Why don't you tell me about her?"

"I can't remember, girl. I'm too damned old and it all happened so long ago. I can't remember yesterday nor nothing much less years gone—"

"Why did you let me go?" she asked. She just said it plainly. And as soon as she said it she regretted it but thought she would never be closer and more comfortable with Carlos than right at this moment. She even thought she might cry when she said it.

"I worked, mi hija. Always working and running around. I owed it to your Lena and wanted her to have such a beautiful young thing. She's your mother, no?"

"Yeah, she's my mother."

"Not Felipa?"

"Yeah, Lena's my mama."

"See how it all works out in the end of things, mi hija? See how it all works out."

LATER WHILE BRUNA PUSHED the old man down the block, Carlos explained to her about his only cousin. It was the only real story he could remember. How Benito R Montoya was buried three times during the Great War before arriving in Costilla, New Mexico, on June 19, 1921. The family drove out to Carbajal Funeral Home to view the casket. Carlos' Grandmother was inconsolable as was Benito's mother though they both insisted on coming. They stood as old man Carbajal explained the procedures and explained how the Army's retrieval service dug the boy up and brought the boy home.

"How could one make it and come back and not the other," Benito's mother cried out loud.

Even Benito's father who worked out in Colorado wondered out loud for the first time, "Didn't you watch out for your cousin?"

Carlos remembered how he sat on the family porch and smoked and held no answer.

ON BRUNA'S SECOND TRIP to visit, the old man spoke regretfully of the world and how change took hold. Carlos said, "I remember when I was a boy in San Luis the calabacitas would crack open and be milky and creamy just like heaven."

"Calabacitas?" Bruna asked.

"Squash," the old man said. "Don't they teach you nothing in them schools, girly? In the fields I would pick them and eat them in my hands."

"What's wrong with them now, viejo?"

"See how you speak to me. No respect," Carlos said. "You must always hold respect."

Later he explained how new companies or "outfits" as he called them took the seeds and ruined them. "Changed the damned taste in everything. Hardly nothing ain't what it was made out to be. Everything is como how they say … corrupted. You know what I mean by 'corrupted,' girly."

"Mama says you just lost your taste buds from years of drinking and smoke."

"Is that what she says about me?"

"That's what she tells me."

"Shit, I can still taste. I didn't change nothing at all. The damn big outfits took what was pure and good and ruined it. The world is what changed."

AS THE TWO SHARED a soda one day Bruna asked the old man, "Do you believe in aliens?"

"I've never seen any."

"So you don't."

"I'm just saying I've never seen anything like in the television box."

"How about spirits or voices?"

"You mean ghosts? Like dead people."

"Yes, I guess so."

"I'm old. I think of dead folks quite a bit. I can feel them. How much I miss them, I mean."

CABRÓNA'S OUT LATE, CARLOS thought, one night after Bruna had gone, mopping the sweat from his own face with a handkerchief which he then proceeded to place into his coverall pocket.

He wheeled into the kitchen and clicked on the evening radio programs. He wheeled and maneuvered about boiling water on the stove top in a little pot. He took out some bread, a tomato and some onions, all while thinking about Felipa and how late it had become. He'd always believed Felipa would desert him, although at times she surprised him with tamales from over on Northern Avenue. He could make her out amongst the children playing around the alley at the far end. A kind of cement walkway would bring her to the door and then to Carlos' bedroom. He'd studied the alley every day after cleaning his stumps and changing his own bandages in those sober days.

Every day he would wheel around the neighborhood and then the house, the only universe for him now. And at seven at night he would clean himself up and wait for his Felipa, coming from the alley after walking or from the front door after being dropped off by a coworker or one of her new found Comadres.

Most days he lay down next to the window from his bedroom and watched for her. The window protected him from the fierce summer heat, and he listened to the neighborhood's sounds. His ears pricked for the slightest rustling of trees and leaves, or the faintest car door or horn. In the distance, perhaps springing up from the neighbor's door or from around a chain link fence, Felipa always appeared: her blue work smock she kept on no matter the weather or the hour. Her short body and wide frame standing near a tree trunk or behind a group of kids. He always kept an eye out for her but today he pulled himself from bed and the window and fixed his own meal because he didn't see her. Later, he cleaned his pot and after turning off the gas burners and then pouring the water into two coffee mugs he went to the window.

That night the wife Felipa returned to the plate of soup prepared by her husband. She spooned it up and, on this occasion, not thinking that it was a meal prepared by her crippled husband and not thinking that in the years since his amputation the man had never managed to prepare much more than a glass of water for himself. Then she readied for bed and Carlos tossed and turned and that night Carlos told his wife he hated to be alone. He told his wife in a sorrowful voice because he knew the woman would fall asleep if not. And as there was no other one to talk about such things, he found himself begging his wife to come home sooner and to call if she would be late. He found his spirits falling and he could sense the bitterness between them. That night Carlos told his wife of his love for her and his daughters and later after Felipa fell in and out of sleep she told her husband she had to work and there was nothing more that she can do about it. She must work nights and longer shifts and there was nothing to do about it. She was tired and in savage humiliation over her work and humiliation in the washing of her work smocks in the bathroom sink. And that night the two silently fall asleep, very quiet by each other's side.

The next night the old man carried on cooking his meals and sitting under the streetlamp for most of the afternoon, studying the neighborhood and the faces. From time to time he napped and slipped into unconsciousness until a car backfire or a dark-haired boy yelled and woke the man.

The old man strained to lift himself up and then he moved indoors to light the fire to brew the tea. Then he ate his bread, and on this rare occasion some meat, onions, and tomatoes, sharing his food with the neighbor's cat he named Sinferosa, which he remembered was an orphaned girl his mother used to feed and care for in his early New Mexico days. He stared at the cat in the window and muttered words of love and admiration for such a pretty little thing. A neighbor happened to overhear the conversation the old man had with the cat this afternoon and yelled to explain, "Oye, Carlos! That cat is deaf and older than you!"

"Hey old cat! Old friend to me!" the old man said and then the neighbor's laughter came and he waited it out patiently and calmly. And from then on he knew the neighbors and kids would not give him a moment of peace with his Sinforosa. He stared at the old girl and through the dirt and sweat of his eyes he could barely make out who from around the corner of his window was laughing and carrying on until finally he had the screen door open wide.

"Be careful, viejo," another neighbor said. "I'll tell your wife about your new woman!"

And wiping the grime from his dirtied fingers and then from his face he thought of his wife and his neighbors and the good fortune to have a full belly and said to himself, "Ay, que cabrón!"

And despite the neighbor's laughter and condemnation he

returned two or three times to see the little cat. He stole from the prepared food he saved for his wife and muttering under his breath about work and the late hours his wife must keep, he stole bread and milk from the ice box for his little Sinforosa.

One afternoon as he looked for the cat on the stoop he saw the deep brown eyes shining furtively and he lifted her to his chest. As they sat and talked Sinforosa pissed down his already stained t-shirt, and it wasn't until the old man spent half the afternoon working hard on his afternoon coffee did the old man notice the smell and the compounding of stains down his side and down his pants and chair.

"Poor old girl," the old man said to himself as he removed his t-shirt and wiped at the stains to his chair.

"And this? What the hell is this?" Felipa asked that night when she returned home to the mess. It is at this moment her eyes overflowed and she remained still. Her eyes streaming and eyelashes soaked. "Can't you keep yourself clean, old man!"

Felipa could not stand the situation any longer. The smell of cat urine to her house and to her old man seemed evidence her world was collapsing. For a month the man seemed to be collapsing. Leaving the small house seemed impossible for him. But tomorrow, when his wife exited for the bus stop, the old man thought, the best thing to do would be to go to some far-off place and wait for the nighttime. To lie down and die. And he told Felipa this thought one night as she washed her face and hands in the kitchen sink.

"And what are you going to do? Like a Goddamn dog in the woods?"

"I don't know," he replied in a loud voice.

And the old woman looked at him in surprise.

Something was waiting for him, he thought. And the next day when his wife left for work and the bus stop after she kissed his oily forehead and instructed him to call Lena and Bruna, the old man took the last piece of bread in the house and rolled more slowly than ever out the door and down to Bessemer Park. He was overwhelmed by the green and the voices and the rush of children to the city pool and to the jungle gyms that lined near the boulevard.

CARLOS SPOKE ABOUT THE PAST. This time no one asked or prompted him. He reminisced. He was delirious, really. He remembered the morning of Benito's return. Carlos had no food or drink and without much sleep packed his bed roll and saddle bags. He took what was left of his last payroll money, carried his saddle and pistola down to the Martinez' corral and livery and bought himself a horse. The steadiest and bridal-wise. He told the men there he was riding west for work and then to farm west of New Mexico and was never going to return though the men believed him to be joking. "How can you leave your people?" the men teased.

As Carlos rode west, he thought on Benito's ways. How he dragged Carlos to Camp Funston in Kansas and how he practically signed Carlos' papers for him. He gave Carlos speeches on duty and honor. He lectured on obligation to the government and to the coming war. Benito ate up the training and the uniforms as Carlos limped along. To Benito it was all a cruel play. Carlos only cared for the horses and the horse training. He learned to shoe and brand and every job at an Army mounting station. His skills for roping and riding came as an asset. The work came natural to Carlos though he never cared for extended hikes and military exercises. It bored him. Benito had affection for the camp and it rubbed off on Carlos for a time until a trip to Fort Riley, Kansas, nearby where Carlos met a young woman who he wanted to marry. He wanted a ranch and a family and spread of animals and more than anything wanted children. He wanted to skip out on the Army and forget the whole damned life after the young girl's green eyes tore through him. But this was all before the journey to the war in France.

Benito stalked Carlos and followed him out to his love's house—her people's house. He kicked the door in and while the family ate and celebrated the engagement and dragged Carlos from the table and from the house. He remembered it all and spoke the words to anyone who cared to hear.

IN HIS CONFUSION he convinced himself that he was chasing for Sinforosa who had been lost for days. "Poor little thing!" he cried over and over again. And he remained for a long time in the shade of a spruce, until the old man thought it time to leave and move on. When his shirt was soaked in August's heat and perspiration, and as he made his way through the weeded vegetation of the empty baseball fields, he had the feeling this would be the last time he would see Sinforosa fleeing around the park all on her own amongst the trees and the careless kids who pay no attention to anything but their own world.

Lena opened the door to her home and Carlos entered the living room with assistance and confusion.

"What is it, Jefe," Lena said, searching around him for signs of Felipa or anyone, in the far end of the street and across Northern Avenue. But she couldn't find anyone.

And before going to her bedroom Lena hesitated a second, but then pushed open the door. In the low light of the early evening populated by the buzzing of crickets and chirping birds, the old man brutally undid the knot of his tie and when he saw Bruna's pictures and her clothes and her dresser, he became embarrassed and furious and hastily threw his tie onto the floor and then struggled to the center of the room.

"Bruna's away with the church, Jefe," Lena lied to the old man. "She's away for the week on a religious retreat. With the church, Jefe."

The old man's hair was a mess, and his face was covered

in spittle and sweat. The old man took hold of his chair and wheeled himself into Lena's bedroom. The old man was waiting for his daughter in the hallway and the daughter said to him before moving on to the kitchen:

"Take a sleep in my bed, Papa! And I'll fix you something to eat. Something to drink. Quieres café?"

Carlos moved across the room, slumped over and with Lena's help struggled onto the double bed, over the knitted serapes and decorative pillows. He was trembling because he was tired and weak from the day, he almost knew what was going to happen and he worried that he did not know many things to say or do. Soon Lena sat next to the old man and wiped at his face and forehead with a cool washcloth after placing the man's food and coffee mug near the bed. Lena slipped her shoes off and she asked the man very softly if he thought she was a good daughter, a strong daughter.

The old man seemed to bend with the question as he breathed quickly and deeply. His mouth unnaturally dropped open and awkward. He hunched and leaned darkly to the woman and slowly nodded and muttered a brief acknowledgment. It looked as if he were hoping to find something in his daughter's brown eyes.

"My hija," he said to her.

Taking Carlos by the hand Lena continued to wipe and care for the man's face and neck under the shade of the evening's coolness. Lena was guiding the cloth to please the old man in hopes he would be able to sleep and dream in peace. From the window they had a view of the neighborhood and the warm evening breeze running freely through the trees.

vecina lady

"Make sure the old man is eating," Felipa had said in the beginning. "Make sure he is eating and taking his pills. And I can only afford a few dollar bills here and there for you."

"That's fine," the vecina lady Gomez said.

"We're on a budget…"

"Of course," the vecina lady said. "I don't need too much."

"Just make sure he eats," Felipa said handing over the keys that had once belonged to Carlos but now just hung near the back door without purpose. "He doesn't get out too much but needs his lunch so he can take his pills," Felipa said.

"I can help him no problem," the vecina lady said. "We can eat lunch together it's no problem."

The first afternoon the two sat silent and watched one another eat and drink but soon they talked. "Tell me about the people in Colmor," the neighbor lady, Mrs. Gomez, asked. When Carlos had his rest and his coffee and rum he liked to talk to her in Spanish. "Tell me about the city."

"No city," Carlos said.

"What?"

"No people. No city," Carlos said. "The last vieja receiving mail died November or December of 1970 or so. No one knows," Carlos said.

"Oh," the vecina lady said. "I didn't know that."

"The newspapers call me about the damned village where I

lived and worked and damned college folks call me about the war. I have nothing to say."

"Don't want to dig around in the past, huh?" the vecina lady asked.

"They say on the box," the viejo Carlos said, thumbing over to the 13" black and white television. "They say right there no mail and no living folks so no town. Pinche Channel 5 News."

"Is that what they say, huh?" the neighbor lady said, pouring herself some coffee.

"My cousin Benito is buried there in the cemetery, Colmor Cemetery, and his head stone is there. He's people so it is a town, I don't care what they say. The only damned thing marking he lived or died—marking he served this country and held a distinguished service cross—the only thing saying he lived and died and now his soul probably living in the same old ranch and visits the same old neighbors and stores out there—visiting the same old ghosts and family. His mother and father dead to influenza and dead to time."

"I never would've thought to ask you on it," the vecina lady said. She was up putting the old man's bologna and the bread together for lunch. "So you believe in ghosts," she said.

"I believe in the sky and the land," Carlos said. "Family and visitors—soldiers—and I tell you they all talk to me and have for years. I guess I just have the ears and eyes for it."

"But I thought you couldn't hear too good," the vecina lady Gomez asked and then she smiled. "I thought your eyes were gone bad because of the machines and saws when you worked in the mountains is what they tell me. I thought that was the reason."

"Shit," Carlos said. "My mama and papa from when I was a boy and the French voices and faces of boys in France—did I tell you I been to France? I once knew all those years and years ago when I was young and stupid and followed my cousin for soldiering and fighting in the war. Benny was the one," Carlos said. "Took years and years for him to find his way home to San Luis. I buried him and dug him up and buried him again and again—three times before coming home to his people in San Luis and the village cemetery down there."

"Dug him up?" the neighbor lady said.

"In the war they buried them and families dug them up to bring them home," Carlos said. "He was a damned fine man—a little rough but straight when it came to soldiering. He could play ball and he could roll a cigarette and sit a horse like no one I ever met. He was a true gentleman."

AFTER THAT THE VECINA LADY, Gomez' wife, came over twice a day, once in the morning right after her job down at the Walmart where they locked her in at night and later in the afternoon with some food. She always warmed coffee on the stovetop and poured cream and sugar for the old man. Sometimes they spoke and other times they did not. They sat and drank sharing a quiet reflection over the smell of brewed coffee. They listened to the rainstorms in the late summer and the children playing after school.

"Thank you again so much for looking in on the viejo," Carlos' grey-haired wife, Felipa, said to the vecina lady. "He needs a good person, a kind person to look in on him while I'm out at work. He needs someone to talk to—too much quiet makes him crazy, stir crazy I think."

"I'm happy to," the vecina lady said. "He reminds me of my own father in New Mexico. He loves to talk about the old times, you know? He'll start in about the old times."

"You speak Spanish?" Felipa asked to the vecina lady.

"I understand what he tells me," she said, "but I have a hard time with the words, you know? Talking to him in Spanish is hard for me so I just listen."

"Just hit him or tap him and say, Hey viejo, in English," Felipa said, acting out the part. "That's what I do."

"Is the old guy hard of hearing or no?" the vecina lady asked.

"Oh, he can hear when he wants to if you know what I'm saying. Just talk loud and if he don't pay attention like I said just give him a hit or a punch in the arm. You know how it is with these old viejos."

"My old man was the same way," the vecina lady said.

"Well, this one is a pretty special one. He's been in the chair for years so I'm used to him, but he can be a real pain to folks who ain't used to him. I have some stories. He's been arrested and a few times for drunk and disorderly."

"No," the vecina lady said, "Carlos?"

"Oh yeah he likes his drink. He likes his beer. They look out for him now and most places won't serve him. He has to go to farther and farther from here to find someone who will serve him. He'll probably ask you for a drink or for something to smoke but just give him coffee and let him be. He'll complain but I think lately he's lost that drive for drinking and getting out to find bars. Just give him his coffee and his lonche and he'll be fine."

"I haven't heard a word about a drink. The viejo licks his lips for water or for coffee, mostly coffee and sometimes he asks for an RC Cola."

"Must've been on his best behavior," Felipa said.

"TELL ME MORE about your Benito?" the vecina lady asked on another lunch visit. Carlos smiled in the way she said, "your Benito" or maybe it was the way she said it softly and kindly. Or maybe it was the rum and the warm air blowing into the apartment and blowing up the drapes. All the units in the projects had no screens in those days and the whole room baked with the whirring of the fans. The heat blew into the kitchen reminding the old man of the llano of his youth—the grassy and treeless plains with the pinon bushes and the heat of late afternoons walking from neighbor to neighbor looking for Benito when the two were boys and ran from one mother and hid from another.

"'Have you seen my Benito?' I would say," Carlos explained to the vecina. "I would go from door to door and ask. Or sometimes I would say, 'Where is my cousin, Benito? His mother is worried and wants him home.' It was miles I would walk. I would hate to go to the neighbor's houses but the old folks, his father Doroteo, would be looking for him. Sometimes I would find him with a girl or with some tobacco he had stolen or most times I would find him behind the schoolhouse off of main street."

"In the San Luis Valley?" the vecina lady Gomez said, interrupting as she fixed the old man's lunch of bologna and cheese. In these final days the viejo wasn't hearing or speaking too well and it was a chore to communicate but Lena's Bruna and the vecina lady Gomez who was religious felt a duty to the neighbor and the viejo.

"No," Carlos said. "Colmor, New Mexico."

"I never heard of that one," the vecina lady said. "Never been there."

"It ain't hardly on no maps," the viejo Carlos said. "The maps are different than the territory is what they teach you in the army."

"When you were in the army?" the vecina lady asked. "My husband Gomez was in the Navy."

"I was trained at Camp Cody in New Mexico in Deming, New Mexico," Carlos said proudly. "I learned soldiering with my cousin."

"The same cousin you were talking about?" the vecina lady asked.

"The same," Carlos said. "You know I spent time with him more than my own brothers—my brothers were older—and Benito and me were the same age. We grew together and slept in the same room. We were of different parents, but we were the same. I never even had a brother like Benito. The brothers I had were old—older and married and gone before I was around and so." Carlos grew silent and stared around the room for a long minute, confused at his surroundings and place. His eyes grew wet and he spoke, "I love him...Benito...I love you...You were my own blood and my own brother and I wish I could find you when you were lost ... I wish I could've found you..."

"WHY DID YOU LEAVE your home?" the vecina lady Gomez asked Carlos the next week after she calmed the viejo's tears and had his lunch down in front of him, green chile peppers in hot sauce, and then she poured a 7-Up for the old man's stomach. She cracked a bag of potato chips and had some lettuce for his bologna sandwich.

"What's that?" Carlos said. He had a chile to his lips, and he smiled with the sharp spike of flavor and heat.

"I said why did you leave your home?" the vecina lady repeated.

"My cousin Benny left to the Army camp in Deming and I followed after him," Carlos said. "I was always following after him and looking for him. He was the handsome one with the nerve and the head I mean brains to make what he wanted happen. He could have anything he wanted. A cattle business, a wife, a contract with the Chicago Cubs. He could've had everything. He could drive before me and he could run and run without tiring and he was taller. And he could talk and talk. He would say to me, 'Don't be quiet, Carlos, with your hands in your pockets.' He would say, 'The world moves to those that can convince it to move.' I was always with my hands in my pockets listening and never saying a word. People would say, 'Don't you talk?'"

"Well that's something that's changed in you," the vecina lady said.

"What's that?"

"You talking and going on about your life. With me anyway. I can't imagine you not talking or not saying anything."

"Felipa tells me I have to get a word in on everything, yes, so Benny, I guess I've learned—took me years and years and so I finally learned, Benny. Soon I'll be with him in San Luis and be able to say those words to him—be able to tell him he was right."

"Tell me how he would talk to people," the vecina lady said.

"Oh, he talked and talked, never in a mean way or a bad way. He was no salesman, but he was straight and honest with folks of the llano. He asked questions and he observed and looked for his opening. He was como—"

"Charming," the vecina lady interrupted.

"Yes," Carlos said. "He was puro charming like a movie actor or a lawyer. He could've had any girl on the llano but he told me he chose himself—he chose discipline. I chose Terricita Marquez and went AWOL and Benny came looking for me."

"You were AWOL, viejo?" the vecina lady said.

"Yes," Carlos said. "I had this girl and had it in my mind I was going to marry her and get a house and own everything I could see around me. A big spread of land on the llano because I thought the land out there was lonely but Benny went looking for me. I was out at the Marquez spread in Colfax County when he found me. He nearly kicked in the door and dragged me onto my heels and said the Army wasn't done with me. I remember he was in uniform and he called me a cabrón and said he didn't care if I married or not but he said I made a commitment to the Army first. And he was right. They threw boys in jail for running out on the Army and he was looking out for me…Benny knew what was right and what was wrong. He used to tell me, there is right and there is wrong. You know this, he would tell me. There is right and there is easy. He knew but I had to learn for myself, I guess…"

—

"I CAN TELL YOU THIS," Carlos said one particular day as the neighbor lady badgered him to talk. He coughed and then wiped at his mouth and nose with his handkerchief. "In its day Colmor was a beautiful jewel. Clean green water and folks invited you to dances or in to their houses to eat—there were no bars on all the doors, the people knew everyone. The people dressed in their best clothes for travelling to church or to the dancehall downtown on Sunday afternoons. The children ran around chasing frogs and the people had a quiet love to them, I can't explain it," Carlos said. "No one rushing around. Not too many cars in them days. No one on Sundays was in a hurry for much except to get home to dinner and family stories about their people and their people's people from before statehood. And after dinner we would sit on the porch and smoke and play cards and watch the wide-open roads and family from Colfax or Mora would visit with their bottles or their pans of desserts. The place came alive and filled with spirit then—and now the place is buried—not even roads anymore—overgrown with weeds and branches—cracked gravel roads leading to nothing and nowhere. I seen the pictures on the box and heard the stories from compadres—my wife's compadres. The place is dying and that world is dying. Soon it will be gone when I'm gone and when I'm dead and buried."

"Don't say things like that, viejo," the vecina lady said. "You're not going anywhere soon and I am here with you."

"THE PEOPLE IN COLMOR were good people," Carlos repeated one afternoon when the vecina lady had tobacco for the old man's pipe. She cleaned up his lunch plate and saucer poured the last of the coffee from the pot and smiled as he brought the pipe to his lips to light the pipe with a match.

"Tell me about your people," the vecina lady said.

"I had an aunt in San Luis who always came over to talk and bring my mother flowers—roses mostly and Indian paintbrush seeds and in the late summer she'd bring green chile to roast. They would bring the green chile to roast on the comal and the home would fill with such a sweet smoky smell."

"Love the smell of roasting chile," the vecina lady said.

"I was a boy and it felt as if each house in each part of the village had chile to roast. It was the wealth of the village. My aunt pulled the meat from the skin and chopped them up with pork for chile pots and the folks' bellies were all filled and warm and then the flour tortillas she made were a gift—I'd never eat as much as when my mother's sister came. The woman would sit and talk in the kitchen around the woodstove while the men stayed on the porch or in the yard and the woman gossiped and gave chisme on all the other women in the village and I remember Josie—that was her name, the comadre—she bragged and told stories of her family though her children were grown and had moved on from the village—maybe to Raton or on to Las Vegas. Maybe Colorado Springs. She had the most gossip and contempt for folks. She made fun of Señor Morales and his oversized suit jackets in church and his wife who wore the same dress over and over. I remember she was always gifting chile and pots of beans—always inviting folks to eat at her spread. It must've been her husband was gone and her kids moved on and she had no one—la viuda, they called her. She was always in black and befriending folks to come over to her house to fix and work on things. She lost her animals and lost her children and only had her garden—tomatoes and chile and things growing in the dry hard earth. She was a horrible woman but when I saw her I knew there would be pots of chile and beans. She delivered food to everyone—and with everyone she sat and gossiped. Later they told me she took up with a man named Mestas—a man who was wealthy from selling and raising cattle. Sold his animals and land and took her to California where she lived away from her village and away from her people. The folks were sad and I missed her cooking and her beautiful green chile—they said she had a child late in life to please Mestas or that was the word and she brought the baby home. Later they said the child was not hers but the bastard son of her husband Mestas who ran off after he sold off her land and cattle. They said she kept the boy as her own and I remember that boy around Colmor in the church school and for the railroad when there was work. They called him Doroteo and he kept long hair. They say he was deaf and dumb and couldn't learn, that is why the husband to Josephine had left, but she was strong and she was large in her life and kept the boy and the responsibility. She took in laundry—sheets and clothes and boiled water to clean them. I remember the white sheets hanging in the yard and that boy of hers helping. My father and the Father Dwyer from church school both had their shirts down—I remember folks saying how could she live without a man or they would say how could a woman raise a boy on her own. Later we brought her chile and tomatoes in the late summer when we had them."

"That's some story," the vecina lady said. "I should bring you tobacco more often. I like that story. Folks should help one another, is what I always say."

CARLOS WAS HAVING a difficult time with memories, what was real. The vecina lady would come by to bring soup or tamales she made and ask the old man questions. "Oye, viejo," she would say. "Tell me about the war or tell me about Colmor, New Mexico?" Most of the time Carlos had no answer—he was prone to sleeping in the warmth of the afternoon sun slumped down in his wheelchair and with his head hung down. The sound of the front door opening or closing would stun the man and it would take a minute or so to fully wake him to the room and his senses. But he was always happy to see and talk to the vecina lady.

"Tell me about the woman in this picture?" she would say. Or she would say, "Tell me about your daughters, viejo?"

It would take a minute for his brain to fire up and think. "What can I tell you?" he would answer. "Colmor, New Mexico, is a beautiful spirit of a town. On the open plains—grassy plains. The town has no real railroad no more. I can't remember the town but I remember I rode the train from Colmor to Deming for my Army mounting training, you know, for soldiering. I took all I owned which was nothing in a box and my family took me down to the station. My mother wore a long black dress like a funeral and kissed me and let me go though at first she forbid me to go. My father and mother fought over whether I should go or not."

"Why didn't she want you to go?" the vecina lady asked.

"Because of the war," Carlos said. "Because I was her baby."

"You were the baby?" the vecina lady laughed and teased Carlos. She poured his coffee and placed his soup with crackers. She took her first sip along with Carlos. "Tell me more about the war, Carlos?"

"I went to the war, yes, and fought in France. My brother was in training with me and he died."

"When did you go? What year was this?"

"Hell if I know," Carlos said. "You want to know so much. You're like my damn Bruna..."

"Your granddaughter?"

"No."

"I thought she was Lena's daughter—your daughter's daughter."

Carlos shook his head. "She comes and asks me at least fifty questions and writes it all down or writes something down in her book. Says it's for school and the family tree."

"That's nice," the vecina lady said. "Good to have family who want your stories, no?"

"If you can remember the stories to tell," the viejo said. "I can't hardly think on my own damn name most times and I have to think and think," he laughed.

"Still, it's good for the young to care on the old. My kids are grown and don't visit. They don't call or write me. I see them on Christmas and that's it—sometimes Thanksgiving. They live in Texas. For their work. My girls are in the army and they stay down there and forget their mama. I can't get out for a visit. I'm too old and hate the car and I ain't about to fly," the vecina lady said. "I ain't about to get myself into a little can and shoot across the sky."

In a little while as Carlos slurped his coffee and his soup and leaned back satisfied with his lunch and the sugar-free cookie the vecina lady put out in front of him, "Say," he said. "Where's the husband? Your man Leo? I ain't seen him in days and days and months and months. Don't see his truck or nothing…Used to come and see me regular."

"Leo ain't Leo I hate to tell you," the vecina lady said.

"What? He ran out on you? He leave you?"

"He's around but he ain't Leo no more."

"Drinking?" Carlos asked.

"No," the vecina lady said. "He's Joanne now. Calls himself Joanne."

Carlos stopped and sipped coffee and thought on this for a second. "I don't know what you're saying, girl."

"Leo is now become Joanne. He wears my clothes and says he wants to be a woman."

"Hay, que cabrón," Carlos said. "What in the hell."

Then the vecina lady got nervous and ashamed and started wiping remnants of soup and crumbs from Carlos' mouth and then the tablecloth. "I haven't told nobody. He's gone to be a woman and won't be back. He ran out on me. He's got an apartment on the east side. I know you spent time with him drinking and bullshitting but I don't want nothing more to do with him. He wears my clothes and wants to be a Joanne and not a Leo. I love him. I have loved him."

"Hay, que cabrón," Carlos repeated.

"TELL ME SOMETHING I ain't heard before about Colmor," the neighbor lady Gomez said on another visit as she warmed the man some soup. She nearly broke down crying as she prepared the food. Perhaps it was because Carlos looked particularly pale and thin and his eyes looked particularly sunken. His shirt and sweater fit around him loose like a blanket and had to be left unbuttoned because of the man's sensitive collar bones. His shirt seemed particularly stained and dirty.

"It's all gone and doesn't matter no more," Carlos said. "The town and people are all gone and no one cares about a dead old spirit of a town. No one gives a damn about the lives there or who lived there no more."

"I care," the vecina lady said. "I care about Colmor. I've been to Colmor when I was a kid."

"You've been to Colmor?" Carlos said.

"I told you, viejo, I grew up near there in Taos. Took the bus over and up to Raton sometimes after trips to Santa Fe or Albuquerque. I got a cousin in Raton. Drove through Colmor a few times. The town ain't much but it's a town."

"That's what I'm telling you. It's a town and needs attention. It's a damn shame in the world people let things die and fall into shit. No one cares for towns or people no more. I had a family and a life in Colmor and there is nothing there. Just a hole in the universe and there is nothing."

The vecina lady shook her head and was sorrowful with Carlos. That's all he was really looking for, she guessed. Perhaps Felipa had heard these stories and laments thousands of times with the details and with the tics of language but mornings and afternoons like this recently Carlos' words and stories were darker and darker. "The boys took a girl from her home near Colmor and killed her and I knew the boys. Rafael and Daryl Quintana. They raised cattle and had horses like all the people around the village and they had land. They took a girl named Gabriella—she was fifteen and short and light skinned, and they took her on a horse with no saddle out on the llano out in the deep plains with no people and no roads—only sage brush and pinon trees and hard earth. They said they were having a picnic—said she came willingly but we all knew. They were evil and silent men. They hurt her. They beat her. They raped her. I don't half know what that was. That's how young I was. She was the great love of my cousin. He wanted to marry her."

"Oh my God, Carlos," the vecina lady said. "You never told me this."

"I've never told this to a soul. Benito knew those brothers and the family traded with them and when he went out to their home and talked to their people and tell them about the girl. I don't remember no sheriff or no law or anything in them days. So Benito goes out there and they lied to him and made him think the girl went with the boys willingly and convinced him. Benny wanted to believe she just left him and not that these boys could do something so awful and bleak out on the llano, that anyone from the village could be so cruel. He cried and cried for her. I tried to tell him she was a whore and that she was bad, but I knew what happened and Benny knew what happened. They took her and they did that to her. We all knew. All the women and the men knew and said nothing. That poor poor girl."

"Oh my God, Carlos."

"So that's why I say that town and those people deserve to be spirits and ghosts. Maybe I deserve it," Carlos repeated. "The things I done in my life. I should've said something but I was young and spiteful and believed she chose those boys over Benny so I never felt bad. But I knew better in my head and in my heart. I knew. When a man sits like I sit. Without legs and without a way of moving around to distract myself and my thoughts

I think and think about shit from past lives. I think on those actions and I know. I know that girl was a victim. I see Bruna about the same age as that poor girl in Colmor on the llano. I worry on her. On Bruna. I worry but there is nothing I can do. She is like me when I was that age. No one could tell me nothing. No one could tell me a thing. I knew better. No one could push me one way or the other," Carlos repeated. "Except for my Benny. I loved him and I hated that girl for what happened to her and what it did to Benny. I know now that's not the way. I should've hated them boys and what they did to Benny. That's what I know now but didn't know it then. I should've let Benny go down there and kill them boys and hurt them. I should've done that then but Benny was no killer or didn't have that in him. He believed every word people told him."

And with that the vecina lady said, "Eat your soup, Carlos. You can't smoke the rest of the afternoon without something in your belly."

THE DAY CARLOS PASSED the vecina lady couldn't sleep and sat in her empty apartment with the lowlight and shadows with her coffee. She couldn't read or listen to the AM radio as most mornings. She sat before sunrise listening to the birds and the buzzing of her furnace and then all the furnace units around the apartment complex. She sipped at bitter coffee and nervously wiped her hands over the Formica tabletop—she thought of the weeks and weeks of conversation with Carlos sitting with the old man, the Viejo, the way she sat with her own grandmother and grandfather. She felt the ache of loss. She had received the call the night before from an upset Felipa. The call came after midnight and Felipa only had a few words of news. Felipa didn't want to waste the vecina lady's time by having to come over when the old man was just gone ... that's how Felipa said it and how the vecina lady always heard it: "just gone".

She thought of saying prayers or baking for the family, but she mostly felt weak and with no energy to move or speak. She had done fine on the phone and then hours after with no sleep or with no rest she dragged herself to bed and then she was up before dawn with coffee and her thoughts. She thought Carlos was the one she had had the most interaction with for months. She spoke to customers, at her diner job and her cleaning job at the grade school, but Carlos was the one she had deeper conversations with about New Mexico and death. She remembered Carlos telling her he was afraid of death but would walk through it and she found that funny because he had no legs. They laughed together about that. He told her one time death would be a relief like taking off a tight shoe. He once told her when his Benny his beloved cousin and brother passed, he imagined him back where he was born. Back inside the llano and the kid around the house and village of Colmor—around the grassless plains of his home and waiting to come on back. He imagined him 12 years old and then 20 years old and on horseback riding the plains in the heat and sunlight waiting to come back to the village, to come back one day to his family and his village. Just waiting for the opportunity. It's a hell of a thing to get old, the vecina lady remembered Carlos said, to see your family die and your friends die—your land change and become something else but it was probably different before you were there. Everyone has people who come and went. I'd rather stay and eat soup with you but the way of things isn't fair and keeps moving. Just a part of that, I guess. I was only halfway here anyway, Carlos said. That's what Benny used to tell me. Because I hated the work and the animals dying. I hated baseball or at least didn't like baseball the way Benny liked baseball. Always wanted something else. I suppose he was right and so I am going back home. Later at the funeral and the services Felipa and Lena—most folks there who spent time with Carlos had no idea who Benny was and no idea about Carlos' people or any of the stories from Colmor. It got to the point the vecina lady wondered if Benny even existed. This was until she talked to the youngest one of Carlos' people, Bruna. She had heard the stories and wrote one of them down in her journal to remember. "I used to think of spending time with the viejo as a waste," Bruna said. "I thought of it as a penance or as a punishment."

"IT'S A SHAME CARLOS' ASHES won't be buried in Colmor the way he wanted. No money for the plot. No money for the transport to New Mexico," the vecina lady said. "The Army is paying for the marker but the plot and the opening of the ground is up to the family, so no Colmor."

The vecina lady brought over some cookies and some chile and pork. She knew it was Carlos' favorite but as Felipa explained to her the money situation and the funeral fees and costs she just sat and didn't say a word. She put out the cookies and her food and sat and hung back as Carlos' people talked. It wasn't until the vecina lady's ex Joanne came in and hugged everyone awkwardly that she turned embarrassed. The woman who was once her husband was in the living room with press on nails and long dyed reddish hair wig. The vecina lady felt embarrassment and shame. She wondered out loud to her ex what he was thinking showing up. She nervously smoked as she talked. She had pulled the man from the apartment and silently spoken her peace.

"I'm not here for you," Joanne said. "I came to pay respects. I knew the viejo and cried too and I talked to him too when we went out. I'm here for him."

They walked back to the vecina's apartment to talk while Felipa's apartment filled with chatter and stories about Carlos and his ways. "The viejo would've hated all this. He would've hated the home filled with relatives he hated and stories he couldn't give two cents on the merits," the vecina lady said.

"I know, huh," Joanne said.

"You're so damned ugly as a woman," the vecina lady said.

"Well, this is how I am now, and I didn't come to get into this with you. You need anything before I get out of here?"

"The bulb in the fridge went out and I don't have the tools to fix it. There's extra food in there too if you want it."

"I ain't doing none of this to you or the kids," Joanne said. "I ain't doing nothing to hurt you or insult you. I'm real now. I wasn't for a long time so maybe that's why I drank so much but I'm real now and I want you to be real and happy too. Maybe you can meet someone who is real for you too."

And with this the vecina lady did something she hated to do—she broke down and cried in front of someone, something she despised. Her people had always said be strong and stand up to things. No tears, her Jefe father would say. But today she broke down for Carlos and Carlos' wife. And her own dead and buried marriage. There was nothing she could do to go back and so she cried. The ugly cry she despised while Joanne hugged and apologized to her over and over. When she recovered she cleaned up her kitchen while Joanne smoked and fixed her fridge and while she sat and watched as was the norm, woman or no woman.

"Things are all changed and I don't know or want to deal with things right now. I don't really want to deal with it."

"I know," Joanne said. "I wanted to tell you I'm moving again to Denver. There's work and a fresh start. I was heading out to California but the money was short, you know. Won't be there for a while. My doctor says to contact everyone I know and let them know but I'll have to wait for more money for more treatments."

"Treatments?"

"I'm taking estrogen."

"I have no money for my doctor in Trinidad anyway so not much to tell."

"I'm not ready to hear any of this."

The vecina lady put on a pot of coffee during the time she had usually cooked for Carlos. "I had hints of this," the vecina lady said. "But no idea you had this inside of you. No idea this is what you were on the inside." Joanne sat silent.

"What will you do now for money?" Joanne said.

"Now that the old man is gone. I've got the call out for work with my aunt and Mrs. James at the hospital. I think they'll call me when they have another viejo available, but I might not keep doing this. I might see if there is something else to do—maybe work at Dundee Cleaners or work at the Walmart."

"I thought you liked sitting with viejos," Joanne said.

"What are we like girlfriends now, Leo?"

"Joanne."

"What?"

"Call me Joanne if you're my friend."

"This is so weird for me. You were my husband and now you have wigs and wear skirts."

"I'm sorry, babe," Joanne said. "It's just the way it is. I've been learning that with a doctor. A therapist I talk with—just the way it is. No, it is what it is," Joanne said.

The neighbor lady told Joanne the viejo Carlos might've been her only friend and she talked to him more than her sister in Denver who she never seemed to connect with when they spoke on the phone.

"I asked my sister to write letters with me—to, you know, write me letters back after I wrote to her and nothing. She sent me a postcard and never wrote me again. Said she would just call if she wanted to talk. I thought we could have that between us but she said no. I had another cousin years ago from New Mexico—back in Mora, and she wrote me every month. I still have those letters and read them out loud sometimes. She told me about the village, the county and the plains and mountains—she wrote me about everything. She told me about everything. She wrote me and told me she hoped I was back home. I wanted to move back after those letters. We don't write no more. I guess people don't do that anymore."

"I guess they don't," Joanne said, packing up her tools and the rest of her clothes and the food the vecina lady had for him.

"People just don't have the patience for it no more, I guess." Later the vecina lady said, "I'm taking the old man's death hard."

"You should miss him," Joanne said. "He was a good soul to talk with."

"I'm alone here now," the vecina lady said. "Talking to the man made me feel better. He had something like from my family I miss. Something I only saw in my own parents, something gone now like my family back in Mora. Back when I was a little moco in New Mexico running around with no shoes and in the dirt. Something back from old times and it seems such a shame it's all lost now."

"I remember you once said that old man was hateful towards women and children, his own children to boot."

"He was just crazy with losing his legs and all. He didn't mean it. I'm sure he didn't mean it. Trapped in that chair all day I'm sure brought out the worst in him."

"He was in that chair from losing his legs because he couldn't stop drinking," Joanne said.

"Well he had a lot to forget, which is what happens to everyone. I'm a Christian and I have forgiveness in my head and in my heart. I have that in me so what can you do. That's what's true and real to me."

ONE WINTER MONTH was one of the worst after Carlos' death and after the vecina lady's husband had ran off and stopped visiting for good. The two women were alone and had to deal with their tragedy. The vecina was used to bad luck, she thought. The kind that manifests itself inside of her apartment. The lock on the front door breaking down, leaky pipes under the kitchen sink and finally the furnace unable to throw heat. And all with no man to fix it. She had a bucket filled with tools in the car and directions from her own uncle she had taken down over the phone. She was in the habit this winter, though, to leave the work—to ignore the problem and walk away. One particular evening she walked down to Felipa's unannounced just to talk. She hoped to have what she found with Carlos—advice from another generation—advice from another grieving woman—advice from a strong woman.

"You should get a boyfriend," Felipa said as she poured weak coffee. "Or maybe a girlfriend. Someone to help you with the work. You don't have to fall in love or nothing—just someone to help fix things. Go to the movies."

"Is it that easy?" the vecina lady said.

"That's what they tell me."

Felipa also had financial advice—maybe just let it go until you can save the money to hire someone or maybe get a credit card. "I see on the TV they always want to give you credit for something or another. You don't need things fixed right now, do you?"

"Well, it's January and the heat is out, Felipa," the vecina lady said. "I might freeze up in the night."

"Well maybe you should stay here? I got Carlos' room and bed for you if you need it."

The idea of sleeping in the old man's bed—the same bed he died in, the same bed he received care and the same bed he sweat and dreamed in—didn't seem to bother the vecina lady. She thought of how she could see her own breath in her apartment and could think of no other place to visit for warmth.

"Don't worry," Felipa said. "I changed the sheets. I have to find you a pillowcase though."

Later that night Felipa brought in a blanket and a pillowcase. The old man's wheelchair and shoeboxes filled with his things were in the corner along with what was left of the old man's clothes. When Felipa said goodnight and left the room the neighbor lady couldn't resist snooping and pulling on one of the old man's flannels—a pale yellow one with the elbows worn through. She held the material to her nose and the smell reminded her of the viejo. She pulled on the old man's Stetson. She found his reading glasses and stared into the mirror before finally settling in to the old man's chair. She made some of his gestures and then pulled his pipe from a shoe box. She mimed tamping and prepping the piece and then she put it into her mouth and acted as if she were enjoying a nice long puff. She smiled and then for a second stared at the viejo's room as the viejo she had come to love.

Felipa screamed when she came back to the room with a glass of water for her guest. She wanted to tell her about the bathroom and the running toilet—she wanted to make sure her guest was okay—she wanted to check in and make sure the girl was not rummaging through the old man's things. And when she saw her dead husband back from the grave and sitting in his room as he always sat she began to cry in a way that surprised the vecina lady and surprised Felipa as well. The woman fell to her knees and wailed.

"HE TALKED ABOUT YOU," Felipa said. "I think he really liked you coming over and passing the time. He liked your coffee better than mine. Said I bought the cheap stuff."

The vecina lady apologized a bit and then her face straightened. "I meant nothing by this. I was just missing the old guy."

"I got him over at Imperial now," Felipa said as she recovered and held herself up at the dresser. "After the church and the viewing, I had his ashes here for a while in the closet and now I'll have his plot at Imperial paid for. His daughter sent money—his social security and army checks came in to help. I don't know how I'll do money-wise but I'll try to make it. I'll try to get along. I worry about the numbers—the money and the bills.

That's one thing he always taught me. He always worked and brought in what we needed when we needed it. He used to say I produce! in a big booming voice. He was from the old ways—the old world you know."

"Like my grandparents," the vecina lady said. "They brought me up and I saw that in him."

"He always liked you and talked of you. Always cared what you thought of everything. He would say, I'll have to ask vecina lady and see what she has to say. I have to tell you," Felipa explained, "because I know you were close. The viejo stopped taking his liver pills. For weeks and weeks stopped taking them. I found him in the morning and he told me not to call an ambulance. Said he didn't want to die in a hospital. Seen enough of hospitals."

That's when the vecina lady broke down crying again. She felt the loss and ached for the man as well as she sat in his clothes and boots.

"Oh, girly," Felipa said. "We shouldn't cry too much for the old man. He had a good long life and had people who cared for him. He's with his people now where he belongs. We all belong with our people. Cry for yourself now. Cry for me," Felipa said. "Cry for your husband who ran off. We're the ones who need it now, you hear? I saw your husband cleaning out your gutters and mowing your lawn. I see he throws out your garbage and cleans up the yard."

"She you mean?"

"Yeah, she."

"She brought in new soil for the plants in the backyard to strengthen the ground for better roots, she says."

"Tomatoes need better soil for better roots. My damned doctor told me not to plant anything or work in the garden. Said they have them at the store."

"Oh, no, not the same."

"That's what I say to him. The tomatoes taste better from

the soil than from the store. Carlos used to say that. See what I mean about having enough of them doctors. The viejo always had lettuce and a garden going for us. No matter how down and out. No matter what a bastard he was. Always wanting to grow something for his people."

viewing

The afternoon following Carlos' passing, the worried Felipa phoned Imperial Mortuary wanting her husband taken to the Sandoval's Funeral Home on Cleveland Street. She remained on hold for the length of five commercials blaring from her television.

"I told yous he wanted immediate cremation," Felipa argued. "I have it in his papers. I have them papers in my hand right now. It was what he wanted."

Lena drove down from work when she got the call. "She stood in the little red bricked house on Crawford Street. "Where were you, cabróna?" Felipa said while she struggled with her coat.

Lena rolled her eyes. "I work," she answered back.

"FOR CHRIST'S SAKE they don't make it easy for a woman to bury her husband. They don't make it easy," Felipa repeated as they drove. "Most uncaring people I ever talked to."

"I thought you said you had his paperwork from Imperial?" Lena said floating the car into the only empty spot of the Sandoval's parking lot.

"I told you," Felipa said. "The neighbor lady tells me Imperial is where to bury him, but Sandoval's is where they will cremate him. I have the paperwork here if you want to see."

Lena shook her head and pushed back at the paperwork being held to her.

"Imperial is a big outfit and Sandoval is run by a family," Felipa said. "That's a big thing for me. I learned that from your father. Your father taught me."

Felipa slipped from the car and was about to enter the place when she noticed Lena still sitting.

"What is it?" Felipa said.

"Jesus," Lena said. "My father is dead can't you give me a damned minute with it."

"They close at 5, cabróna."

INSIDE, THE OLDEST SANDOVAL BOY with his slicked back hair and dark grey suit coat came forward and explained to Felipa and Lena about a viewing.

"There ain't no viewing," Felipa said. "I told you he wanted immediate cremation."

"He means for us," Lena said. "Right now. That is what you're saying, right?"

"Many families ask us if they can spend time with their loved one before the funeral service."

"There ain't going to be no service," Felipa said but the boy continued on.

"This reflection time can be very important to help with the grieving process as it helps the bereaved face the reality of death while also allowing for quiet time to reflect, remember and say your goodbyes," the Sandoval boy explained. "But it will take us some time."

"Do they have you memorize that?" Lena said. "Sounds like they have you memorize that."

"It can be here or in a chapel," the Sandoval boy said.

"There ain't going to be a chapel," Felipa said. "I told you Carlos wanted immediate cremation."

"Is that what the old man wanted?" Lena put to Felipa.

"That's what I am telling you," Felipa said.

In a minute, as the women sat side-by-side and waited, Felipa asked if Bruna would be around to type up the obituary. Felipa had the form in her file filled with paperwork. "They got a form," Felipa said. "They think of everything except for how you are going to pay for the damned thing."

"We'll figure out the cost," Lena said not really knowing where the dollar bills would come from.

"But can Bruna do it?" Felipa said. "I know she was always good with the typewriter. With the words, I mean."

"If I see her, I will ask her."

"If?"

"Haven't seen her in months," Lena said.

"Cabróna," Felipa said. "That damned girl worries me."

"BECAUSE IT IS FRIDAY, I'm afraid the cremation won't take place until Monday or Tuesday morning," the Sandoval boy explained.

"So immediate, Felipa said, "don't mean immediate."

"I'm afraid, no."

"Every Goddamn place has their pinche rules," Felipa said exhaling. "Everything is a big pinche lie."

"Please, Felipa," Lena repeated. "You sound just like him."

"Who?" Felipa said affronted.

"Carlos!"

"Well, I should hope so," she said throwing her hands up. "I lived with the man for nearly 30 years!"

"You'll need an urn as well," the Sandoval boy said later while Felipa sobbed into her handkerchief. "If not, the remains may be returned to you in a container, which may be a cardboard box."

"Well, of course we will need an urn," Felipa said.

AT THE YELLOW FRONT on Northern Avenue, Felipa and Lena walked the aisles unsure as to what they were looking for.

"Can't believe they want to charge a family a hundred and fifty damned dollars for a damned urn," Felipa said. "They make money off the family hurting."

"Family?" Lena said.

"What's that?" Felipa said.

"You're the one who wanted him at Sandoval's.'

"They take payments," Felipa said.

"I just don't want it to be no cardboard box," Lena corrected. "He was a bastard, but he deserves more than a cardboard box."

"Who told you that?"

"The friendly undertaker said."

"The Sandoval boy called Carlos a bastard?"

"No, that is what I am calling him. I'm also saying a damned dog or a bastard should get more than a cardboard box."

"Is that what you think of him? Of your father?" Felipa repeated clutching her purse. "That he's a bastard."

"Of course not," Lena said in a daze under the harsh store lighting. "He was a bastard and he was my father and I loved him. But my grandmother always called him a bastard."

"I never knew your people," Felipa said.

"Well, my mother never let my grandmother forget. Never loved a man more is what my mama used to say."

"Your mama?"

"My mama was a whore," Lena said. "That's what they used to say. That's what he used to say sometimes. You ever hear him say that? You ever hear him call my mama names?"

Felipa only nodded and looked out toward the parking lot.

"Carlos and his damned mouth," Lena said.

"That was just his way," Felipa said. "He didn't mean it. Don't make it more than just words. You're a lot like him too."

"What do you mean?"

"You're like him too," Felipa said. "I see you. How you are. You say things you don't mean."

"I'm nothing like him."

"Let's see. You blow all your money on cigarettes. You take your drinks at the bar. You call him a bastard. You say what you don't mean. I see you, Lena. I see him in you."

Lena just shrugged and shook her head.

"You know when I met the man," Felipa said with a quick smile. "There was no one who could ride a horse and rope a steer like him. It's like he was born to it. I never told him but I loved to watch him. I used to smell his clothes. They smelled like grass and sweat. I loved it. Never told him though. Never said what I meant. I can tell you that now. And he could work. Just like you work. I see you, Lena. I know you were at work this morning. You never miss a day. I know. You're his daughter that's for damned sure."

At the checkout the two women stood close while Nancy Gonzales' youngest girl chewed gum and entered in the numbers of the forest green metal urn found in the home and garden aisle.

"Did you find everything you were looking for today?" the teenaged Gonzales girl said as she wrapped up the sad looking purchase.

BACK AT SANDOVAL'S, when Felipa came out of the viewing room, from her private viewing of her husband's body, she waved Lena inside, saying, "That's not him. That's not my husband."

And when Lena entered, she nearly had the same idea. That skinny pale and legless old man is not Carlos, she thought. This thing drained, bathed, and left rotting under white lights looked nothing like the man she knew.

It's funny, Lena thought, but the last time she saw her father alive, Lena gave the man a bowl of cheap ramen noodles and then helped him to lie down and rest in her bedroom. I'll be sure to see you soon was the last thing she had said.

She touched his stubbled cheek, kissed his forehead, and with wet eyes whispered to him, "My poor poor, papa. Nothing but stories now."

bruna's boy

Bruna had come to Huerfano because Lena had a new man, a steelworker named Luis F. Romero, living with her. It was the cousins in New Mexico who told her about the man. Bruna insisted, "I'm sure they'll have something for us."

I had ridden in the shelf behind the back seat of her Nightwatch Blue Dodge 400 and stared up into the night skies until the old woman's narrow streets were soaked in rain, and when the red-haired Lena took one look and found our tired, pale faces at her doorstep, she immediately set her ancient plates onto the table. My stomach burned with hunger.

I sat in an oversized t-shirt that first morning. I transformed the footstool on the floor into a massive steering wheel. I created a reality of a highway and traffic, dashing in and out of racing lanes. I wore gifted boxer shorts and undershirt, Lena's old man's clothes because I had nothing of my own. I used their toothbrushes and their baking soda to clean my teeth. The Tia was more a stranger than family, but I focused on the food and the smells, the sounds of Lena's soft voice.

THAT MORNING THE SUN was coming through the windows and glazing the breakfast table and the Tia had her morning coffee and her first cigarette. There she was in her housecoat and her pink apron. Her lips were newly red, and her hair had been quickly made up and covered. She always wore a handkerchief on her head same as the woman who had raised her.

She had filled the black plastic lunch box for the old man heading out for another day of fishing–she had filled his thermos and packed a bag with elaborate cakes and breads to ease the man's sorrow through the day. She placed it all out of the boy's reach and patted the bag with a smile. She flicked her ashes in the sink and stole a second Marlboro red from the pack she carried in her apron. "Oh, lord in heaven," she sighed in between puffs as she moved from task to task. She hummed to the radio and listened quietly to the morning weather. She smiled at the news of sunny skies and warm temperatures. There was a familiar strain in her temples as she smoked–she now had one more mouth to feed.

Half irritably the old woman thought that the old man would need answers; for now she put the whole problem away as she continued her routine, sitting with her hands turned palms upward in her lap and listening to the mid-morning sounds, trucks passing and the far musical cry of a train down toward the Arkansas River. When it was all but light out, her grey-haired old man entered and leaned near the old woman's ear and said, "She didn't even have clothes for him?" Then my Tia Lena put her finger to her lips and shushed him.

IN THE AFTERNOON the bowlegged Tia Lena dragged her lawn chair from the garage, and the legs scraped at the concrete as she huffed and worked to move herself and the chair. The sounds of the summer traffic cried past, then the wind from the trees swirled up and down the narrow driveway.

"Oh, Manito," she said to me. "These will fry up real bueno."

After the old woman pulled her supplies from the kitchen, she sat me by her side. In the garage she puffed on her cigarette and whistled as she drank from her 7-Up can. We sipped and shared, and soon she dropped her cigarette ashes into the empty.

She pulled the bloody plastic bag of trout from the refrigerator and turned a basket over to use as a workspace for the work of cleaning our dinner. She had her way with a knife. She sliced at the bellies and at the insides and then dropped the bag of fish guts across the street into the Bessemer Ditch. Around lunchtime she seasoned a heavy cast iron frying pan and then fried up the trout with potatoes and onions.

The woman's common law man, the grey-haired boyfriend, stood and watched the woman work and later cook. Every once in while he pulled his leather pouch. He tamped the pipe slowly and carefully with his ancient finger, keeping the embers burning. He wiped at his neck with a handkerchief, and he had no care for television or magazines and no interest in the Tia's telenovelas. He sat on the porch with his Bible or with his evening edition newspaper. He took care to run a comb through his hair before sitting at the dinner table and he took even great care with his coffee and milk.

Tia Lena had the old man's more ragged white t-shirts for me. She pulled them from the mothball-smelling closet and had them over my head in no time when I spilled food.

"Wear this man's shirts," the Tia whispered to me. "Wear his underwear. But he ain't nothing to you. He ain't blood. Remember that."

"The way I see it," Romero said and then he puffed at his pipe, "I'm about all this boy has." And with that he put a fifty-cent piece into the pocket of the borrowed t-shirt and then patted it with a sly smile.

"This boy is no Romero," she told me and then she kissed me. She handed me a beaded charm she insisted belonged to her father. "The boy here is a Montoya."

"WHY ARE YOU HANGING your face to the floor, boy?" my red-haired aunt said to me.

"That man in those picture frames was your grandfather and he lost all his wives except for Felipa," Bruna added after sleeping nearly all day, and just before she finished a cigarette and then fixed herself another to light. "She was the last, no?"

Tia Lena nodded and agreed. Then she grabbed at my chin and cheeks: "He looked like this little one here, Bruna. Looks like your little Relles Junior here."

"Just happens to look like him. But I don't think he remembers," my mother answered as I shook my head. "I thought my boy would remember."

"I would come home from work, Manito," the old woman said. "And then I'd find bottle after bottle from that man. I'd pour one out, and in no time, I'd find another. I remember he never worried too much about work. I remember he drank," she continued. "Wine. Always wine. He would come over and bring his bottle. When he visited, you know. He would howl at the moon in them days. Something awful. Then he'd get into my purse and run out to the liquor store for another bottle. I couldn't keep up with him."

"And didn't you say he went crazy and tried to take his own house down?" Bruna said.

"One night I woke up to sledgehammers and light bulbs smashing. He was tearing the house apart around him."

"Drunk off his ass again," Bruna added.

"We were all sleeping. Me and Felipa and the sister. Felipa's sister was always around. And he was a carpenter and said he was working but we thought he would tear it all down around us."

"I never liked him," Bruna said. "He could've killed you, Mama."

"That was your father. No matter what you think of him he was still your father. Whether he raised you or no."

"But you say he was a bastard? Said he called you a whore."

"Worse than that."

"All that hell he gave you in his life. Why didn't you hate him? That's what I'd like to know. I would've hated him."

"Because he was my papa," Lena said. The old woman paused and made sure we had clean forks and glasses of milk to drain. Then she looked at my mother, wiped at her apron: "That man's hell gave me you."

OVER DINNER, my crimson-haired aunt Lena sat and told stories over bowls of green chile and mugs of sugary coffee. "My poor Papa Carlos," she said. "God rest his soul."

This was all right before my mother ran off, when my aunt cooked and cared for me, and before I found myself living in Lena's neighborhood.

"Mean old bastard," my mother said. She stabbed and scraped at every dirty plate from the kitchen table and then wiped down the counters.

"Shame on you!" my Tia answered. "Don't say such things to the boy! He needs to know about his people!" Then she tamped out her latest cigarette. And before lighting another, she advised us to locate family for ourselves. To always look for family for ourselves.

"He's dead and gone," my mother said, exasperated.

My aunt shook her head and threw up her hands. "Your father was a builder and a soldier. In the villages of the San Luis Valley. The man is there. That is where you can find him. The place of his birth."

"We buried him at Roselawn. Don't you remember?" my mother said. "Nothing left of him. House out on Franklin Street burned down and ashes. The man is in the ground!"

"No," Lena said. "He's there!"

My mother held her hand to her forehead. She said, "You're scaring me. Can't you see what's real no more? That's fool as all hell."

When it was just me and my aunt sitting close again and whispering, she nestled her leathery hand into mine. "Promise me," Lena insisted until I finally nodded and smiled. "Good boy, mi hijo. You go see about my father."

About the Author

John Paul Jaramillo holds an MFA in creative writing (fiction) from Oregon State University. His debut story collection *The House of Order* was named a 2013 Int'l Latino Book Award Finalist, and his novel *Little Mocos* is now available from Twelve Winters Press. In 2013 *Latino Boom: An Anthology of U.S. Latino Literature* listed Jaramillo as one of its Top 10 New Latino Authors to Watch and Read. Currently, he works as Professor of English at Lincoln Land Community College in Springfield, Illinois.